THE GOOD GIRL

MICHELLE DUNNE

BLOODHOUND
— BOOKS —

For Ted and Billy
Remembered always, with love.

"Dads are most ordinary men, turned by love into heroes, adventurers, storytellers, and singers of song."
– Pam Brown

CHAPTER ONE

S tanding on her doorstep with her brown cardigan pulled
tightly across her chest, Grace Murphy didn't look like
someone who had a man, sitting in his own filth, slowly dying in
her spare room. The cable ties which bit into his wrists and
ankles had opened the skin around them and some of those
wounds were festering now. But Grace wasn't worried about
them, or him. He was exactly where he was supposed to be.
And she was just a woman, watching a fat slug hauling itself
around the inside of an ancient dog bowl, which sat beside her
wheelie bin. It had been there since before she moved in and a
lot longer by the looks of it. Maybe the previous tenants, or the
ones before them had had a dog. Or maybe it was just another
piece of junk that they'd accumulated, but either way, it was
hers now and she had a good use for it.

The slug hadn't been alone in the bowl during the night.
She could tell by the silver trails leading this way and that in an
apparent random design and it was dotted with the excretions of
other creatures who had long since gone. She waved politely at a
neighbour who was crossing the unkempt green area, around
which the equally unkempt estate was built. Then she bent to

pick up the bowl. She brought it level with her face to get a closer look at the slug. Grace had never been squeamish about things like that. If anything, she liked slugs. Yes, they were slimy and disgusting. But they never pretended not to be and that was something to be admired.

'You know what, buddy? You can stay,' she said with a smile as she carefully carried it inside. She placed the bowl and its contents carefully on top of a clean tea towel, on her kitchen counter. Then she covered the slug and everything else in there, with dry dog food. Not the good stuff, mind you. The own brand one from Aldi. Three euros for three kilograms. It was a bargain really, especially as Grace didn't own a dog. If she did, she'd feed him nothing but the best. Dogs were special. Everyone knew that.

She took a measuring jug from the cupboard and emptied four sachets of powder into it. She added the required amount of water, mixed it up and poured it over the food. Then she crushed a small white pill and added it like powdered sugar on top. Whether or not he'd stopped noticing she couldn't say, but he'd certainly stopped objecting. He must have realised that to continue doing so was a waste of precious energy.

She washed her hands and carried the meal upstairs to the smallest of the three cold bedrooms. She placed it gently on the floor while she unlocked the padlock, slid open both deadbolts and let herself in. She ignored the muffled sounds coming from him. They'd grown weaker over the past few days as he seemed to resign himself to his situation. The smell didn't bother her either. He'd soiled himself so many times that his once white boxers had become a part of him over time. This was one side effect of the drugs she'd been feeding him and she wasn't the least bit unhappy about it. It gave her pleasure to imagine the condition of the skin on his buttocks now. Open, raw wounds were what she imagined. The thought made the smell almost pleasant.

A sheet of thick plastic was spread out, covering the floor entirely so that he wouldn't ruin her carpet. The room was dark too, but that was by design. Grace had painted the windowpanes black. Not that anyone could see in this particular window at the back of her house facing some trees. But you'd never know who might be up in those trees. Nothing was unusual in Grace's estate. But mainly she did it so that his world would be as dark and cold as it should be.

She placed the bowl on the foldable table in front of him. *His* bowl. His eyes no longer spoke to her. They once tried to tell her what a *good guy* he was. Then they let her know how much he hated her. They'd pleaded with her for a while, but now they were dead. They suited him best that way. She moved behind him and pulled the gag out of his mouth.

'You have three minutes.' Her voice was flat and held no emotion.

As he dropped his head into the bowl and chewed loudly, she counted down one hundred and eighty seconds in her head. It seemed like a lifetime to her, but no doubt it felt like a lot less for him as he jammed the only food he would see for a few days, down his throat. She lowered her eyes to where his wrists were tightly bound at the back of the hard wooden chair. Blood was crusted around the black cable ties and there were little bubbles of pus in places. His ankles weren't faring any better, while his swollen feet rested in the fetid pool that surrounded him.

'This is your own fault, you know that.'

He stopped chewing and his head shook slowly. Then his shoulders started to shake. Again. He could cry all he wanted. His tears wouldn't draw one ounce of sympathy from her.

'Two and a half minutes.'

The chewing resumed and the sound mixed with his gasps and grunts might have been funny in another context. He'd start gagging soon. He always did. He was quite predictable. Once she was satisfied that his time was up, she removed the bowl. He'd only gotten through a small amount of the food, but the powdered pieces were gone from on top. There was, however, a pool of liquid remaining at the bottom. Putting her hand on his forehead, she pushed his head back and brought the edge of the bowl to his lips. She blocked his nose and poured every drop of it down his throat, making him gag and choke while covering his face with soggy dog food. She picked up the gag again. It was a pair of old, opaque tights in purple. She hadn't bothered to wash them.

'Pl... please!!'

She muffled his weak protests and left, carrying the bowl without another word.

CHAPTER TWO

Grace enjoyed the short walk to work, through the estate, across the green and over the road. The fresh air helped clear her head. Blow off the cobwebs, as they say, and set her up for the day ahead. She was senior barista at *Jake's* café and she enjoyed the responsibility that came with that. Really she was the manager there, but such a title would probably come with an increase in pay. Even the idea might cause Jake's entire body to blister. It might even give him a stroke. But Grace didn't mind. She didn't need a title and she didn't need much more money than was necessary to cover her bills and eat relatively well. Plus, she really did enjoy the work and the routine that it gave her.

Jake himself was okay too, though nobody else seemed to think so. He was a small round man who was hated by his customers. He was aware of this because most of them were happy to tell him. That's what Grace liked about this part of Cork city; people said what they meant. But knowing it, didn't make Jake understand it any better. Grace tried to explain it to him once, that people don't like to be patronised. Saying to someone, *Wow, I love your hair*, when they feel like they've been skull-dragged through life, isn't going to make them buy an extra croissant with their coffee. It's going to make them want to punch him, kick him, possibly rob him and then go somewhere else for their cuppa. He responded with something derogatory, which he would only mumble incoherently because he was too much of a gentleman to say it aloud. Or at least that's what he'd said at the time.

Grace saw the real man though. When he wasn't trying to be lick-arsey with the sole intention of getting an added sale, he was a hard worker who treated Grace as a person of value. There were two other *Jake's* coffee shops in the city and the Heatherhill one was his least favourite by far. So Jake spent as little time as possible on the premises. He trusted Grace to look after the place and that meant something to her. He came each evening at closing time to sort out the day's takings, he paid her promptly each week and most importantly, he never bothered her. Therefore, Jake was all right.

Like she did every other morning, Grace arrived to open up at eight sharp. The man at home was already forgotten by then. She turned everything on, took delivery of that day's pastries and pre-packed sandwiches and displayed them all neatly. *Jake's* was the cleanest coffee shop in Cork and that was thanks to Grace. It was also possibly the smallest. As soon as you stepped inside the door, it was just two more steps to the counter. He'd managed to squeeze two small tables, a bench against the wall and three chairs into the premises, which was impressive. But that whole area, more often than not, was taken up with just one woman. Maggie Hayes. She was the first customer of the day, every day, and she had a tendency to linger.

'All right, Gracie, my love?' Maggie croaked as she ambled through the door at twenty past eight, pulling her two-wheeled shopping trolly behind her. As always, it got jammed in the door frame and as always, she wasn't gentle about getting it unstuck.

'One of these days you might actually steer that thing in here without trying to take the door off the hinges, Maggie.' Grace smiled at the woman.

Maggie responded with a fit of coughing. Also nothing new. She was wearing the same brown fur coat that she always wore, whatever the weather. It was genuine mink, she'd said. No doubt that was what she was told by the guy who sold it to her for a fiver down the Coal Quay, twenty-three years ago.

'The usual?'

'You know what, Grace? I feel like going all out today. Give me one of them expresso things.'

'An espresso? Are you sure?'

'Yeah! One of the things you see all the posh ones drinking in town.' She smiled. So many of Maggie's teeth were missing that you could see right down her throat if she smiled brightly enough. But at eighty-odd years of age, she couldn't care less.

'If that's what you want, Mag. Have a seat and I'll bring it over.'

While Grace prepared the drink, which she knew would be returned to her immediately after she'd served it, her next customers arrived. Three boisterous teenage boys, who should be on their way to school, but probably weren't. She didn't know their names, but they came in from time to time.

'A tea and a bottle of Coke there when you're ready,' one of them called from the door.

'And your phone number!' his friend called jovially, before ducking back outside and out of sight.

Maggie hacked out a laugh. 'You're a brave boy hiding behind the door, aren't ya? Ya little shit.'

The boys were laughing, Maggie was choking slightly and Grace smiled at them all. She was good-looking enough, she knew that. It had been a problem for most of her life. Even as a young child, she was taller than the others, thin, bordering on

7

scrawny and naturally blonde with bright-green eyes. But she was twenty-seven now. She knew how to use it and how to handle her looks, so comments like that, from boys like these, didn't bother her much. Not that Grace had much in common with other twenty-seven-year-old women. Her life had made her age so quickly that, compared to them, she might as well be a hundred and twenty-seven. But most days, that didn't bother her either.

'Four five six, eight five three seven.'

'Is that really your number?' The tea-and-Coke lad asked, surprised and still laughing.

'Call it and see.'

The boy hiding outside stuck his head around the door and waved his phone. 'Jesus Christ, that was Heatherhill Garda Station!'

'Exactly. Now bother me again and see where it gets you.'

'I'll have a Coke too, please?' he replied, not at all sheepish. 'I can't believe you made me call the cops on myself. That's a first.'

Grace went and placed Maggie's espresso on her table while she was exchanging banter with the boys. Then she went to retrieve three Cokes from the fridge, knowing that the third boy would eventually order the same as his friends, whether he actually wanted Coke at half eight in the morning, or not.

'What the fuck is that, Grace?' Maggie pointed indignantly at the tiny cup in front of her.

The boys didn't try very hard to muffle their laughter.

'It's an espresso, Maggie.' Grace placed the Cokes on the counter and went about pouring the boys' tea into a takeaway cup. She didn't have long to wait for Maggie's retort.

'I'm not paying two euro and forty cents for a thimble full of cat piss.'

'Two sixty,' Grace replied with a smile.

'Two euros and sixty cents for that!' Maggie was about to lift off. 'Where's the fluffy stuff on the top? Where's my chocolate dust? What in the name of sweet Jesus is this thing?'

'Give me one minute to sort these lads out, Mag, and I'll get you your cappuccino.'

'Oh for fuck's sake, just give me my cup of tea. At least I know what I'm getting with that.'

Grace could hear the boys laughing and doing their best impersonation of Maggie as they bundled themselves out the door and right, past the small strip of shops. Everyone knew Maggie. She was one of the characters in the area and there were several others, good and bad.

Jake's was in an area that was deemed to be *rough* by other Corkonians. It had a high rate of unemployment et cetera, et cetera but Grace liked the idea of what you see is what you get. People around here had enough to be putting up with. They didn't have time to waste putting on a show for anyone else's benefit, so they seldom did. Grace respected that. Far too many dangerous people wore nice suits and drove expensive cars and were respected by everyone. Not here. Here you could see the danger coming from a mile away, once you knew what you were looking for. And here, people looked out for their own.

Grace poured a cappuccino and she poured a tea, then she took both over to Maggie. 'Here, taste your fluffy coffee and if you don't like it, here's your tea.'

Maggie smiled a wrinkly smile and gently pinched Grace's cheek. 'You're a good girl, Gracie.' Her pinch ended in a small slap and left a sticky residue on Grace's skin.

'So I'm told.'

'But you'd want to have a word with fatso about them yolks. Whatever he's trying to pass them off as, they're rip-off dribbles of cat piss that he's trying to pawn off on hard-working people.

He's not in the South of France now. This is Cork. He won't get away with pulling stunts that like here.'

'I'll tell him.'

Grace looked up to see Mary-Assumpta pushing her pink, souped-up buggy through the door.

Mary-Assumpta was nineteen years old and another regular at *Jake's*. There was a new baby in the buggy, which Grace thought looked unsuitable for a newborn. But she didn't actually know about these things, so she decided to keep her mouth shut. The buggy to be fair, had all the bells and whistles, including a cow-print hood and matching muff and it took another bit of life out of Jake's door as it made its way through it. Behind the buggy, toddled a little girl, the previous owner of said buggy. She trailed distractedly behind her mother and her new sister. All three were well dressed in Nike and Adidas, but still managed to look unkempt, as they always did.

'Give's a cuppa tea there please, Grace, and a Coke... do you want Coke, Ella-Mai?'

Ella-Mai was preoccupied with something she'd just picked up off the ground outside.

'Yeah, she'll have a Coke.'

Ella-Mai was tasting whatever was in her hand now.

'How's the small one?' Maggie bellowed.

Ella-Mai was no longer *the small one*. At two years old, she'd lost that status. She also had an older brother, three-year-old Willie. Their mother wasn't much more than a *small one* herself when she started having babies and a father had never presented with any of the children. If Mary-Assumpta was in any way bitter about this, she never showed it.

'Come in out of the cold, love,' said Maggie, struggling around to the inside bench, making room for Mary-Assumpta and her brood.

'Papers!' Peter from the Spar called in the door, as he

dropped *The Echo* and *The Examiner* on top of the bin and left again without so much as stepping inside. The man was always in a rush.

Ella-Mai picked up *The Echo* after it slid off the bin and landed on the floor and she began pulling it apart in earnest. Pages flew everywhere and the front page landed face up at Mary-Assumpta's feet. She turned her head to read the urgent-looking headline.

Wife of missing Cork man, Terry Reynolds pleads for help in tracing her "best friend"

Below the headline was a large picture of a smiling red-haired man.

Mary-Assumpta snorted out a laugh. 'Girl, your *best friend* is after running off with his bit on the side. You've been traded in.'

'I don't know,' Maggie added, with an ominous tone. 'None of his bank cards are after being used since he disappeared. I have yet to meet a bit on the side who's stupid enough to foot the bill as well.'

Mary-Assumpta picked up the page, more curious now. 'He's been missing for nearly three weeks it says and you're right, Maggie. None of his bank accounts have been used. It says he just went out to lunch and never came back and that he worked in an accountant's office.' She looked thoughtfully at Maggie for a second, as she uncapped a bottle of Coke. She handed it to Ella-Mai, who drank like her life depended on it. 'Probably one of them tiger kidnappings so,' she said. 'You know the ones where they take rich fellas hostage and make them hand over all their money.'

Maggie nodded but looked sceptical.

'That, or his bit on the side had a fella of her own and he

found out and went after this Reynolds character,' Mary-Assumpta continued. 'Or maybe he was gay! His wife just found out and did him in for wasting all those years of her life. Now she's on the paper acting all innocent.'

Maggie looked at Grace, one pencilled-on eyebrow raised. 'Christ, listen to Miss Marple over there.'

'You hear of stuff like that happening all the time, Maggie. I read about it on Facebook.'

'Facebook.' Maggie snorted. 'Sure, that's run by robots. What do they know about anything?'

'What do you think, Grace? What's his story, would you say?' She turned the page so that Terry Reynolds was smiling up at Grace now.

'I wouldn't have a clue.' Grace went behind the counter. 'But people rarely disappear for no reason.'

'You're right there, Grace.' Maggie nodded solemnly. 'You're right there.'

'Yeah, but I mean...'

'Listen, people go missing all the time, Mary-Assumpta.' Maggie seemed eager to move on now. 'Some people just want to fuck off and live a new life. So off they go. Some throw themselves in the river. Others are shagging their secretaries, as you say. He'll turn up or he won't. Either way, rain will still pour in through my roof all winter long, you'll keep popping out sprogs and our tea will still get made by the notorious Gracie Murphy. In other words, it won't make a blind bit of difference to us either way.'

'What makes Grace so notorious?'

Subject changed. Mission accomplished.

'What, you never heard about the eejit who came in here three years ago, wearing a Harry Potter mask, with a breadknife for a wand?'

Grace sprayed the surfaces behind the counter and cleaned.

'No.'

'It was Gracie's second day on the job. Fatso was in here, going on as if pouring boiling water on top of a teabag was rocket science, when in comes this fella. Turned out, it was one of the Burkes. Anyway, he started waving the breadknife around the place, demanding money. I mean, I don't know what his plan was. Was he going to lie one of us down flat on the table and start cutting us into doorsteps, or what?'

'What happened?'

'Gracie there came out from behind the counter, as if she were going to hand over everything to him. Then in the blink of an eye, t'was she was holding the breadknife and Harry Potter was pinned to that wall there.'

'No way! What happened then?'

'He started crying, so I went across the road and got his mam. Jake found his star employee and no one's tried to rob this place since.'

'Christ, Grace, you're a bit of a dark horse. But they always say, it's the quiet ones you'd want to watch.'

'Just luck, Mary-Assumpta.'

'Hmmm. I read that on Facebook once. That a woman can lift up a car full of people if a child is trapped under it.'

Mary-Assumpta was off on another tangent.

'So you're saying what? That Jake was her child?'

'No, Maggie. I'm saying that you were all like her children on the day. She was protecting. That's women's instinct. It's what we do.'

'Let me guess; Facebook?'

'Are you on Facebook, Maggie?' Mary-Assumpta picked up her phone and began a search.

'What do you think, love?'

'What about you, Grace?'

'Not me.'

'But you're still youngish. Shouldn't you be on Facebook?'

'I don't need it. I have you in here morning, noon and night telling me everything that's on there.'

'But you can meet people on there. Men like. You could probably do with one of those.'

'And you could do with less of those.' Maggie cackled.

Ella-Mai was becoming more and more hyper now. 'I'm thinking of getting my tubes tied,' Mary-Assumpta said, looking at her. As if she understood what her mother was saying, Ella-Mai threw herself to the ground and launched into a massive tantrum. Mary-Assumpta rolled her eyes and got to her feet. 'She's been doing this constantly. I don't know what's wrong with her. I think she has ADHD or something.'

'You don't think it might just be a dose of TOCS?' Maggie asked.

Mary-Assumpta turned to look at Maggie, very interested in the explanation to come. She sat back down. 'TOCS, Maggie? What's that? It sounds like some kind of creepy-crawlies!'

'Toddler-on-coke-syndrome. TOCS.'

Mary-Assumpta rolled her eyes again and got up. She grabbed Ella-Mai and pulled her to her feet, then she wrestled herself and her children out the door. Quite honestly, Grace was glad to see them go. She didn't mind chit-chat but she struggled the more it dragged on. Especially with people who had no regard for boundaries. People who took a lack of response as their cue to ask more questions. Grace did like Mary-Assumpta, but she had her limits.

She was glad to have Maggie though. She was a shield for Grace, taking the brunt of other people, which she seemed to enjoy. But Maggie looked at her in a strange way sometimes. Kind of a deep stare when she thought Grace wasn't looking and that was unsettling. But Grace was a people watcher too, so she noticed that Maggie looked at a lot of people like she knew something about them. Something that they didn't want anyone else to know. It was like this quirky old woman in the five-euro mink could see into the souls of certain people. But of course that wasn't true. If Maggie could see into Grace's soul, then she wouldn't continue to pass her days here. She couldn't spend so much time in the company of someone like Grace Murphy and if she could, then what did that say about Maggie?

CHAPTER THREE

CORK, 2005

'Grace? Are you awake?' Amber's voice was only a whisper now, but even at its loudest, it was small and weak. Just like her.

Grace pulled her matted old blanket aside and shuffled up against the wall, making room for her little sister. Amber climbed in and pressed her cold, damp body against her. She'd been wetting the bed for a while now and though Grace did what she could to wash her sheets and nighties, they hadn't had a bar of soap in the house for months. Everything that they wore carried the Murphy stench. That's what it was called in Grace's school. Not that she went there much. What was the point when their teachers came from another planet? One where people could think about numbers and words and things that happened hundreds of years ago. Anyway, teachers didn't want Grace in their classrooms any more than she wanted to be there. They had no idea what to do with her, or how to hide their discomfort around her. It was easier for them to ignore her, so that's what they did most of the time, which she guessed suited everybody just fine. Most of the other kids came from the same planet as Grace, but they relished the chance to prove that their lives weren't quite as shit as hers. She couldn't blame them for that. But Grace didn't need the constant reminders. Nor did she need stories about Bethlehem or Ancient Egypt. What was she going to do, move there?

She pulled her sister close. Amber was shivering with the cold and Grace wrapped her skinny body around her as best she could. There was something stuck to Amber's foot and it tickled Grace's shin annoyingly. Something that had clung to her as she made the very short journey from her tiny bedroom to Grace's. She reached down and pulled it off. A tissue, or paper napkin that had been picked up somewhere. There was no point in cleaning up the rubbish in their rooms anymore, because there was nowhere to put it. Black refuse sacks, bulging at the seams, were piled high in one corner of the kitchen. Some of the bags had split and the contents leaked out onto the linoleum floor. The house next door had been boarded up for years, so their mother used to just toss the bags over the small wall and into that garden. But the council had started renovating it last month and had threatened to have them evicted if the rubbish tipping continued. So that was the end of that. Grace didn't understand the ins and outs of refuse collection. She just knew that it didn't apply to them. Nothing did, it seemed.

Grace and Amber stiffened when they heard the front door opening downstairs and a clatter of footsteps rushing inside. Somehow the frigid night air seemed to sweep in, up the stairs, under their bedroom door and wrap itself around them in the seconds before the door slammed shut again. Grace jumped out of bed and pinned her ear to her closed door, the threadbare carpet sticky and cold against her bare feet.

Her mother's shrill voice travelled all around the house. She was drunk as always. A man's voice responded to something she'd said. Grace couldn't make out what he was saying, but she didn't need to. She moved silently across the room and pulled the small bedside locker across the floor and shoved it against the door. Then she climbed in alongside her sister again and spooned their bodies together.

'It's okay,' she said, matter-of-factly. At ten years old, Grace was the big sister. The protector. 'Go to sleep.'

'I'm hungry,' Amber murmured.

'Sleep makes hunger disappear.' She injected a smile into her voice and kissed the back of her sister's head. Grace was hungry too. She'd been hungry for days.

Grace lay awake on full alert, as Amber eventually dozed off alongside her. About an hour passed before footsteps and giggling came up the stairs. Someone bumped noisily against the paper-thin wall of their bedroom and Grace stopped breathing momentarily. Then the door to the next bedroom closed with a bang.

It didn't take long for the metal-framed bed to start hitting the wall and vibrating through them. Seconds after that, their mother's dramatic moans began scratching Grace's ears and Grace closed her eyes, happy. Now she could sleep.

———

Grace woke the next morning, not long after the sun came up. She could see her breath in the air, playing with Amber's. She'd wet herself again. She'd wet both of them and they were freezing. But Amber was still asleep.

Grace crept out of bed and took the blanket with her. Then she expertly slid the wet sheet out from under her sister. She unbuttoned her nightdress and slipped it down over her shoulders and removed her underwear, all without waking her. Either she'd become incredibly good at something so strange, or her baby sister was growing so weak that she couldn't bring herself to wake on a freezing cold morning, even when drenched to the skin.

Grace picked up an old towel that she always kept in her room. Like them, it hadn't been washed in a very long time, but it was dry. She used it to pat Amber's mottled skin and then she dragged a spare blanket across the floor. Like everything else, it too fell into the same category as the towel. She rolled her sister in the blanket, so that it came between her and the wetness on the mattress. She kissed her on the head, pulled the locker aside and left her to sleep for as long as she needed to.

Downstairs, Grace went about cleaning up. Eight empty cans of Stella, cigarette butts from the overflowing ashtray and one from the arm of the battered sofa, which was rescued from a skip once and had miraculously *not* gone up in flames on many occasions. It seemed last night was another such occasion. She moved to the kitchen next, which Grace honestly couldn't smell anymore. They say you become accustomed to these things and Grace supposed that was true. She wondered what Miss Curley would think of it, if she were to knock on the door and ask Grace's mother why Grace and Amber weren't coming to school. Not that Curley Wurley would ever think to do that.

There was an empty chip bag on the kitchen table. Grace tore it open and licked it hungrily. There was some dried-in ketchup and she could still smell the vinegar. She licked until the paper disintegrated on her tongue and she immediately felt guilty because Amber didn't get any. She quickly wrapped the cigarette butts in the paper and opened one of the black bags and stuffed them inside. She shoved the cans in on top and knotted the bag again. She picked up her mother's shoes from the hall and placed them neatly under the stairs, straightened the cushions on the couch and wiped down the kitchen table with her hand.

It would be many hours before their mother surfaced, but

some mornings she surprised Grace by coming down early. If she did, and there was any evidence of the *night before* lying around, then Grace was in for it. She'd cracked Grace's rib with the handle of their sweeping brush once, because one of her assholes commented on the fact that she lived like a pig. They hadn't had a full-length sweeping brush since.

When she'd finished tidying up as best she could, Grace quietly left the house. The rest of the estate was still sleeping as she hurried up the road to Reilly's shop. The bread man would be doing his deliveries shortly and she liked to be in the vicinity before his van got there. Reilly's was the building on the gable end of a strip of small businesses, most long abandoned and boarded up. On the other end of the strip was a small pub called The Robin's Bill. Or as it was more affectionately known, The Rob and Kill. Grace stood out of sight from the shop door and waited. She had a long coat on over the urine-soaked T-shirt that she'd woken in, but embarrassment had no place in Grace's life. Had she gone back upstairs to change, she would have risked waking their mother and for what? So that she could look good for the bread man?

The van pulled up and opened its side door, practically up against the front door of the shop. Grace muttered under her breath. They were expecting her, so they wouldn't make it easy.

'Go home, Grace, and stop trying to rob me blind, ya little runt,' Eamonn Reilly said without even looking at her. The man was as old as he was cranky.

'I'm not doing anything, Mr Reilly. I'm just standing here minding my own business. It's a free world, you know.'

'Sure you are. Go on, Grace, get.'

Grace moved off, but didn't go too far. Amber needed to eat.

The bread man was called Seán. She knew that because Mr Reilly always made a point of putting everyone's name into each sentence that he spoke to them. *Good morning, Seán. How are you today, Seán? Lovely day, isn't it, Seán?* Seán was old too, but not nearly as old as Reilly. He was a bit weird if anything. He was staring at her, but out the side of his eye, like looking directly at her might turn him to stone. He made her feel like a strange new attraction at the wildlife park and she wondered briefly what his own life must be like, if he found her so fascinating. Or maybe it was Bell's palsy? One of the Burkes had that once.

'Ignore her, Seán,' Mr Reilly continued, as if she couldn't hear him. 'Grace is a chancer, that's all. But she's harmless, so she won't bite you unless you ask. Now her mother on the other hand! Well she's another story.' He threw his head back and laughed.

Grace edged her way towards the van again, but as Seán carried trays of bread inside the shop, Reilly stood by the open doors, looking right at Grace. She wouldn't give him the satisfaction of asking him for some bread only for him to say no, so she moved off again. She'd wait until he was finished with Seán and gone back inside. Then she'd run in and grab something else while he was putting the loaves on the shelves. Whatever was right inside the door would do. Usually that was just the bruised apples and juiceless oranges, but even if that was the best she could do, it would be better than nothing. Either way, she was bringing her sister some breakfast. Grace was faster than old Eamonn Reilly. She knew that much for sure, so good luck to him trying to stop her.

The van door slid shut with a thud and Seán said his goodbyes to Mr Reilly. Grace watched as he got in and started his engine. Again she found herself wondering where he might be going next and what awaited him at home at the end of his day. Probably a wife and a big dinner she imagined.

He turned the van around and headed past her to where the car park exited onto the main road. He stopped there for a minute, before reversing back to where she was bracing herself for the corner shop dash.

He rolled down his window. 'Hey.'

'What?' Grace took a step further away from the van, which put her flat against the wall.

'Here.' He held a fresh crusty loaf towards her. One of the round ones.

She looked all around her, then she reached through the window, grabbed the loaf from his hand and ran. Grace Murphy was a lot of things, but she wasn't stupid. There was no such thing as a free lunch. Or breakfast, she knew that. No man gave a girl a brand-new loaf of bread without wanting something in return. She laughed as she ran down the road and through her estate. She was far too clever for that eejit.

CHAPTER FOUR

G race entered the house as silently as she could and for a few seconds she stood in the hall with her back to the front door, listening. There were no sounds, which meant their mother was still asleep. Grace crept upstairs. There were many creaks and groans in the steep narrow stairs, but Grace knew them all by heart and she knew how to avoid most of them. She crept past her mother's room, past her own and into her sister's, closing the door gently behind her.

'Amber,' she whispered in her sister's ear. When she didn't wake immediately, she shook her gently by the shoulders. Amber's bones protruded everywhere and Grace was convinced that it must hurt her to be touched, so she was always gentle when she did touch her. Grace was probably just as skinny, but she was used to it. She didn't feel it much, only when she was so hungry that it felt like her stomach was resting against her spine.

'Amber, wake up. I have breakfast.'

Amber stirred and rolled onto her back. Her arms were wedged inside the blanket that she was rolled up in.

Grace broke off a chunk of the fresh loaf and as she did, the crust cracked and flaked into her lap and onto the bed. She scrambled to pick up the small pieces before they ended up in the wet patch. She pulled the coat across her lap and rested the broken crusts in a small pile there.

Amber struggled to free her arms and then she grabbed a chunk of bread from Grace.

'Easy now, don't eat it too fast. You'll get sick.'

Amber nodded and forced herself to slow down. Grace was her big sister. In Amber's eyes, she was always right and there was nothing she didn't know. If Grace said something was true, then Amber would never question it again. She didn't need to.

'How'd you get it?'

'You won't believe it, but the bread man *gave* it to me!'

Amber smiled and took another bite.

'Yeah but, Amber, you know that's okay because it's me. If a bread man ever tries to hand you a loaf of bread, you just run away, okay?'

'What? Why?'

'Because, Amber, there's no such thing as a free loaf of bread. You think that fella didn't want something in return? But see I'm too clever for that eejit. And I'm fast. He wasn't going to catch me. Not by the time he turned his van around and all that. I was home and dry before he even knew I was gone. But you're much smaller than I am, so if you're hungry, you come to me. You hear me? Don't trust anyone who tries to give you something for free.'

Amber nodded unquestioningly and then she stopped chewing when they heard a sound coming from the room next door. Grace broke off a smaller chunk of bread and ate it quickly. She handed the rest to Amber. 'Eat as much as you need and hide the rest. Put it in the wardrobe, right at the back.'

Amber nodded with her mouth full and Grace got up and hurried back downstairs. She got there just as her mother's bedroom door opened. A second later the bathroom door slammed shut. Her guest would have left not long after he'd arrived and was probably at home with his family by now. Or maybe he was teaching a class in one of the nearby schools. Or saying Mass. He could be lying in a single bed surrounded by cats, but Grace didn't care where he was, so long as it wasn't here, in her kitchen. That was always a small mercy this early in the morning. Grace put on the kettle and pulled a chipped mug out of the press. The inside was stained brown, which she did her level best to scrub off, but it just wouldn't budge. She pulled a teabag from the box and placed it in the mug. When the kettle boiled, she waited until she heard her mother's footsteps on the stairs before pouring the water in on top of the teabag.

'Hi, Mam,' Grace offered with a smile.

'Give me my tea, Gracie. I'm parched.'

Liz Murphy looked as rough as usual in the harsh morning light. Last night's smudged mascara wasn't washed off properly before the new layer was applied and lipstick seemed to have seeped into the premature wrinkles around her mouth. Grace went to the fridge. The inside was bare expect for a pint carton of milk, three days past its expiry date. The carton had little black marks all the way down along it, where their mother would keep tabs on how much was being used. She would mark it again once she'd poured some in her tea. This was her tea milk and was not for general consumption.

Grace placed the milk and the cup of tea, bag still in, in front of her.

'Good girl.'

Grace hovered for a bit, watching as the milk coloured the tea and little white bits started to float on top. She imagined the heat of it as it worked its way down the throat and into the stomach, warming the whole body from the inside.

'What is wrong with you, Grace? You look like one of them special needs fellas, gawping at me like that.'

25

Grace turned away and busied herself by putting the teabags back in the cupboard.

'Give me those for a second.'

Grace turned and handed the box to her mother. She peered inside and then fingered through the neat rows of teabags, stuck together in twos.

'Two, four, six, eight, nine,' she whispered. Then she looked up at Grace and smiled. 'Now you can put them away.'

'Mam.'

'What?' She stuck a cigarette in her mouth and lit it.

'Can I have money for some washing powder?'

She blew out a long stream of smoke and squinted at Grace. 'Washing powder?' She said the words like they were in a language she didn't understand.

'It's just that Amber has wet the...'

'If she can't stop pissing herself, then really, she *should* have to wear it, shouldn't she? What is it, is she too lazy to get off her arse and go to the toilet, like a normal person? Or is she just too thick to figure it out?'

'She's small, Mam, and she...'

'She's ten years old!' she screeched.

'*I'm* ten, Mam. Amber is only six.'

Her mother pounced across the table and slapped Grace so hard, her teeth rattled.

'When dear little Amber gets off her arse and gets a job, then she can have all the washing powder she wants.' She got up and went to the hall taking her tea with her. 'The only thing the two of you are good for, is bleeding me bloody dry. *I want, I want, I want.* That's all I ever hear from you, you ungrateful little runt.'

Grace could hear her putting on her shoes. She'd be gone any second and Grace had no real idea when they'd see her again. It could be late tonight, or it could be next week.

'What about some food, Mam? Amber is starving,' Grace called after her.

Even at ten years old, she hated the desperation that dripped from her own voice. But she *was* desperate. There was nothing she could do to disguise it. Their mother would eat today. She always did. But aside from the loaf of bread, Grace had no idea when their next meal would come or what it would consist of.

The only response that came her way was the slamming of the front door.

There was a very strong possibility that Liz would throw the remaining tea in her cup onto the dead grass outside, rather than let Grace or Amber drink it. But she'd leave the mug on the doorstep. She usually did. It was one thing to waste what little supplies they had. But it was another thing to have to waste money on a new mug.

Grace and Amber sat huddled together on the matted and blackened old couch in their front room, as evening rolled around once more. They hadn't seen or heard from their mother in three days and all that was left of the loaf of bread, was a rock-hard heel. Grace used a knife to cut it unevenly in two and she gave the bigger piece to her sister.

'I'm starving, Grace.'

'I know. I'll head out after this and get something, okay?'

Amber nodded and as they went about trying to chew their bread, there was a knock on the front door. They both froze. Amber glanced at Grace. 'Who's that?' she whispered, the bread still between her teeth.

Grace shrugged but didn't move. It was probably one of the neighbours coming to complain about something. They hadn't done anything to warrant a complaint, but that never stopped them.

Another knock, sounding less patient now. Grace got up reluctantly and went to the window. She looked out through the net curtains.

'Who is it?' Amber asked again.

'Some fella with a big square-looking bag.' Grace looked back at her sister. Then she made the decision to answer the door.

'Is this number sixteen?' said the man, sounding very stressed.

Theirs was number eleven, but she wasn't about to tell him that because his big square bag had the word, *pizza* on it and she could smell its contents from where she stood. 'Yeah, thanks.'

'Sorry for the delay. Our delivery driver called in sick, so we have a massive backlog. I'm having to deliver these things myself and you wouldn't know where you're going in these estates! They all bloody look the same.'

'It's grand. My dad was just about to ring and complain, but you're here now. Thanks.' She took the box that he held towards her, stepped back inside and slammed the door before he had a chance to realise his mistake.

Amber was sitting on the very edge of the couch when Grace went back inside. She was bouncing slightly and looked at Grace like she didn't quite trust herself to speak. But she did. 'What is it?'

'Amber,' Grace said with a beaming smile, 'we just struck gold. It's only a bloody pizza!'

'Open it, Grace! I can smell it from here.'

They pulled open the box and they both laughed, almost delirious at the glorious sight. Grace shovelled up a slice and handed it to Amber who was eating it before Grace could reach for a slice of her own.

'Have you ever had pizza before, Grace?' Amber asks with her mouth rammed with food.

Grace shook her head, taking another mouthful of their ham and pineapple feast. 'If there's such a place as heaven, then everything up there is made of pizza.' She grinned.

Amber giggled and then neither of them spoke again until they'd finished the whole thing. Once they had, they slouched like two fat slugs. Eventually Grace bolted upright, remembering. She folded the pizza box in on itself as many times as she could and nudged Amber, who was dozing contently beside her.

'I'll get rid of this. She might come home and smell it.' She stood up. 'Actually, let's go to bed, just in case.' Grace's instinct was telling her that something so good couldn't possibly happen without consequence. Something bad would follow. It had to. She went to the kitchen and to the side of the rubbish-bag mountain. She pulled an old bag out of the middle of the pile and opened the knot. She flinched at the smell, but she stuffed the box inside and shoved the bag back in, pulling others over on top of it. She turned off the kitchen light and went to meet Amber, who was waiting at the foot of the stairs. The pair hurried up and into Amber's room.

Grace helped Amber to change quickly and then she tucked her sister under the blanket. She sat on the edge of her unwashed bed and stroked her hair until she fell asleep, which didn't take long. With such a full belly, Grace was sleepy too, so when the sound of Amber's soft snores wafted over her, Grace got up slowly and tip-toed to her own room. She climbed into bed and minutes later, she too was fast asleep.

Their heavenly treat had warmed them. It filled their bellies and it made them sleep soundly in their own beds that night. So soundly that Grace didn't wake when the front door opened. Nor did she hear the lone footsteps on the stairs. It was only when her bedroom door opened and a man stepped inside that she finally came to. She squinted as the landing light shone behind him, silhouetting him in her doorway, until he stepped further inside and closed the door behind him.

She didn't need to see his face to know who it was. It was *him*. The one who would stroke her hair and whisper in her ear that she was a *good girl*. Her tears came immediately. 'No.' She cried softly.

'Shhh...' He sat on the edge of her bed and ran his fingers through her hair. 'Be a good girl now.'

CHAPTER FIVE

PRESENT DAY

It was after four thirty and the last of the day's customers were gone. There were two fruit scones left and a twisty apple pastry thingy. Grace put them in a takeaway bag and into her handbag. Jake never minded when she did that. Or maybe he didn't know. She didn't actively try to hide it from him and it was never mentioned either way. Though it normally took place before he arrived at a quarter to five to close out the till.

Grace took the spray bottle of surface cleaner and not for the first time that day, she scrubbed every surface until it shone. She swept and mopped the floor and even cleaned the bin after emptying it. Perhaps this was a trade-off of sorts. As long as Grace was in charge, Jake would never have to worry about health inspectors, or unsightly leftovers. Not that Grace wanted to eat fruit scones for dinner. Tonight she was making tagliatelle, with king prawns from Aldi and she was looking forward to the cooking of it as much as the eating of it.

'Hello, Miss Grace. How'd the day go?' Jake arrived and gave the place a quick once-over as he came through the door. Then he smiled and continued around the counter to the till.

She liked that he called her Miss Grace. She'd never been *Miss* anything.

'The usual. Steady enough, lots of tea and Coke were drank. Maggie asked me to tell you to stop ripping off hard-working people with tiny cups of cat piss. Or something to that effect. You're not in the South of France now, she said. You're in Cork and Cork people won't stand for it.'

'Did she order an *expresso* again?'

'She did.'

'Next time she does that, just give her a cappuccino. If you have to call an ambulance for her, people around here will assume it was food poisoning and that'll be the end of me. And it *will* happen. She'll blow her top and hit the floor, mark my words.'

'Right. I'll do that. Do you need me for anything else?'

'Go on away home, Miss Grace, and thank you.'

See? Jake was all right.

Grace took her time on the short stroll back to her estate, enjoying the fresh air. One of these days she was going to take up walking. She saw other people doing it sometimes. Not really going anywhere. Just walking for the sake of walking. Although most of them looked like they were in pain and who knows, maybe they were. But people still talked about the virtues of *a good walk* and they couldn't all be wrong.

The house where Grace grew up was in the same estate that she lived in now. It was directly facing her on the opposite side of the green. Both houses were identical to all the others, with black roof slates continuing down past their bedroom windows. The lower part of the wall had originally been pebble-dashed, but naturally the pebbles were long gone. Now all the houses looked acne-scarred. Amber still lived in their childhood home; if you could call what Amber did, living. Grace stopped outside the house. Someone had dumped a refuse sack, bulging with household waste, into the garden, but at least the bag was intact. Grace knew exactly whose rubbish it was and she would return it to them on her way home.

There was no point in knocking because Amber wouldn't answer. So Grace used her key and let herself in, picking up the mail in the hall as she did. She flicked through it; mostly junk mail and an electricity bill for forty-two euro. Grace put the bill in her bag and brought the rest inside with her, destined for the small kitchen bin.

'Amber, it's me,' she called out as she walked through to the kitchen, which these days was kept as clean as it could be. Though there were stains on the lino that a blow-torch would struggle to remove.

There was no response from Amber.

She went into the sitting room and there was her sister, sleeping in the armchair. On a small table beside her was a filthy-looking cotton ball, resting on Amber's browned teaspoon, which was both twisted and bent. A used syringe had been discarded beside it.

Grace walked over and gently removed the rubber tube from around Amber's skinny arm. She leaned in close to hear her breathing, then tenderly pushed her hair back from her face, tucking it behind her ears. She kissed her on the forehead, then she stood up and looked around. The place was a mess. Grace pushed up her sleeves and got to work, cleaning. She chatted to Amber as she did.

'You should have seen Mary-Assumpta trying to wrangle Ella-Mai out the door today, Amber. It was so funny. She was after a load of Coke and was having an absolute meltdown! Peter from Spar came in too. Remember you used to like him?

He's still nice. He flew past in the morning and just banged the papers on top of the bin, like he always does. But then he came back at lunchtime and ordered his usual; a takeaway Americano with three sugars. His mam isn't too well, he said. She's in the hospital, but I can't remember what he said is wrong with her. Jake didn't see me taking the scones tonight, but you know, I don't think he'd mind even if he did. He's all right as far as they go. He always calls me Miss Grace, like I'm royalty or something. He's fierce thick though. You should hear some of the things he says to the customers. I tell him he should just not come in when anyone's there, but sometimes he can't help himself.'

Grace was aware that she was rambling and just as aware that Amber wasn't listening. She talked to her out of habit because she had no idea if Amber could hear her when she was high or not. She liked to think that she at least knew her big sister was there.

She stopped talking finally and looked affectionately at her. Then she lowered her voice to a whisper and said, 'Okay, sweetheart, I'll leave you to rest. I'm making tagliatelle with the nice prawns from Aldi. Come over when you wake up and if not, I'll bring you some tomorrow on my way to work, okay? Maybe you can have it for your lunch.'

She kissed Amber on the top of the head and watched her for a moment longer. She was out for the count and wouldn't come round for some time. Before she left, Grace buttered the two scones, using the little individually wrapped pats of butter that she'd also taken from *Jake's*. She put jam on one, also from *Jake's* and left the other with just butter. Sometimes Amber liked jam. Sometimes she didn't. She placed both on a plate and put them on the table, moving the heroin paraphernalia to the side as she did. She knew better than to take them away. It broke Grace's heart, but Amber needed it.

When she left, she took the bag of rubbish from the garden with her. She walked three doors up, ripped open the bag and scattered its contents over the low garden wall of their lifelong neighbours, the Bradys. Nine children had grown up in that three-bedroom house at the same time as Grace and Amber were growing up in theirs. At least two of them still lived there along with children of their own. Mrs Brady liked to think she was cleverer than anyone else and she also liked to think that people were afraid of her. Some were. But Grace was not.

'I think you left something at our house, Mrs Brady,' Grace called, as she threw the empty bag over the wall on top of its contents.

It never occurred to Grace to stop calling it *our* house when she now lived in her own house. But for as long as Amber was there, it would be home.

The front door swung open and one of the younger Bradys came barrelling out. She was Amber's age and three times her size. She was carrying one of her children on her hip. Before she had a chance to start screaming, as the Bradys were prone to doing, Grace spoke calmly.

'Before you start, Melanie, be thankful that it's just in your garden. The next time you go near our house, whatever you leave there will be shoved so far up your arse, you'll taste it for a month.'

Melanie opened and closed her mouth a few times but didn't say anything as Grace walked away. Though Grace went to great lengths to carry herself in a way that was as far removed from her mother as possible, people around here still gave her a wide berth. Those who grew up here with her, were wary of her. It was good in a way. It meant that they didn't bother her. And people around here bothered *everyone*. It was in their nature. But that one incident when she was fourteen years old had changed everything in that regard. Nobody made any reference to the Murphy Stench after that, and no one spoke back to her. She'd be surprised if another bag of Brady rubbish showed up in their garden, but you could never be sure.

Rather than crossing the green to go home, Grace walked the long way around it to avoid the four teenage girls who were involved in a vicious fight in the middle of the grassy area. Clumps of hair were being pulled from one girl's head, while another was on the ground taking kicks to the ribs. Their boyfriends were filming and cheering on their girls. They took no notice of Grace as she passed, and she didn't take a whole lot of notice of them. Just enough to be able to tell Amber about it tomorrow.

All the fresh air she'd gotten on the walk home was of little value to her when she stepped inside her own front door and was hit with the smell. It was *him*. She walked through the downstairs, opening windows as she went. Then she took the stairs two at a time and let herself into the small bedroom.

He'd vomited up his breakfast and by the looks of it, had made another huge mess in his boxers. There was a lot of blood in it, but she suspected there wasn't much else in there left to come out. He was not a well man.

'And that's why you don't get the good stuff,' she said, almost pleasantly.

His chin was resting on his chest and he didn't respond. But the rise and fall of his ribcage betrayed the fact that he was still alive.

She tipped the table so that its watery contents flowed onto the plastic groundsheet and then she put the table to the side. She moved behind his chair and started rolling up the plastic. Just like she had with Amber all those years ago, she was able to pull the sheet out from under the four legs of his chair, though with more difficulty than Amber's bedsheet. She had to shove him this way and that and he neither fought nor helped. She pulled in the four corners to contain the human waste within and then balled it up. She placed it carefully on the floor out on the landing. Behind the man was a large roll of industrial plastic leaning vertically in the corner, beside the window. Two more were rolled horizontally on the floor. She pulled on the vertical one until she'd unrolled enough to cover the floor once more. Having him here was one thing. Having him stink up her house was another. Maybe it was time to let him go. Maybe he'd learned his lesson.

'Hey.' She started rolling fresh plastic on the floor. When she got to the legs of the chair she stopped. 'Lift your chair and I'll get you some water.'

He didn't respond.

'Hey.' She slapped his face. 'You want water, don't you?'

Of course he did. He hadn't had a drink in days, aside from the water splashed on his dry dog food. But that wasn't water exactly. He started to move his head, almost imperceptibly at first, but it was enough for her to push on.

'That's it. You can do it. Lift the front legs of your chair, then the back and I'll get you the biggest drink of water you've ever seen.'

His head came up just enough that their eyes met. There was no life left in his.

'Did you hear me? I'll get you some water and then... I'll let you go. Just lift your chair.'

There was something just then. A glimmer of hope maybe. He made three attempts and finally lifted the legs enough for her to drag the plastic sheet under.

'Now the back.'

Again, it took some effort on his part, but he managed it. And so did she.

'There.' She straightened out the sheet, pushing it into the four corners of the room and smoothing it out. 'All clean.'

'Wa... pl...'

'Water. Yes, I know. It was *my* idea, remember.'

Grace left the room, sliding the bolt across and replacing the padlock before going downstairs. She filled a half-pint glass of water. She swirled it around for a while, looking into the clear liquid which essentially held the power of life and death. She slipped in two pills, the green ones this time and she waited for them to dissolve. It didn't take long. She took her time going back upstairs and as she let herself into his room again, she could tell that he was surprised to see her.

'You didn't think I'd come back, did you?' She placed the glass of water on the table in front of him. 'Unlike most people in this world, I always keep my word. Enjoy your water. You've earned it. Good boy.'

Before going back downstairs, she hauled the old plastic sheet into the bath and ran the shower over it. She watched the water turn murky as it washed human waste down the drain. Once it was relatively clean, she balled it up and brought it with her downstairs and outside to the bin.

Back in her kitchen, Grace scrubbed her hands and went about making prawn tagliatelle. She used lots of garlic, dried herbs and the prawns from Aldi. She dropped the dried pasta nests into a pot of water, enough for Amber too. She might call tonight and if she didn't, then Grace, true to her word, would deliver some to her on her way to work in the morning.

As the prawns sizzled in hot oil on the pan, she didn't wonder if the smell was reaching the man upstairs or what effect it might be having on him. She never wondered about him. She didn't think about him at all, except for when she had to go and see him. She mixed the cooked pasta with the prawns and garlic oil and filled two plates, each with a mountain of food. Her table was always set for two. She placed the plates with care and started eating. She never waited for Amber because she could turn up at any time. *If* she turned up at all. But Grace always had enough food for her sister. She made sure of it. She'd promised Amber once that she would never go hungry again and Grace Murphy always kept her promises.

That night, just like every other night, Grace was settling into bed by nine o'clock. She didn't own a television and she liked to wake feeling fresh, early in the morning. Amber hadn't shown up, but she still might, so the spare bed was made up as always. Just in case. She smoothed down her freshly washed and pressed pyjamas and pulled the covers up to her nose. She inhaled the scent of cotton-fresh fabric softener. The good one. She smiled and closed her eyes. Grace never had trouble falling asleep, safe in the knowledge that both her house and her bed were her own. But her night's sleep wasn't what she'd hoped it would be and when she woke the next morning, she didn't feel well rested at all. Not like she usually did. Her sheets were a mess and she didn't feel well. She brought her hands to her face and rubbed her eyes, which made her thumb sting a little. There was a fresh cut there. She sat up and her whole body ached. This happened sometimes and she'd learned not to give it too much thought. But she resolved to go to bed at eight o'clock that night, to make up for it.

It was only six now and not yet bright outside, but she got up and slowly dressed anyway. Every part of her hurt. But she was awake, so there was no point lying there being lazy about it. As she made her way out onto the landing, she looked at the door to the small bedroom. The padlock was gone, the bolts were open and the door was ajar. She stopped still but her eyes darted around the small landing, to the bathroom on one side of her, the banister in front and back to the spare room again. Her breathing quickened and her heartbeat thumped louder than before. She stepped slowly backwards, into her own room and picked up the wrought-iron poker that she kept beside her bed. Her hands were clammy, so she gripped it tightly with both.

If he was still in the house, then he'd be silently waiting for her. Her breath came in jagged bursts as she forced herself to move again. A long time ago she'd vowed never to be a prisoner in her own bedroom again, so with the poker held high, ready to strike, she walked slowly onto the landing and towards the spare room, glancing over her shoulder and down the stairs the whole time. When she reached the door, she steeled herself, just for a moment and then pushed it fully open with her foot. She dropped the poker on the floor and her hands fell limp by her sides. The plastic floor covering had been rolled up and was lying neatly on the floor under the window. The chair at the centre of the room was vacant and the room had been cleaned. The man and all traces of him, were gone.

CHAPTER SIX

It was Thursday and Grace didn't work on Thursdays. Or Sundays. Sometimes she liked having days off, but other times she didn't. She didn't have a choice on a Sunday because *Jake's* was closed. But she often popped in to help out on Thursdays. Beyoncé, who insists she was *not* named after the singer, worked there on a Thursday. Jake paid her in cash for the day, so she could continue to claim the dole, meaning that he didn't have to pay her contributions either. That made it a win–win for both of them. But it wasn't a win for Grace because Beyoncé was useless. Grace had to spend most of her Friday mornings cleaning up the mess she somehow managed to make, every single time. Grace was doing herself a favour by going in on her day off. That's what she told herself.

But not today because she had things to do. She was taking the bus to town, so she started walking early. She liked to be at the bus stop in plenty of time. She popped into Amber's on the way, as promised, with a plastic container full of tagliatelle. Amber wasn't home, and the remains of yesterday's scones were still in the sitting room. Grace tidied them up and washed the plate. She left a note for Amber asking her to call over later on the promise of shepherd's pie. That was Amber's favourite and Grace made it really well. As she left again, she made a mental note to put the bin out for Amber when she was on her way home that evening. It wouldn't be collected until morning, but they came early even by Grace's standards. She knew the neighbours would squeeze as much as they could into it between the time Grace rolled it out to the kerb and the time the bin lorry came, but she didn't mind that too much. So long as they closed the lid and didn't bring any extra charges upon them, it was okay. Maybe they too had a rubbish mountain in their kitchen and just needed some help to get it down, like they had once. Grace was happy to help people like that, once they didn't take advantage.

She left Amber's house after a quick tidy up and hurried to catch the bus. As she passed Heatherhill Garda Station on the way to her stop, she saw Jerry, just about to get into a squad car.

'Hi, Jerry,' she called across the road and waved. She liked Jerry. He was nice.

He smiled and waved back. Then he closed the car door again and crossed the road to her. 'Grace, how are you?'

'Aren't you a bit old to still be cruising around in a squad car, Jerry?' she asked with a smile.

'You know, some people still call me Detective Inspector Hughes, Grace.'

'And some people still call me *Miss* Grace, Jerry.'

He laughed quietly. 'How are you, girl? I hear you're practically running that place for Jake?'

'I'm not practically doing anything. I *am* running it. It would literally be closed down by now if I wasn't.'

'That's brilliant. I'm very proud of you.'

There was a pause then and she knew he was going to ask her something. He always did because he was nosy by nature. But she didn't mind that. It was just another thing about Jerry.

Like the fact that he always told her that he was proud of her. He was the only person she'd ever met who said that. Which meant that he probably said it to everyone. Some people say, *Hello, how are you, goodbye.* Jerry said, *Hello, I'm proud of you, question, question, question, goodbye.* That was just him.

'How's your mam?'

'I wouldn't know. We don't see her much, but she's still around. You'll probably see her somewhere on your travels today.'

'I haven't for a while.'

'Yeah well. She always turns up eventually.'

'And what about Amber? How's she doing?'

'Amber's great. She's on the go all the time but I was talking to her only last night. We had tagliatelle.'

'One of my favourites. Chicken?'

'Prawns from Aldi.'

He nodded approvingly.

She heard the bus before she turned to see it coming to a stop just up the road.

'That's my bus, Jerry. Don't you go getting yourself in any trouble today.'

'I won't if you won't.' He smiled again, but he didn't walk away. Instead, he just stood there, watching her as she hurried to the bus and climbed on board. He was still there as the bus lumbered past a minute later, so she waved out the window and he waved back looking sadder than he had a minute ago. Grace worried that his work got to him sometimes and he really wasn't a young man. She'd known him most of her life and she could honestly say that Detective Inspector Jerry Hughes had *never* been a young man.

———

Patrick Street in the city centre was busy as always. It was almost nine o'clock and people were rushing around with cardboard coffee cups in their hands, probably late for work. Others were about to commence their shopping, while some stragglers were clearing their belongings out of the doorways where they'd slept the night before. Grace wasn't in a hurry to go anywhere. Her plan consisted of a trip to the English Market to buy minced meat for Amber's shepherd's pie. When it came to food, the English Market had the best of everything, which was exactly what her sister deserved. But first she made her way to the ATM beside Penneys. There was a short queue, but she didn't mind the wait. She took out the purse that she'd paid almost nine euro for in Penneys two months ago. She still felt enormous pride to be seen with it. It was cream with one blue stripe, one pink stripe and some coloured diamante around the edges. It really was lovely.

When it was her turn at the machine, she took the first bank card out of her purse and withdrew two hundred euro, just like she did every Thursday. That was Amber's social welfare money. Grace saved the other six euro on Amber's behalf. She might need savings someday. Then she took her own card out and withdrew a further two hundred, leaving her with a hundred and ten euro from her wages, which would pay some bills. She would try to save the ten this week if she could. It was good to have savings, she thought. She tucked all the money into her diamante purse, with Amber's folded neatly in the back section and Grace's opened out in the front. Then she made her way to the Princes Street entrance to the English Market.

As she always did, she stopped just inside to look around and savour the sound and smells. On the mezzanine above her, The Farmgate Café were serving coffee and fresh food and Grace made a mental note to go up there, purely for professional reasons, before she left. But for now she made a start on the butchers. There were several in the English Market and she wasn't one to make rash decisions when it came to her ingredients. This would be her most important decision of the day and important decisions took time. The first counter she stopped at was manned by a grumpy-looking bald man who made no attempt to offer his assistance, as she stood there perusing his display. The English Market was renowned for its friendly atmosphere and warm hospitality and that bald man went against all of that. He would not be rewarded with Grace's business today.

The second one was called O'Farrell's Butchers. There were three people working behind the glass display, two men and one woman. Two were laughing among themselves and one was laughing with a customer. An old woman with a wheelie shopping bag like Maggie's. Grace would buy her mince from them she decided.

'Ah, you're back!' The man who was laughing, not with the Maggie customer, gave Grace his immediate attention, abandoning his colleague. Though she didn't seem to mind. 'How did you enjoy your chicken curry last week?'

He remembered her. 'It was nice,' Grace replied with a smile. 'My sister said that I didn't make it hot enough, but we both agreed that the chicken was lovely.'

He rubbed his hands together and beamed. His name tag said Kevin and she guessed that his surname was O'Farrell judging by the level of pride that he took in his work.

'Brilliant! So what are we having tonight?'

'Shepherd's pie. It's Amber's favourite.'

'I think that sister of yours is a very lucky woman. So you'll be looking for this lovely bit of lamb right here?' He slipped his hand into a plastic glove and shovelled up a thick slice. 'Will I mince this beauty for you?'

She nodded enthusiastically. Now here was someone who knew the importance of dinner.

'One moment please, madame.' He hurried away with the lamb and sang out, '*Olé, Olé, Olé, Olé,*' unselfconsciously as he put it through the mincer.

That song held memories for Grace. One of her earliest memories as it happened. She was in The Rob and Kill one night, presumably with her mother because Grace was very young at the time. She had no idea what happened or how her nose got broken, but she remembered what seemed like thousands of people all around her, singing that song. Her mother fixed Grace's nose herself a day or so later and now Amber told Grace that she whistled in her sleep to this day. Still, Grace found herself humming along with Kevin.

'There you go, my lovely. Now Lilly has some gorgeous carrots over there, fresh out of the ground. They'd go lovely with that shepherd's pie.'

Grace knew Lilly's vegetable stand and that would be her next stop. Fresh veggies were important. Amber needed a wholesome dinner to make her feel like herself again and fresh carrots with the dirt still on them were exactly right.

'Thanks. Bye.'

'See you next time. Yes, my love, what can I get you?' Kevin's goodbye to Grace took him straight to his next customer, who was treated with the same enthusiasm. Grace liked that. He saw her just like he saw everyone else.

Lilly was also one of the friendly and hospitable ones in the market, but she was a bit more harried about it. Like she was crazy busy but would deal with you as best she could. Even though Grace was the only person at her stand. She spent some time examining various bunches of carrots before settling on a bunch of six. She also counted some loose potatoes into a small plastic bag, again examining each one before packing it away. She paid Lilly and left.

The Farmgate was next. She made her way up the stairs and wandered through the always busy café. She pretended that she was looking for someone, but really she was looking at their display. How they presented their scones and pastries and their fresh meats and salads. *Jake's* didn't have those, but it was still nice to look; to compare the two. It was like comparing day and night, but Grace still thought that it was an important thing to do.

'Are you all right, love? Are you looking for a table?' asked a woman in her fifties wearing a neat Farmgate uniform.

'Not just yet,' Grace replied. 'I'm just checking to see if my friend is here.' She enjoyed the lie. It made her feel like one of those secret shoppers that she'd heard about once. She was spying on them, and they would never know.

'Right you are.' The woman carried on with whatever she was doing, which was no doubt several things at once. She seemed that type.

That's when Grace spotted him. She stopped in her tracks and stared. It couldn't be. She walked slowly in his direction to get a better look. He was sitting opposite a blonde woman in a business suit. He too wore a suit and yes, it was him.

'Did you find your friend?' The same waitress again.

But Grace didn't hear her. How the hell was he here, looking like nothing had happened?

'Hey?' The woman touched her arm and Grace jumped. 'Sorry, love, I didn't mean to startle you. I said, did you find your friend?'

Grace shook her head.

'Well that table behind you is free now if you want a cuppa while you're waiting.'

Grace never bought coffee in any of these places. To do so

would be taking one step closer to putting herself out of a job, surely. But she had to stay. She had to know that this healthy, happy-looking man without a care in the world, wasn't *him*.

Grace nodded and sat down heavily in the chair closest to her. 'Americano.'

'Right.' The waitress sounded a little more clipped now and Grace caught herself.

'Please,' she called after her.

The smile returned to the woman's face. She was just like Grace and she deserved the words *please* and *thank you*. Just like Grace.

He was sitting on the opposite side of the mezzanine facing her. Between them was the gaping void that looked down over the traders below. He was smiling politely at the woman across from him. He nodded and chatted and gestured with his hands to make his point, whatever it was. How was he smiling and chatting and nodding and eating a fruit scone like he was perfectly fine and had learned no recent life lessons at all?

Grace's stomach ached now. He was causing her pain and she didn't like it. *He's* the one who should be in pain, not her.

'There you go, love.' Her Americano landed in front of her.

This time she couldn't bring herself to say *thank you*, or anything else. It felt like a huge clump of hair had become lodged in her gut. This couldn't be happening. Grace had turned him into a sorry mess over the past three weeks by emptying the entire contents of his body onto the floor. The drugs, the lack of food, the pressure of being tied up in the same position day in, day out. The white noise that she'd played for him every single night; a crying baby. He himself had cried for days at a time and was practically catatonic the last time she'd seen him, which was only last night. How was he here, eating, smiling, doing business or whatever the hell was going on at the table opposite hers?

He lifted his head and looked directly at Grace now. She was staring back, but there was nothing. No hint of fear. No panic in his eyes. He was grinning. Defiant.

Grace could physically feel her features changing; her eyes darkening, her mouth sliding into another shape. If the waitress returned, she would wonder where the other girl had gone, but the waitress no longer existed to Grace. No one did. Just him.

The woman was first to get to her feet. She reached across the table to him, as he stood too. He smiled and nodded as he shook her proffered hand, but as she walked away from their table, his smile vanished. He picked up his phone and made a call. This conversation was much more serious. But still, not serious enough. There was no fear in it. No regret or reflection or any of the extreme feelings that he should be afflicted with. He was back to business as usual and Grace had once again failed her precious sister.

Minutes later he got up to leave and as he walked towards her, Grace turned in her seat to make sure that he saw her as he passed. He was still talking on the phone and again, he looked right at her. Then he just looked away again and headed for the stairs, like he'd never seen her before in his life.

Nothing.

She got up and followed him. He was jogging down the stairs, but she took her time. He talked and talked as he thundered up Princes Street. She thought about how pleasant he'd been with the woman who'd had breakfast with him and how quickly his demeanour had changed once she left. That was the only part that made any sense, because of course he did have at least two personalities. The one that he showed to those who knew him and the one that he showed to those who *really* knew him. Grace followed him onto Oliver Plunkett Street which wasn't as busy as it would be a couple of hours from now. She could see all the way to both ends, so when he turned right, she took a second to throw up in a bin. She could feel the hairball dislodge itself and though it felt rough coming up her throat and it scraped its way through her mouth, it finally landed in the bin. A new one would form. She knew it would, but she was fine now. Or at least, she would be.

At the top of Oliver Plunkett Street, he turned left onto the Grand Parade and she jogged to catch up, not wanting to lose sight of him. He took another left onto South Mall. The business end of the city. He finally ended his call as he jogged up the steps and in the front door of one of the grand old buildings. Grace crossed the street and stood facing the same steps. The nameplate suggested that there were several different businesses operating out of the same building, but none of them were clear on what type of business they conducted. Just a bunch of pretentious-sounding names with double-barrel surnames, except for one; Alan Manning, Auctioneer.

He did not belong in such a place and he would regret his behaviour today; pretending that he didn't know her. That he'd never destroyed her family and that she in turn hadn't destroyed him. She'd shown him compassion that he had not deserved. She wouldn't make the same mistake twice.

CHAPTER SEVEN

CORK, 2005

'Is my mam here?'

The uniformed Garda manning the desk at Bridewell Garda Station looked up from his newspaper, or whatever it was that he was pretending to concentrate so hard on. He gave her the same smile that he always did. It seemed like he was a permanent fixture behind that desk.

'Hiya, Grace. Why don't you have a seat over there?'

'No thanks. I just want to know if she's here. I can't stay because my dad will be wondering where I am.'

'Your dad is at home, is he?'

The look on his face wasn't an unkind one, but it was one that Grace didn't like all the same. It was the same look that some of her teachers used on her when they heard other kids talking about the Murphy Stench.

Grace nodded in reply but was already regretting coming in here. Her mother would kill her if she found out, but Grace didn't have a choice. Amber was sick. She'd been coughing for days and last night she coughed so hard that she threw up everywhere. It happened again a couple of hours later and once more this morning. The place was a mess and so was Amber.

She needed a doctor or at the very least, she needed some medicine and so Grace needed money. She'd made two attempts to steal it on the way here, but was chased off both times. Shopkeepers everywhere seemed to know her and made it their business to follow her around whenever she set foot inside their door.

The Garda came out from behind the desk, placed a hand on Grace's shoulder and led her to a plastic chair. He sat down beside her. 'My name is Garda Hughes, Grace. But you can call me Jerry.'

'I know. You told me that before.'

'You remember? It's been a while since we met. I thought you might have forgotten me.'

Grace didn't like that he was sitting beside her and she instinctively shuffled away, onto the next seat in the row. Garda Hughes didn't follow her. But he did notice the move and again, she regretted coming in here. She didn't like that about him. He always seemed to be watching and *noticing* but saying nothing.

'When was the last time you saw your mother, Grace?' is what he *did* say. Just like last time.

'This morning. I just forgot my lunch money for school and I thought she might be here.'

He nodded solemnly. 'How much does your lunch cost?'

She eyed him now and took her time answering. 'About twenty euro.'

He just looked at her for a moment while she waited to see if he'd challenge her. Grace had no idea how much a person's lunch might cost, but twenty euro was the small fortune she needed today. Finally, his thinking face turned to a knowing face and he just nodded and rooted in his pocket. He pulled out a ten-euro note and another seven in change. He wrapped the change up in the note and held the now small bundle towards her. She looked at it for a second, knowing that if she took it, she would owe him something in return. She also knew that if she didn't take it, then Amber was going to puke on everything they owned and they still didn't have washing powder. Assuming she hadn't already done that. Grace had been gone for over three hours now and had searched all their mother's usual haunts. Or at least the ones she knew of.

'Call this an investment in the future of Cork city, Grace. Have a good lunch, so you can work hard at school in the afternoon and when you go on to college, you can make the city that I love an even better place for everyone.'

Clearly Garda Hughes was a bit wrong in the head. But fools were easily parted with their money. That's what her mother always said, but Grace hadn't seen it in action until now. She held out her hand and took his seventeen euro. She tried not to laugh about the fact that she would *never* pay him back or make Cork any better than it already was. But he wouldn't find that out for years, so she was away scot-free.

'Thanks.' She smiled as she got to her feet.

'Now before you go, Grace,' he stood with her and she immediately felt like he'd lured her into a false sense of security, 'I want you to remember my name; Garda Jerry Hughes. I'm going to give you a card with my number on it and I want you to ring me, or call in here to see me any time you want. Even if it's the middle of the night and it doesn't matter what the reason is. Whatever it is, you will never be in trouble with me if you do, okay?'

She stared blankly at him. Then he handed her a small rectangular card with the An Garda Síochána logo on it, along with his name and phone number.

'If you call and I'm not here, you can ask for me and someone will find me for you. The second thing is, you're very late for school.' He smiled, but it wasn't a real smile. Or a happy one.

As Grace left the Garda station, she felt a bit better about going there. She didn't think Jerry would dob her in to her mother and she'd gotten the money she needed. More actually. She was sure that if she made the trip out to Aldi she could get their cheap washing powder *and* Amber's medicine *and* maybe something to eat! Thanks to Jerry Hughes, Grace was loaded!

Grace bypassed Boots pharmacy in town, knowing full well that if you shopped somewhere that didn't have the name of a family over the door, then you were an idiot who was going to pay twice as much for the same thing. She knew where there was a tiny chemist that didn't even have a proper cash register. Just an old wooden drawer and an even older man who looked like he never left the place. He also looked like he knew everything there was to know about medicine. She'd go there.

'I need some cough medicine, please?' Grace said when she approached the counter. The place was too small for anyone to have to follow her around, watching to make sure she didn't steal anything. But it was also too small to steal anything. The counter was literally inside the front door and all the supplies were behind a glass partition.

'For what kind of cough?' he asked.

The coughy kind, she thought, but that probably wasn't the answer he was looking for. And she wanted to get the right medicine for Amber. 'The kind that makes you throw up.'

He raised his eyebrows. 'Who is it for?'

'My mother.'

'Does she smoke?'

'No.'

He raised his eyebrows again.

'Does she have asthma?'

Who coughs out of their ass? She shook her head.

'Does it sound wet or dry?'

54

How many kinds of cough are there? 'It was wet when she was getting sick.'

Again with the eyebrows, but finally he made his way behind the glass divide and started rooting around back there. 'Give her this and tell her to take it three times a day.' He handed her a tall pink-and-white box that felt worryingly heavy. She wondered how much change she'd get from her seventeen euro.

He held another box towards her. 'And she can take this to settle her stomach.'

She looked at the two boxes without a price tag between them. 'And how much do they cost?'

He eyed her to her toes and back up again, taking in her shabby clothes and possibly getting the odour from where he stood. 'Have you a fiver for the two?'

'One fiver or two?'

'One.'

Now it was Grace who raised her eyebrows. She'd have loads of money left over. Grace knew that Aldi had a concentrated liquid washing powder that would do a whopping forty-two washes for two euro and twenty-nine cents. That left her with...

'Well? Have you the one fiver or haven't you?'

She nodded and turned her back to him while she counted out five of the coins that Jerry had given her. If he saw how much she really had then he might be tempted to change his mind. She handed over the money, took the two boxes off the counter and promptly left without waiting for a bag.

It took her almost two hours to walk to Aldi, buy what they needed and then walk home. She was worried that Amber might have destroyed the house by the time she got there. If her mother came home and found vomit everywhere, they were done for. It would be equally bad if she was already at home when Grace came through the door carrying a bottle of washing detergent, two loaves of bread, a jar of jam and a twelve pack of Okey Dokey crisps. One way or another Liz would get it out of Grace that she'd gotten the money from Garda Jerry Hughes and then Grace wouldn't see straight for a week. She'd also take the remaining seven euro and seventy-two cents out of Grace's pocket and that would be the last she'd see of it.

But luckily, none of those things happened. Amber was still doing her best to cough a perfectly good lung up onto the couch, but she'd failed to regurgitate anything more than she had that morning. Probably because there wasn't anything left inside her to come out.

'Is she home?' Grace stuck her head around the sitting-room door.

Amber shook her head in a fit of coughing that sounded more like a dog barking.

'Come on then!' She let the excitement come through in her voice as she motioned for her sister to follow her upstairs, her coat bulging with all the goodies that were concealed inside it. She hadn't forked out for a plastic bag. She wasn't stupid.

Amber's eyes grew wide and she seemed to get a new lease on life as she scrambled to her feet and up the stairs ahead of Grace. She was headed for Grace's room.

'No, your room,' Grace called and Amber continued on and burst through her own bedroom door.

They dived onto the bed and Grace dropped everything in a pile. She pulled open the wrapping on one of the loaves and using all the strength she had, managed to open the jar of strawberry jam and the pair of them started gouging it out with rolled up slices of bread. One after another after another until more than half the loaf was gone. Then they lay down, smiling contently.

After a few minutes of happy silence, Amber wriggled closer to her big sister and rested her head on Grace's shoulder. 'Thanks, Grace.'

Grace turned and kissed the top of her head. Amber started coughing again and Grace sat up. She pulled the pink-and-white cough mixture towards her and did her best to read the instructions. She had no idea how much 5ml was and couldn't understand why the instructions on something as important as medicine couldn't be written in clear English.

'Here, open up.' She opened the bottle and then put a hand on Amber's forehead to tilt her head back. She held the bottle to her lips and let her drink. But not too much. She guessed 5ml would be about a mouthful because that made sense.

After she swallowed, Amber licked her sticky lips. She liked the taste of it.

'Now have some of this.' Grace picked up the blue bottle, which also instructed that she take 5ml.

Amber tilted her head again and opened her mouth. She swallowed but wasn't as enamoured with this one. Her face contorted.

Grace sniffed the bottle and took a small swig. She was right. It tasted like chalk.

'Now lie down and rest. This will make you better.'

Amber did as she was told, like she always did and Grace lay down beside her. The two cuddled close. Grace would wait until Amber fell asleep and then she'd start by washing the blankets and sheets that were festering in the wardrobe in the corner of the room.

'Grace?'

'Hmm?'

'Why do we always eat in my room and not yours?'

Grace opened her eyes and looked up at the ceiling. She never wanted her sister to know why she hated her own bedroom and everything in there. From the bed itself, to the cracks on the ceiling, the squeaky springs and the broken spring that dug into her back at times when she was already in so much pain.

'Your room is nicer.'

Amber was happy with that. She snuggled in a little closer and closed her eyes and before she knew it, Grace too was nodding off.

By the time she woke, it was getting dark outside. She scrambled out of the bed as gently as she could so as not to wake Amber, but something had woken Grace. If it was the arrival of their mother, then any second now she was going to come through the bedroom door, see the groceries on their bed and take it all away from them, along with their leftover money. She grabbed everything up in her arms and hurried to the wardrobe.

The smell hit her as soon as she opened the door, so she pulled out the soiled blankets, sheets and nightdresses and shoved the food inside. She closed the door quietly and stood still, listening.

The doorbell rang.

Was that the sound that had woken her? She crept to the window and pulled the grey net curtain aside just enough that she could see out, without whoever was out there seeing her.

She was looking down at a woman's head. She had an unruly mop of curly brown hair and a very large handbag on her shoulder. Grace dropped the curtain again and slouched down under the sill. It was social services. That woman had been to their house more than once, but it was always because someone had called them. Someone telling tales. Grace didn't like any of the social workers that she'd met. They all just wanted the same thing; to take Grace away from Amber and this woman was no different. If anything, she was the worst of all of them and Grace could think of only one person who could have called her. Garda Jerry Hughes and his poxy seventeen euro.

'Liz?' the woman called in the letterbox. She always did that too.

The doorbell rang three more times. Then she heard the woman talking to someone outside and Grace stuck her head up again to look out. Mrs bloody Brady.

She couldn't hear what was being said, but Mrs Brady looked like she had plenty to say. As always. She was hanging them all out to dry and it would be just her style. Most of the neighbours around here covered for them over the years. Saying that they just saw the girls leaving with their mammy, or that they were at school or gone on holidays. Whatever they had to say to get rid of them. But Mrs Brady was intent on getting them caught. She hated their mother and she hated Grace too. But she could say whatever she wanted because no social worker was getting in here tonight.

'What the hell do you want now?'

Grace stiffened at the sound of her mother's voice. Her words were crystal clear because she was so loud, but Grace couldn't hear what the other woman said in response.

'Please, God, don't let her tell on me,' Grace whispered forcefully with her eyes closed. 'Please, please, PLEASE, God!'

The front door opened and Grace scrambled back to the bed. She climbed in alongside Amber and closed her eyes tight. She could hear both of their voices more clearly now as they stepped inside the hall.

'Where are your daughters, Mrs Murphy?'

'They're in bed. Where do you think they are at this hour?'

'And where have you been?'

'That's none of your goddamn business. But seeing as you're such a nosy bitch, I was at the shop.'

'And you left the girls at home by themselves while you went?'

'It's across the fucking road, woman! It's not a million miles away, I can practically see my house from there.'

'And what did you buy?'

No doubt Liz was empty-handed.

'Fags. I'd offer you one, but I don't want to be accused of trying to kill you. You seem to like accusing me of things.'

'I'd like to speak to Grace.'

'Like I said; she's in bed. Asleep.'

'Show me, please.'

Grace could hear her mother's loud sigh as she stepped into the hall and started stomping up the stairs. She knew better than to get as abusive as she'd like to with the social workers. It didn't work out well for her that one time when she did hit one of them. Grace and Amber spent the next month in a group home in Heatherhill and had never lived it down. Mrs Brady in particular had a field day with it.

Grace heard her own bedroom door being opened and she imagined a silent rage building inside of her mother as she looked in at the empty bed. She was worrying now that her daughters were about to make a liar out of her.

'They must be in Amber's room,' she said, sounding suddenly overly pleasant.

Their door opened. Grace kept her eyes shut tight.

'There, see. What did I tell you?'

'Mrs Murphy, can you get the smell in your children's bedrooms?'

'Oh that's Amber. She's pissing everywhere these days. It's a phase, what can I say?'

'And you're not at all worried that your six-year-old is wetting the bed?'

Grace could almost feel her mother's body stiffen and the pause before she spoke was loaded with the threat of violence. 'Well, *Mizz* Logan, if you could find a man who was willing to knock you up, then you'd discover for yourself that a child will do whatever the fuck a child wants to do! What, you think I want her pissing all over my house? I spend my life cleaning this place and she spends her life stinking it back up again. I've done everything in my power to make sure she knows how to use the toilet and that she's not to piss in her pants. But she's a child, so she goes and does it anyway. You wouldn't know about that because you know nothing about being a mother. You give and you give and you get nothing in return. You hear me? Never mind all these celebrities who go on about children being the most rewarding things in the world. They can say that because they have ten nannies looking after them. But this is the real world, *Mizz* Logan. They give you nothing but trouble.'

There was another long pause then, before their mother spoke again.

'But God knows, I love them. For my sins, I do.'

'Let's continue this downstairs,' the woman whispered.

'I don't see what else we have to talk about.'

The bedroom door closed again, but Grace could still hear them through the paper-thin walls.

'Who called you this time?'

'You know I can't tell you that, Liz. But I'm worried that you weren't just at the shop and that the girls have been home alone for some time.'

'Can you prove that?'

They were almost back in the hall now and Grace started another prayer. 'Please, God...' but she didn't know what to ask for. As much as she wanted the woman gone, she was terrified now about what would happen once she did leave. 'Please, God, let Mam be so tired that she just falls asleep on the couch. Please don't let her come back upstairs and please don't let the couch go on fire.'

She rolled onto her side and hugged Amber before creeping silently out of the bed and into her own room. She closed Amber's door fully and left her own open. If her mother did come back upstairs, she'd find Grace first and Amber could sleep on.

The front door finally closed and Miss Logan was gone. Grace listened to her mother's footsteps as they slowly click-clacked towards the kitchen. She didn't seem to be in any particular hurry and as her mother moved around the kitchen, sounds of water being poured into the kettle made Grace relax slightly. She was making herself a cup of tea. The sound of the kettle boiling made Grace's shoulders sag with relief. She pulled aside her blanket and climbed under, fully dressed. The house was freezing and now that the immediate threat had passed, she tried to remember what Amber was wearing. Would she be warm enough during the night?

She heard her mother's footsteps on the stairs, but they were slow and relaxed. She was bringing a cup of tea into bed with her. She didn't often do that, but it must mean that she was much calmer than Grace expected her to be. She came and stood at Grace's door. She was silhouetted by the light on the landing behind her. She was holding something large and round. It was the huge pot that came with the house.

The realisation dawned on Grace a fraction of a second too late and the scalding water gushed over her legs sending a searing pain right through her body, the likes of which she'd never experienced before. Her scream was a blood-curdling sound and ordinarily she might have worried that Mrs Brady would be on the phone again. But Grace wasn't thinking about anything. Even the pain wasn't anything that she could make sense of and the sound just kept on coming. She hardly noticed her mother walking away from her door, just as calmly as she'd arrived at it.

Amber came running in, but Grace couldn't focus on her. Not until she pulled back the blankets and lifted the legs of Grace's tracksuit pants, taking a layer of skin off both of her shins as she did. That was the last thing Grace remembered before she passed out.

CHAPTER EIGHT

PRESENT DAY

Grace hung around the South Mall for nearly five hours, but he didn't come back outside. Maybe he knew she was waiting for him. Or maybe he was in there, catching up on all the work he'd missed over the past three weeks. Like he'd been away on a holiday and now needed to make up time. It was almost three in the afternoon and Grace couldn't wait any longer. She had to get back to make dinner for Amber.

Despite putting a rush on herself, it still took over an hour to get home. But Amber knew as well as anyone that it was all uphill from town, so she'd understand why Grace was late. When she got there, she pulled the bin back inside Amber's gate and around the back of the house, before letting herself in the back door. The kitchen was empty and clean, so Amber hadn't cooked. It had been a very long time since she had, so that was no surprise.

'Amber?' Grace called. 'You home?'

There was no response. Grace went to the cupboard and took the USA biscuit tin down from the highest shelf. The tin was so old that the colour had almost completely faded off. She popped the lid and put Amber's dole money inside. She placed the tin back on the shelf and closed the cupboard.

'I'm sorry I'm late. I got held up in town, but I'm going to run over now and make a start on the shepherd's pie.' She walked through to the sitting room and stopped when she saw Amber lying face down on the couch. Grace's breath always caught when she saw Amber sleeping. There were so many times when they were young that she worried her sister might never wake up. She still worried about that sometimes. But Amber told her once that every time she closed her eyes, she prayed that she wouldn't have to open them again. Grace stopped mentioning it after that. She didn't like to put ideas in her sister's head.

'Amber?' She lowered her voice, not wanting to startle her.

She moved and Grace's heart started beating again.

'Amber? I'm making dinner.'

Amber's bent-up spoon was on the arm of the couch and the syringe was on the floor. Grace started gathering them up. She pulled Amber's hair back off her face. Her beauty was still very clear to Grace. Her sister was the most beautiful girl in the world. Her brown eyes were like saucers and her hair, even as greasy as it was now, was the colour of milk chocolate. Grace and Amber had different fathers, or so they were told. They'd never met anyone who claimed to be a father to either of them, but it made no difference. Grace and Amber were two halves of one thing. They didn't need anyone to tell them what they were or were not. Even now, she looked beautiful to Grace. But Amber wouldn't be coming for shepherd's pie tonight.

'It'll be on the table for you in an hour, Amber. You come over anytime you feel well enough. If not, I'll bring it here later.' She sat on the edge of the couch and stroked her sister's hair. 'I promised you that you'd never be hungry again and you won't.

Just get yourself well enough to eat, okay? I'll take care of everything else.'

The remains of yesterday's tagliatelle were on the coffee table and Grace cleaned up before she left. The estate was relatively quiet as she made her way home, taking her time now that she no longer had a reason to rush. Once inside her own front door, she went about preparing the food, which always took Grace's full attention. She had been thinking about *him* all the way from the South Mall to Amber's house and she would get back to him later. But for now, the food was the most important thing and she made it exactly how Amber liked it; with extra gravy and extra butter on the potatoes. But as soon as the dish went into the oven and the timer was set, Grace opened the browser on her phone and started her search for Alan Manning, Auctioneer. Sure enough, there he was. Alan Manning. That's who he was passing himself off as now.

Even from her screen, he was mocking her with his smile. His was the kind that had been cultivated over time, to make people believe that he was a trustworthy guy. Someone you could hand your house keys over to, because he would look after you and your best interests. His smile was designed to hide the beast inside, but Grace saw him clearly. Soon he would see *her* clearly too. Only this time she'd make sure he would never forget.

Amber didn't come that night either, which was probably just as well. Grace needed to think. True to her word, she went to bed at eight o clock, but it wouldn't make up for the rough night's sleep she'd had the night before. She lay there for hours, staring at the ceiling and having imaginary conversations with Alan Manning. It wouldn't be as simple as pretending that she wanted to sell her house. He'd been to her house and he'd nearly died there. Despite his nonchalance in the English Market, she was certain that he wouldn't set foot inside her door again. Not voluntarily at least. No. She'd have to come up with another way to pay back all that was owed to him. And she would. Grace was resourceful. She always had been and when she least expected it, the answer would come.

Eventually she did drift off to sleep and when she woke the next morning she had a rare feeling of dread about having to go to work. She'd never been the kind of person who dreaded Mondays or anything like that. She loved the normality of getting up and going to work. Earning her money and spending it however she liked. But every minute she wasted pouring coffee was another minute that Alan Manning got to walk the streets, as if he deserved to do so. Still, she had no choice. She had to go to work, and in the end, she was damn glad that she did.

CHAPTER NINE

People always said things like, *What's for you, won't pass you by* or *What's meant to be, will be* and for the first fourteen years of her life, Grace didn't believe any of that to be true. But now, she knew that it was. The universe looked out for Grace and today was another fine example of that. Maggie had been a gift in Grace's life for some time now. Like her, Maggie had always been around Heatherhill. Grace's earliest memory of her was when Maggie swung her handbag at Mr Reilly's head, as he was about to pick up the phone to call the Guards on Grace. She was about twelve at the time and had been caught red-handed, legging it with a box of Cornflakes. Again. Thanks to Maggie, she not only got away, but she managed to grab a bag of apples as she ran out the door. The locals thought she was a bit mad and maybe she was. But there was good mad and bad mad, and Maggie was definitely good mad.

These days she shielded Grace from other people, whether it was her intention to or not. It probably wasn't. Maggie was just passing her days, same as everyone else. But now she was about to prove her worth once more.

Mary-Assumpta was prattling on about her latest

infatuation. A boy by the name of Nigel who had been in her class at school. While Mary-Assumpta left school at the age of sixteen, Nigel not only completed his leaving cert, but he was now a student at UCC. He was studying medicine and she was trying to re-connect with him on Facebook. Nigel had blocked her and now she was sure that Facebook actually *was* run by robots and that Maggie had been right all along.

That's when it happened. Out of nowhere and with no new signs that something might be wrong, Maggie just keeled over. She slid off her seat and onto the floor with a dull thud.

'Maggie!' Mary-Assumpta screeched, pulling Grace out of her own thoughts.

'Maggie?' Grace repeated and hurried out from behind the counter. She knelt down beside her and lifted Maggie's head and shoulders onto her lap. She lowered her ear to Maggie's mouth. She was breathing.

'Mary-Assumpta, call an ambulance.'

'I have no credit!' she replied, panicked.

'It's free. Dial 999 now, Mary-Assumpta, and tell them to hurry.'

Grace was calm. She always was in a crisis, but she wasn't happy. She didn't want Maggie to die, so she spoke softly to her. 'Maggie? It's okay. You're going to be fine. An ambulance is on the way...'

'I don't know! I'm not a bloody doctor, am I?' Mary-Assumpta was still screeching, but it was directed at ambulance control now. Ella-Mai, picking up on her mother's panic, had joined in.

Grace did her best to tune them out and focus on Maggie. She stroked her head and continued to talk softly to her. Maggie opened her eyes and looked pitifully up at Grace. She was mumbling incoherently and moving her head from side to side, but she made no move to get up.

'Here! Over here!!' Mary-Assumpta ran outside, across the small car park and onto the road, waving her arms in the air.

Grace lifted her head and saw an ambulance sitting in traffic at the lights out front. Its blue lights weren't flashing and it didn't look to be in a hurry, so it probably wasn't their ambulance. But it soon would be if Mary-Assumpta had anything to do with it.

Sure enough, the lights started to flash and traffic started to part. One of the paramedics hopped out and hurried towards *Jake's* while the other brought the ambulance around.

'What's happened here, ladies?' he asked in an easy manner as he came inside. He had the tables shoved aside and had Maggie lying flat on the floor in a matter of seconds, with his medical bag open.

Grace stood and got out of the way as the second paramedic entered and promptly took her place beside Maggie. She'd parked the ambulance directly outside and the dramatic scene had attracted a small crowd to the door. Grace went and closed it on them, but soon there was a row of squashed faces in cupped hands, pressed against the glass. Grace thought briefly about Jake's concerns and wondered if they really would pass a tale of food poisoning down through the grapevine. Could they really put Jake out of business and Grace out of a job with their rumours? She was snapped out of her rambling train of thought by Mary-Assumpta, who was giving the most dramatic account of Maggie's collapse imaginable. It included gasps for air, a gurgle and an earth-shattering bang as her head hit the tiled floor. Grace didn't interrupt her flow. The more serious it sounded, the better her chances of getting proper care, surely. Grace did not want Maggie to die. She glanced back up at the row of spectators. Nor did she want *Jake's* to be shut down.

The paramedics worked on Maggie for what felt like an eternity and Maggie was waking up and nodding off continuously throughout. Eventually, they loaded her into the back of the ambulance and drove away and that's when Grace realised that she needn't have worried about any rumours. Mary-Assumpta, thrilled to have an audience, started retelling her account of things before the ambulance moved at all. By the time she was done with her day, the whole of Heatherhill would know exactly what happened. More importantly, they would know that Maggie hadn't eaten a thing.

Almost an hour after they placed the call, their *actual* ambulance arrived. Mary-Assumpta screeched at them for a full five minutes about the fact that Maggie would be dead if she'd had to wait on them and how they wouldn't turn up this late if the call had come from Maryborough. Grace supposed she had a point. Absent-mindedly she picked Maggie's old tote bag up off the floor and brought it behind the counter. She bundled it onto the shelf beneath the till, which was a mistake as the contents started to fall out onto the floor. A bundle of not-so-new tissues, a small fake fur purse, a tennis ball, a half-eaten chocolate digestive and a bundle of keys that wouldn't look out of place hanging from a prison warden's belt. Grace bundled everything back into the bag, but paused as she picked up the hefty bunch of keys.

'Thank you, Maggie,' she whispered.

CHAPTER TEN

MAGGIE – PRESENT DAY

Before she'd even opened her eyes, Maggie knew that something was wrong. Her body wasn't protesting anything and that was just the first sign. The second was that her uncharacteristically quiet limbs felt like they were cocooned in a cloud, which of course meant that she couldn't be dead. If she were, then she wouldn't be anywhere near the clouds. No. If Margaret Leonora Hayes was dead, then her arse would be on fire, sure as God.

Another clue that something was amiss was the feeling that she was being watched intently, which was why she hadn't opened her eyes just yet. Someone was breathing beside her and she could feel eyes drilling into her face. She instantly regretted her attempt to stretch her arthritic fingers because it caused her hand to flinch dramatically. Or rather, the cannula sticking out of her hand caused her to flinch dramatically when it was disturbed by her movement.

'You're back.'

'Shit,' Maggie mumbled in response to the woman. 'Have you really got nothing better to do?' she asked, opening her eyes and then squinting against the light.

Louisa smiled. 'What could be better than seeing Maggie Hayes beat death yet again?'

Louisa Jennings was a psychiatric nurse who Maggie seriously believed had been stalking her for two decades or more. She seemed to appear out of thin air whenever anything like this happened. Maggie's legs flailed as she tried to haul herself into a sitting position.

'What are you doing?' Louisa asked, patiently.

'I have to go.'

'Go where?'

'How's that your business?' She flopped back on the bed, spent. 'You know, the whole country is cribbing about a crisis in the health service. So how is it that you seem to have all the time in the world to harass me!'

'She'll be all right without you for a few days, Maggie.'

Maggie turned away from the woman and went looking for a jug of water that she believed should be on a table beside her. 'What are you on about? What hospital am I in? Shouldn't there at least be a jug of bloody water beside my bed?'

'Mercy University Hospital and the water is beside you – on my side. And I'm on about Grace, as well you know.'

'Do you work here now? Or are you my visitor?'

'Both.'

'Well in that case, I'm within my rights to ask you most politely, to fuck off.'

'Have you been taking your medication?'

'That's not your business either, is it?'

'I've checked and it seems like you have. You've certainly been filling your prescriptions, which is good.'

'Jesus, woman! Any chance you might get a real job for yourself and leave me in peace?'

'I'll go, Maggie. I just want to make sure you're taking care of yourself, as well as...'

'Go. You're giving me an ulcer.'

Louisa stood and gathered her coat, but her face didn't harden an inch. Maggie honestly believed that it was impossible to offend some people and Louisa happened to be one of them. And Maggie would know; she'd been trying to lose the woman for years.

'It's good to know you're all right, Maggie.' She smiled pleasantly and then she left.

Maggie stopped fussing about the water and lay back on her pillow; the likes of which she only ever encountered in hospital. The softness of it, and the crisp white pillowcase were things that she didn't want to get too used to, so again she attempted to get up. Again, she failed.

'Hello, Maggie.' A smiling young doctor whipped back the curtain surrounding her trolly. His jeans were tight enough to lessen his chances of fatherhood and he was holding a clipboard. She'd met him before and it seemed he remembered her.

'Can someone call me a taxi?'

'No, but I can get you a rap on the knuckles for not taking your meds, young lady.'

She shook her head, rolled her eyes and mumbled something, but even she didn't really know what.

'Your heart nearly came out through your fur coat, girl.' He was still smiling at her and Maggie didn't like it. She didn't like the sympathy that these kids had for her and their efforts to conceal it only made it more obvious. And more infuriating. What did they know about anything?

'I need to get home.'

'And we need the trolly back. But you'll be here for a while yet.'

'I won't. I'm a grown woman, I can leave if I want.'

'Fine. But will you at least stay until tomorrow? Take some medication and see how you feel in the morning. Please.'

She let out a long sigh, moan, mumble combination and acquiesced, but only because she didn't feel like she could stand, let alone take the required number of steps to reach the front door. 'I do take my medication,' she grumbled like a petulant child. 'I only missed a day or two.'

'That's all it takes sometimes.' The smiling doctor, who was beginning to grate on her, proffered a minute plastic cup with some tablets inside. She didn't bother asking what they were. She just threw them in her mouth and took the water that he held towards her with his other hand.

'Good. Now don't give the care assistants any trouble and don't abscond or I'll come looking for you.'

He left in a bit of a flourish and Maggie rolled her eyes, but as soon as he was gone, her whole body sagged and her mind was once again assailed by thoughts of Grace Murphy. Grace was the reason why Maggie had to get better and get out of this goddamn hospital bed. She was also the reason why Maggie would eventually burn in hell when she finally did go ahead and die.

CHAPTER ELEVEN

'Cuppa?' Garda Mike Duggan placed a cup of milky tea on the desk beside his boss.

'Cheers,' Jerry replied automatically.

'See anything new?'

Jerry had photos of the three missing Cork men spread out on the desk in front of him. William Jones from Douglas, Joe Ferrier from Wilton and Terry Reynolds from Blackpool. An office manager, a salesman and an accountant. Three men with nothing in common except for the fact that they were missing.

'Tell me everything you know,' Jerry said, and he sat back and picked up his tea. He closed his eyes as his colleague started talking.

'William Jones, fifty-one years old from Douglas, originally from Passage West and working in a recruitment office on Oliver Plunkett Street. Separated from his wife of fifteen years, two daughters, both living with their mother. William rows with Shandon boat club and volunteers with Cork River Rescues. No online dating profiles, no closeted love affairs, no red flags. Joe Ferrier, forty-nine years old and living in Wilton. Happily married for twenty-two years, no kids and has a job selling insurance. Joe lost a twin brother to suicide at the age of nineteen and up until the time he disappeared, he spent most of his nights patrolling the bridges in town. Literally talking people down as far as I know. All round good guy and then there's fifty-three-year-old Terry Reynolds. An accountant from Blackpool, with an office on Grand Parade, Terry is on his second marriage. His first wife is happily living with her Spanish toyboy in the Costa del Sol. No ill will. Terry, however, is also active on several dating apps, despite his new wife. Had several hookups in the weeks before he disappeared and surprisingly, none of them used their real identities.'

'He's the odd one out.' Jerry opened his eyes.

'How you do mean?'

'A volunteer with Cork River Rescues and a guy who spends his nights talking people off ledges. There's every chance their paths may have crossed, or at least, they may have crossed paths with the same person. But Terry Reynolds?' He picked up the photo of Terry and studied it. Something about the man seemed familiar, but he couldn't place him. He didn't have a record, but Jerry was sure they'd met before. 'What do you have in common with these lads?' he said, almost to himself, but Mike answered almost flippantly.

'Well, they all wear suits to work.'

'Jerry?' Detective Paul Jenson popped his head in the door. 'Just spotted an ambulance outside *Jake's* a few minutes ago. Thought you might like to know.'

Jerry pulled out his mobile and found *Jake's* number.

'*Jake's*?'

'Hello, Grace.' His shoulders sagged at hearing her voice. 'Everything all right up there?'

'Jesus, Jerry, is nothing private anymore?'

He could hear a smile in her voice. 'Just checking in, that's all.'

'Well, as you don't seem to have any real crimes to be working on, Maggie keeled over and if you ask me, it was the butler in the kitchen with the candlestick.'

'Smart arse.'

'Are you coming up for lunch?'

'Not today. Contrary to popular belief, I actually do have some real crimes to solve.'

'Well, don't give yourself a heart attack or anything.'

'I'll do my best. Bye, Grace.'

Paul was smiling after having probably heard most of the conversation. 'She's all right then?'

'Grace Murphy is always all right,' Mike Duggan responded sarcastically.

Jerry looked at him, but didn't say anything. 'I need a bit of air.' He walked out, leaving the young Garda looking after him.

'What did I say?' he mumbled to Paul as Jerry left.

'How long are you on the job now, Mike?'

'Four years,' Mike responded, defensively.

Paul nodded, unimpressed. 'Well, I hope you never have to come upon a situation that'll change your life the way Grace Murphy changed his.'

Mike didn't respond as Paul left. He had the background information on Grace; they all did, but he didn't understand Jerry Hughes' interest in the woman. She was a tinker who used the fact that she had a shitty mother as an excuse for everything.

'The young lad is in there trying to figure out why anyone gives a shit about Grace.' Paul leaned on the bonnet of the squad car, beside his old partner and lit a cigarette for each of them.

Jerry grinned. 'Do you think he'll ever figure it out?'

Paul inhaled deeply. 'Not until he comes across his own one.'

'God knows, there's a lot more just like her scattered around this city, Paul.'

'Christ, I hope not.'

They smoked in silence for a few minutes.

'What are you thinking about those lads? Anything jumping out at you?'

Jerry took another drag and shook his head, blowing out a long stream of smoke. Christ, it tasted good. He'd been off the smokes for more than six years, but he liked to have one from time to time when he was working a case. They helped him to think. 'I feel like I've seen Terry Reynolds before, but I can't place where.' He looked at the half-smoked cigarette and lowered it back to his side. 'Mind you, I'm probably spending too much time staring at their faces. He's not in any of our systems so I don't know why I think I know him.' He shrugged and shook his head again. 'The boy did say something that wasn't entirely thick though.'

'Yeah? Like what?'

'They do all wear suits to work.' He crushed his butt under the sole of his boot and stood up. 'Anyway, they won't find themselves I suppose.'

Jerry went back to work, knowing that Paul would now spend some time looking into possible ways that Terry Reynolds and Jerry could have crossed paths. He and Paul had worked together for most of their careers and each of them followed the other's hunches, regardless of where they might lead. Often it was nowhere. But now that the feeling of familiarity had struck him, Jerry couldn't shake it, which begged the question, who was Terry Reynolds, really? Who were any of them?

CHAPTER TWELVE

G race carried two takeaway cups of coffee as she walked towards Maggie's ramshackle home at six thirty the following evening. She went out of her way to buy them at the petrol station, rather than at *Jake's* or Spar. She was wearing the black blazer jacket that she saved for times like this, with black jeans and boots. Her hair was tied back in a tight bun, which in itself made her almost unrecognisable. Grace never pulled her hair back like that. She wore a pair of reading glasses from the café's lost and found to complete the look of sophistication. She looked exactly like the kind of person who might need to meet with her auctioneer about a spare piece of property.

And there he was, walking around the front of the house, sizing it up. Maggie's place was a farmhouse, so ancient that the farm had been reduced to the patch of dead grass to the rear of the two-storey building. Several housing estates took up the remainder of the land as the city had grown around it over the past few decades. The roof was sagging and one of the upstairs sash windows didn't look like it closed properly. Just looking at the front of the house could trigger a fit of depression, like a bleak old haunted house from a Halloween movie. Grace had no idea if Maggie somehow owned this building or if she'd just been squatting there for most of her life. But she seriously doubted that there were deeds attached to the place. Still, Alan Manning didn't need to know any of that.

'Hi!' Grace smiled and offered him a cup. 'I guessed Americano with two sugars. We might need the warmth in there.' She turned on the charm and could immediately tell that it was the right tactic. His face broke into a smile as he took the cup from her.

'You guessed right, thank you. So...' he waved the cup in the direction of the house, 'this place belonged to your aunt?'

Grace nodded and pulled the bunch of keys out of her pocket. 'She passed away a while back and left this to me. To be honest, I haven't been in here in a very long time, so I'm not sure how bad it is.' She'd been to Maggie's house earlier that day, so Grace knew exactly how bad it was. She also knew which of the keys fit the front door lock, like a good niece would. She found it quickly and unlocked the door.

'Well, there's a big market for fixer-uppers at the moment. It's in a great location and actually,' he stepped back and looked at the house again, 'I imagine it has the potential to be divided up into a couple of rentable spaces.'

He took a sip of his coffee.

'Sounds good.' Grace shouldered open the door and stepped inside. The first thing to hit both of them was the smell. It was dark and very damp and possibly colder inside than it was outside. No wonder Maggie spent so much time at *Jake's*. Anywhere would be less depressing than this. It didn't seem to bother Alan Manning much though. He was well used to slumming it. Alan removed the lid from his coffee and took another, longer gulp this time. It would cool rapidly, just like them and he looked happy to let the aroma take over from the damp, mouldy stench. He swallowed and brought the cup to his lips again. Grace smiled.

He talked continuously as they walked through the house and made the perilous trip up the rotting staircase to the second floor, which clearly Maggie didn't do very often, because it was home to several multi-legged creatures, including a couple of ferrets. Frankly, it was unfit for human habitation.

'You don't remember me, do you?' Grace asked when they got back to the kitchen some fifteen minutes later.

He turned to look at her. 'Oh I'm sorry. Have we met before?' He put his hand to his head.

Grace nodded. 'I can see how you might not remember. Are you feeling okay?'

His face started to change. A hint of suspicion followed by a glimmer of disbelief as he looked at his cup. Grace liked this part. The slow, dawning realisation. He fell against the small table, which of course moved promptly out of his way and he hit the floor with a thump.

'I do believe you've been roofied, *Alan*,' Grace said, leaning over him. 'Or whatever you're calling yourself these days.' His eyes were open and he looked confused and a little panicked. But she'd given him enough that he wouldn't give her any trouble.

He'd lost a lot of weight, thanks to her, so it didn't take much to get him into the sleeping bag. Just some minor dragging and rolling and once he was zipped inside, she took his car keys from his pocket and went outside. She pulled the door closed behind her, but didn't feel the need to lock it. She wasn't worried about him somehow escaping while she sat in his parked car and reversed it right up to the front step. Aside from the council estate behind her, Maggie didn't have any neighbours as such. But by the time they were ready to leave, it was dark, cold and raining pretty hard. No one would be sticking their noses out in this. Still, Grace stood outside for a few minutes to make sure.

Soon it was a little darker and really bucketing down. She went back inside and slid the sleeping bag, feet first, towards the front door. She used a fireman's lift of sorts to get him into the boot of his own car. Grace learned the importance of physical strength at a young age, when she didn't have any. Not that she dressed in Lycra and frequented a gym with a wall of mirrors or anything like that. But she did have an old tractor tyre in her back garden, that she'd recovered from a bonfire a few years back. And the old mayonnaise buckets from *Jake's* which she'd filled with sand and rocks. She practised on these a few times a week, not so that she could look chiselled and fit. But so she'd never be the weaker target again.

It was a very short drive from Maggie's house to Grace's. She didn't drive through the estate though. Instead, she parked on the footpath near the back of the estate. Grace's was the third house in. She pulled the wheelbarrow out of the overgrown grass, where she'd left it, along with an old curtain, a giant teddy bear and a clear plastic bag full of aluminium cans for recycling. She removed the sodden teddy, curtain and bag from the wheelbarrow and dragged Alan, covered head to toe in his sleeping bag out of the boot and into the wheelbarrow. She bent his knees and wedged his feet inside. She quickly bundled the curtain on top and lay the bag of cans and the giant teddy across his body. She left the driver's side door open and the keys in the ignition as she shoved the wheelbarrow through her estate and in through her front door, knowing that no one would care what rubbish Grace Murphy was bringing to or from her house in a rusty wheelbarrow in the pissing rain. She also knew that the car would be gone in a matter of minutes and she was right on all counts.

CHAPTER THIRTEEN

The man was upset and he was alternating between anger, fear and self-justification. Right now he was feeling the need to justify why it had taken him almost two weeks to report his boyfriend missing.

'He wasn't my boyfriend! Well, I mean he *was,* but we broke up.' He pushed his glasses up along his nose, even though they hadn't slid. Not since he'd shoved them up five seconds earlier. It was a nervous tic, Jerry guessed.

'So when did you last see him, Mister Jacobs?'

'On the day we broke up. Two weeks ago, yesterday.'

'And what makes you think he's gone missing?' Mike asked. 'Maybe he's just not answering your calls.'

'He called me from work that day to say that he'd left his wallet at my place the night before. We had a fight, broke up and he left in a hurry. I told him he'd also left his AirPods and that I wanted my front door key back. He could use Google pay in place of his wallet and he would be in no hurry to return my key because he could be a fucker that way. But he'd just bought those AirPods and there's no way he'd leave them to me. His phone started going to voicemail so I called his work. The secretary said he hadn't been in for almost two weeks and she couldn't reach him.'

Jerry raised his eyebrows. 'He doesn't turn up to work for two weeks and his secretary doesn't think to call someone?'

He bobbed his head from side to side. 'Technically she's not *his* secretary. They do hot desks there. I'm not sure if she's a secretary exactly, but she looks after the place and answers calls at a main switchboard-type thing and then she can let you know if whoever you're looking for is there today. Alan was hot-desking there for a few months, but then a little cubby of an office came free and he decided to take it. He only put his nameplate up outside the week before.'

'So this manager would have been used to seeing him coming and going irregularly?'

Leonard Jacobs shrugged his shoulders. 'He worked from home as much as he worked in there, so yeah. I suppose she would.'

'Maybe he's just busy working from home then?'

'Detective, Alan and I have been together for six years. We break up regularly. A week is the longest we ever stay apart and we'll always respond eventually, even if it's a bitchy remark or a *screw you* text. His family haven't heard from him, not that that means much, but neither have any of his friends. His phone is dead. Whatever else happens, that does not. Alan can't breathe without his phone in his hand. Nobody has heard from him. He's missing.'

The desk sergeant placed a printed photograph of Alan Manning on the desk in front of Jerry. He studied it closely. There was something familiar about him too.

'Was he involved with any charities or outreach?'

Leonard snorted. 'No.'

'Any frontline work, rescue services, work with the homeless; anything like that?'

85

'Alan didn't have a strong stomach, so no, nothing like that. He was an auctioneer. When it came to homes, he was all about the people who had them and the commission that he could get for them.'

'Has he ever had dealings with the Gardaí, that you know of?'

'What kind of dealings?'

'Any kind. Has he ever been in court for any reason? Has he ever been the victim of a crime? Has he ever been accused of a crime? Did he have any reason at all to cross paths with the likes of myself or my colleagues?'

The man shrugged and shook his head. 'Not that I know of.'

Jerry nodded and studied the photo of Alan Manning again. 'Okay, Mister Jacobs. We have your information. We'll send someone around to take a look through his stuff in a while and we'll take it from here. In the meantime, if Alan should get in touch, please do let us know. Otherwise, we'll speak to you again in due course.'

Jerry and Mike got to their feet and so did a worried and slightly bewildered Leonard Jacobs. He seemed reluctant to leave which wasn't unusual. Often the victim of a crime, or indeed their family members felt that as soon as they left, it became a waiting game. A feeling of powerlessness came with leaving a Garda station with assurances like *We'll speak to you again in due course.* Jerry walked them as far as the door of the interview room and let Mike take him the rest of the way. He returned minutes later with Paul in tow.

'Another one?' Paul asked, as Jerry added Alan Manning's photo to the whiteboard, beside the other three.

'Take a look at them, Paul. Why do they look familiar?'

'Probably because you've been staring at them for months now,' Mike replied and perhaps he was right.

'Alan Manning is not involved in any frontline work and

he's gay. Again, nothing in common with these other men, but they are linked somehow.'

'Well,' Mike sat back against the desk, 'I suppose they all have the same colour hair.'

Jerry looked at him and then looked back at the photos. They did. A cross between ginger and blond. What was that called?

'And they're all around the same size and shape,' Paul added.

'And age bracket,' Jerry mumbled. 'Fifty-three, fifty-four, forty-nine and fifty-one.'

They sat quietly looking at the photographic line-up until Jerry spoke again. 'And they all wear suits. Good man, Mike.'

Mike looked at him. 'Seriously? You think someone is killing these guys off for being old ginger codgers in badly cut suits?'

'Who said anything about killing them off?'

'So where are they? Big boys like them aren't that easy to hide.'

'Where are they indeed?'

CHAPTER FOURTEEN

GARDA JERRY HUGHES – 2009

'Hi, Jerry!'

'Oh, here comes trouble,' Jerry responded with a smile.

It wasn't quite accurate to say that he looked forward to seeing her strut into the station, like she owned the place. But it brought him a certain peace. Grace had been coming in at least once a week for over four years, ever since he'd given her money for her non-existent school lunch when she was ten. She came in her old, ill-fitting and dirty clothes with a head of hair that you wouldn't see on a scarecrow. Sometimes she came bruised or walking in way that told him she was hurting. But she always gave the kind of excuse that befitted the child that she was. He'd send social services on those days, but by the time they actually went to the house or gained access to Grace, the bruises were gone and nothing was done. But she always left the Bridewell Garda Station with some form of food in her belly and some cash in her pocket. Nothing that would make up for the life the poor child was living. But at the very least, he wanted her to leave feeling like she'd had a small win that day, which to be fair, wasn't too much to ask. Not for a child who was so used to losing.

'Guess what?' She was beaming.

'What?'

'It's my birthday today! I'm fourteen. I'm an adult now.'

She sat on the row of plastic chairs and he could smell her from where he stood behind the desk. His heart broke for the child, as it did every time he saw her. But he didn't show her that.

'Christ, Grace, you're nearly as old as I am.' He smiled. He scribbled a note on a yellow Post-it and handed it to the young Garda who'd come to them from Templemore Training College that very morning.

The young lad looked at the note and then looked at Jerry, who glared at him in response. Grace was talking a mile a minute and didn't seem to notice the exchange, until the young Garda hurried past her and left the station.

'Where's he going in such a hurry? What was that look about, Jerry? What did he do to piss you off?' Then she jumped to her feet. 'Or was that about my mam? Is she okay? Did you send him out to get her?'

'You know, Grace, you'd make a great detective. All that time you've been gabbing like you're powered by Duracell, but still taking in everything around you. But to answer your questions; he's going to the shop, he didn't do anything to piss me off, *yet*; it wasn't about your mam and I didn't send him out to get her. And before you ask, no, I haven't seen your mother. Has she not been home?'

'Course she has,' she responded defensively. 'It's just that she gave me her last tenner to go get a chicken and some potatoes for dinner, but I've lost it.'

'Oh, well that's no good, is it?' He reached in his pocket and took out the tenner that had been rolled up in there for the past two days, waiting for her. 'Here. Some chicken money. Call it...'

'An investment in the future of the city that you love,' Grace said, finishing the sentence for him as she walked over to the desk and took the money with a flourish.

'Exactly.'

The young Garda returned a few minutes later carrying a plastic carrier bag.

'What'll I...' he began.

'Do I really need to explain, Martin?' Jerry responded. 'Because if I do, you'll be on the next bus back to Templemore. I'll stick on the kettle. Cuppa, Gracie?'

'Yes please.' She sat back down. 'Just so you know, Martin; I'm allowed in here whenever I like,' she said, matter-of-factly. 'You're new, so you might not know that. But I am, aren't I, Jerry?'

'That's right,' Jerry replied solemnly.

Finally, Martin smiled and nodded at Jerry. He took the chocolate Swiss roll out of the bag, stuck some candles in it and lit them up. Then he joined Jerry in singing the only 'Happy Birthday' that fourteen-year-old Grace Murphy was likely to get, and the look on her face was all the explanation that the young Garda needed. She lit up like a Christmas tree.

Two slices of Swiss roll and a mug of hot tea later, Jerry boxed up the remaining cake. 'Take that home to your sister.' He handed the bag to Grace. 'Get straight home now, Grace. It'll be getting dark soon.' Jerry knew better than to offer Grace a lift home. Even a lift *nearly* home could land her in trouble and Lord knows, she had enough of that. The Bridewell was a safe haven for Grace. The first sign of her getting pally with the cops and Liz Murphy would put a violent stop to it.

She stood up and wiped the crumbs off her jumper. 'Bye then.'

'See ya, Gracie.'

'Nice to meet you, Grace,' Martin said with a genuine smile and with that, she was gone.

———

Two hours after Grace left the Bridewell, Jerry and Martin were on patrol when the call came through dispatch. Reports of screaming from inside a house. The address that followed was one that Jerry knew by heart. It was Grace's house. Blue lights and Jerry's heavy boot propelled them through the city as they responded to the call in record time. The car screeched to a halt outside the Murphy house and the noise from inside could still be heard over the shouts and calls of the neighbours who had gathered on the green outside.

'Someone's being killed in there!' a woman shouted out from the crowd.

It certainly sounded that way and there was more than one person screaming inside. Jerry ran at the door, his shoulder colliding with it but it didn't budge. He used his fists and started pounding as hard as he could, but no one answered. The screams didn't sound like they were coming from a human being.

'Grace! Liz? Open up, it's the Gardaí!' he roared and began shouldering the door to no avail. 'Unlock the fucking door!' he shouted, his voice catching in his throat.

He looked around, feeling his own panic rise in his chest. He grabbed a brick that rested in the weeds at the front of the house and he used it to smash the pane of glass in the front door.

He stuck his hand through, catching it on a shard of glass and opening the skin on his palm before he could unlock the door and stumble into the hall. Martin, to his credit, ran back to the car and called for back-up.

What greeted Jerry inside that house would change his life forever. A fourteen-year-old girl, drenched in blood and wailing like a feral animal. A man in a suit lying on the floor, his face a bloody pulp. Liz Murphy, also bloody and screaming with her hands to her head.

'Grace,' Jerry said softly, though his voice shook. He held his hand out towards her but didn't go any closer. 'It's me, Grace. It's Jerry. Can you look at me?'

Grace had stopped screaming, but she was breathing very heavily. A low guttural sound came from her belly and out through her clenched teeth. Her eyes were wild. This was not the cheeky little birthday girl who'd left the station with her cake and a smile two hours earlier. She looked demonic, standing there holding a cast-iron poker in her hand with blood dripping from its end. Another siren could be heard approaching.

There was a sharp intake of air behind him as Martin stepped into the hall and quickly covered his face with both hands. Just like that, he was in the deepest end of his chosen new career.

'Jesus, Mary and Joseph, she's after killing a fella!' One of the neighbours was in the door behind Martin, who realised his mistake too late.

He turned and shoved the woman back outside, but the damage was done. In that moment, Grace Murphy's notoriety was cemented in history, regardless of what had actually happened in that house, on that day and all the days leading up to it. Martin seemed only too happy to remain outside and deal with crowd control, while inside, Jerry was in hell. But at that moment he still didn't know that the scene before him was only the preamble to the nightmare.

'Grace?' His voice was softer than he'd ever heard it. 'Grace, my love; look at me. Please.'

She did.

'It's okay, Grace.' He held out his hand and looked at the poker.

Slowly and silently she handed it to him.

'That's the girl. It's okay. I'm going to check his neck; see what's going on with him.' He nodded towards the man on the floor but was careful not to show too much sympathy towards him. Whatever had happened here, he doubted very much that the man on the floor was an innocent bystander and Grace needed Jerry to be on *her* side for now.

'She fucking...' Liz screeched.

'Shut up, Liz,' Jerry said, in the same soft tone. 'Are you hurt?'

'Yes, I'm fucking hurt! She...'

'You'll be seen to in a minute. Martin!' he called.

Martin reluctantly came to the door.

'Bring Mrs Murphy out to the car until an ambulance gets here. Tell them we'll be needing three ambulances.' He leaned down and felt the carotid artery of the man on the floor. He was alive, but barely. 'The first one is for him. Then Gracie.'

'It's the fucking squad car she should be going in!' Liz was hysterical, but even her voice shook now and that was something. It took a lot to spook Liz Murphy, but the look on her face said that she was afraid of her daughter. She was used to it being the other way around and she looked deeply disturbed by her new reality.

'Get her outside, Martin, and tell the ambulances to get a move on.'

Martin wrestled Liz out the door and pulled it closed

behind him, to keep the neighbours at bay. He had the sense to put it on the latch so that help could get in when they arrived.

Grace was still standing in the same spot she'd been occupying when Jerry arrived. Still staring at the floor, her squared shoulders moving up and down with her breathing and her hand still holding an imaginary poker. 'Where are you hurt, Grace? What did he do to you?'

She didn't respond. She didn't move.

Then Jerry heard a sound from upstairs. At first he wasn't sure he'd actually heard it. It had gone from deafeningly noisy to eerily quiet in the space of a few minutes. But then he heard it again.

'Is Amber here, Grace?'

She still didn't respond in any way. Her face was completely blank.

The front door opened and Garda Stephanie Casey stepped inside. She too stopped short, but recovered herself with the professionalism that she was known for.

'Grace, this is my friend, Stephanie. She's going to stay right here with you for just a minute, while I go and check on your sister. Is that okay?'

Stephanie nodded, but Grace was gone. Her body was still there, unmoving before him, but the little girl was gone.

'No one other than a paramedic gets through that door, Steph.'

'Go,' she whispered, 'find the other one.' Stephanie had lost all colour from her face and looked suddenly unwell.

He moved slowly towards the stairs, his stomach rising higher with each step that he took. At the top of the stairs, he glanced in the open bathroom door. It was filthy, but empty as was Liz's room. He gently pushed open the door to Grace's room. There was nowhere for his sadness to spread tonight. His fear was too great. Fear of what he was about to find, because he knew that he was about to find something awful. Something that would make a child beat a man almost to death with a poker. He paused outside Amber's bedroom and took a breath. He knocked gently, hoping for a response that he knew wouldn't come. He took another breath and slowly opened the door.

Ten-year-old Amber Murphy was lying on her side on her heavily soiled bed. The sight of her told him everything he needed to know. 'Jesus.' Jerry covered his mouth with his hand and hot tears burst from him as he ran to her. 'Amber?' He took off his coat and covered her broken body. 'Steph!' he called, and his voice cracked dramatically. 'Steph!'

'Yes, Jerry?' she replied calmly from the bottom of the stairs, but he could hear the dread in her tone.

'Get a fucking ambulance here NOW! And no one gets in it before Amber Murphy. Not that fucker on the floor; NOBODY!' He was crying, something he'd never done on the job before, and she could probably hear that. But she wouldn't question his authority.

Steph was straight on the radio. Back in the Bridewell, they joked that Jerry had a stomach of steel. He could walk into any scene or come upon any situation and handle it like no one else could. Then go and eat his lunch as if it was nothing. He was certainly not a man who cried. That all changed in Amber Murphy's bedroom that day and when Steph called his name again, as a question this time, loaded with apprehension, he responded with, 'Don't come up.'

Jerry would never be the same after this, but while the whole world should know what happened here, and what that beast had done, no one else should ever have to see it.

CHAPTER FIFTEEN

PRESENT DAY

She'd done the roast potatoes in goose fat and made the gravy from the roast chicken's juices. The peas were from a tin, but she didn't think Maggie would mind that too much. She had thought about doing a lasagne, but Maggie was more of a meat and veg kind of woman. Actually, Maggie was a beans straight from the tin kind of woman, but Grace imagined that if someone were to offer Maggie the dinner of her dreams, like on death row, right before they kill you, she'd ask for a Sunday roast with all the trimmings.

Grace made enough for her own dinner and a plate for Amber. The rest she dished up onto two paper plates and covered them with tin foil. When Maggie came coughing and spluttering through the door of *Jake's* the next morning, Grace was glad that she'd gone to the trouble.

'Welcome back, Maggie.' Grace smiled at her as she all but fell into her usual seat, with her back to the wall and the large window beside her.

'What a fucking hullabaloo.' Maggie waved away her greeting. 'Promise me this, Grace; next time I go down in a heap, just leave me. Don't call those fucking butchers to cart me off in that yellow box on wheels. I tell ya, I was worse off inside in that hospital. I'm sure I picked up five new diseases in there and the so-called *doctors*! Sure, they don't know their arse from their elbows. Still in nappies, half of them and the other half can't speak Cork.'

'So you enjoyed your stay then?'

Maggie hacked and choked for a full three minutes. 'See? I'm fucking worse.'

'Tea, coffee or cat piss, Mag?'

'Christ, gi'me tea, Grace. Nice and safe.'

There was a storm forecast and it was starting to rage outside. Rain blew sideways past the open door, which banged shut, causing the pane of glass to shake, but not shatter. It was going to be a quiet day, so Grace poured herself an Americano and went to join Maggie. She really was glad to have her back. Grace felt safer somehow when she was there. She put their cups on the table and went back behind the counter to fetch the plates of roast dinner.

'Here.' She placed them on the table in front of Maggie and sat down opposite her.

'What are those?' Maggie lifted the tinfoil on one.

'The chicken is from the English Market and I roasted the spuds in goose fat.'

'You made these for me?'

Grace nodded and Maggie looked like she might cry. But she had a coughing fit instead.

Grace drank her coffee and eventually, Maggie tackled her tea.

'Don't die on me, Mag,' Grace mumbled.

Maggie looked surprised. 'Well... I mean, I probably will at some stage, Gracie. I've been mocking the Reaper for a few years now and he's getting really fed up with me.'

'He's no match for you.'

Maggie looked at Grace for a long minute before speaking again. 'Do you remember the first time you met me, Grace?'

Grace had to think about that one. She felt like she'd known Maggie, to see at least, for most of her life. 'No. Well, aside from when you clocked old Reilly on the head with your handbag.' She grinned and looked at the bag resting on top of Maggie's shopping trolly. 'That one there, if I'm not mistaken.'

Maggie chuckled mischievously. 'Ah, I knew you since you were born. But I only really noticed you properly, that day.'

'What, when you caught me robbing Reilly?'

'Everyone robbed that mean bastard. No. Your fourteenth birthday.'

Grace got to her feet and took her cup with her. Everyone in Ireland got to know Grace Murphy on the day of her fourteenth birthday. No one gave a shit before that.

'I did a spell in there myself, you know,' Maggie continued, as if Grace hadn't walked away and signalled the end of the conversation. 'In the big Dublin nuthouse.'

Grace didn't respond. She didn't want to talk about this.

'No place for a child, that.'

'I survived,' Grace mumbled.

'That's what you are, Grace. A survivor. Like me.'

'Is this your way of telling me that my roast dinner is just another thing that you'll have to survive?' She didn't want to fight with Maggie. She needed her to keep passing her days as a buffer between Grace and the rest of the world.

Maggie grinned. 'No one's ever made me a dinner like this before.'

'Well, they have now. And one for tomorrow too.'

'Oh, neither of these will survive the night, Gracie. I'm going to have myself a fucking feast. Thank you, my love.'

'Lock her down, Grace.' Jake came barrelling through the door looking like he'd been washed in with the tide.

'What? Why?'

'This storm is going to cause carnage. I'm closing everywhere early.'

'But I'll still get paid, Jake.'

'You will if you help me with the sandbags.'

Grace dumped what was left of her coffee down the sink. 'And you'll drive Maggie home?'

Jake stopped what he was doing, looked at Maggie and sighed dramatically. 'Fine. Now start closing up shop. I want to get home before the worst of it hits and puts the city under water. Have you seen how high the tide is?'

'Now why the fuck would either of us be looking out at the tide, Fatso?' Maggie asked.

'Can't see the tide from here, Jake,' Grace answered, to save him having to respond to Maggie.

'Well, like I said; the city'll be underwater in a couple of hours, so let's get this done.'

Forty minutes later, *Jake's* was shuttered with sandbags built up outside. Not that they were likely to flood this high up, but that wasn't her call to make. Jake had reluctantly taken Maggie, her shopping cart and her dinners home and now Grace battled the raging wind and rain as she headed for Amber's house, with a third roast chicken dinner.

'Amber?' Grace slammed the door shut behind her, but the rain still followed her inside, leaving a small puddle on the hall floor. There was no response from Amber.

Grace went through to the kitchen and into the living room. Still no Amber. She went back out into the hall and from the bottom of the stairs, she shouted up, 'Amber, you up there?' No response. 'Damn it,' Grace muttered under her breath. She never went upstairs in this house anymore. Not since the day she left it. She hated it up there and so did Amber, which is why she almost always slept on the couch or in the armchair downstairs. But Grace needed to know that her sister was home and safe with the weather picking up the way it was.

The stairs creaked as she stood on the bottom step and in her mind she heard all the different creaks and groans that each step made. They played in her head like a long-forgotten tune. One of those godforsaken ones that, once you heard it, it would be stuck on a loop in your head forever more. Slowly, she did the old familiar dance, avoiding the musical steps like she'd done as a child. 'Am... Amber?' she called, her discomfort rising with each upward step. She passed her mother's open bedroom door without looking in. Amber would never go in there. She closed her eyes and passed her old tomb. Then she stopped at Amber's door and knocked hesitantly. 'Amber?'

No response. She shoved open the door with her foot. The room was untouched from when she was a child. The smell was still there, but it had changed with time. The old wardrobe where they'd hidden food among their soiled clothes and blankets. Amber's metal-framed bed, stained mattress and an old woollen blanket balled on top. She wasn't there. Grace pulled the door closed and pressed herself against the wall, breathing heavily with... relief, maybe? Yes, relief.

If Amber had come upstairs in this house, it would probably be to kill herself. They had no other reason to come up. Grace had been asking Amber to come live with her for years, but she wouldn't. For reasons only she knew, Amber would never leave their hellish childhood home. She hurried back downstairs and only when she reached the kitchen did she take out her phone. She tried Amber's number first, knowing that it would go to voicemail. Then she dialled the only other number she knew by heart.

'Grace, everything all right?'

'Are you working today, Jerry?'

'I'm always working, Grace. What's up? Are you okay?'

'If you're down around town, can you keep an eye out for Amber? She's not at home and according to Jake, the city is going to be underwater in a couple of hours. What if she's passed out somewhere?'

'I haven't seen her around for a while.'

'She's around all right. She's doing her best to kick the gear, but it's not easy for her.'

'When was the last time you saw her?'

'Yesterday morning. I brought her food on my way to work and she was home then. I just called with dinner and there's no sign of her, which means she's downtown.'

'Okay, Grace. I'll take the car for a spin in a little while. I have stuff to do downtown anyway so I'll keep my eyes peeled.'

'Thanks, Jerry.'

'Mind yourself, Grace.'

CHAPTER SIXTEEN

'Can you hear that?' Grace stood in the doorway of the box room.

He didn't respond. He'd been weakened by his last visit to her house and it seemed this time, his body wasn't holding up as well. He couldn't even lift his head.

'Because of you, my sister is out in that weather. She's sticking a needle in her arm so that she can forget what you did to her.'

He dragged his head up now and tried to speak, but his voice had abandoned him. He'd only choke on his own lies anyway.

'I let you go. You should have learned from it, but you didn't. Instead, you swanned around the city like you still own it. Like you own everyone in it.' She walked over to him and shoved two pills into his mouth, clamped his jaw shut and blocked his nose until he started thrashing. 'You don't own me,' she said through gritted teeth. 'Do you hear me?'

He struggled as hard as his restraints and weakened body would allow.

'I said, do you hear me?' she shouted. Grace didn't normally shout, but she was worried about her sister and that was his fault.

She let go of him and he started shaking.

'Go on. Shake, shit yourself, cry, see if I care. I'm not letting you go this time, you might as well know that.' She went up to him again, stepping in the fetid pool around him. 'Who's a good girl now, hmm?'

CHAPTER SEVENTEEN

Jerry had no real reason to go downtown and it would be traffic carnage in this weather. But he needed a break from staring at the faces of the missing men and rummaging through their lives. By now he was almost convinced he'd met them all at some stage. That they *all* looked familiar, even though he'd never clapped eyes on any of them before in his life. That had been pretty much confirmed. None of them had had run-ins with the law and before they'd gone missing, he'd never heard any of their names before. So why did he feel like he somehow knew each of them?

'This case is trying to tell me something,' he mumbled to Mike.

'Oh yeah? What's it trying to tell you?'

'That I've been doing this crap for too long. Maybe it's time to take my ass out to pasture on the Costa del Sol, what do you think?' He stood up and pulled his jacket off the back of the chair.

Wisely, Mike didn't answer that. Instead he asked, 'Where are we off to?'

'I just need to take a break. Maybe go look for some trouble downtown for a while. You can stay put if you want, it's miserable out there.'

'Well, I was just about to root my Nespresso pods out of my desk drawer.'

'You're a miserable little shit, you know that?' Jerry laughed. 'Hiding the bloody coffee.'

'Correction; hiding *my* expensive bloody coffee.' He grinned. 'You sure you want to head out in that?'

'Enjoy your illicit coffee, you mean bastard. I'll bring you back a chicken-fillet roll?'

'You're a good man, Jerry. Enjoy the spin.'

It seemed people lacked the common sense to get out of the city while they had the chance, because the quays were a mess. Jerry sat in his squad car, bumper to bumper, keeping his eyes open for Amber Murphy. But even the homeless and addicts were out of sight for the most part. He wanted to find her, in whatever state she might be in, just to know that she was still alive. He worried about her almost as much as Grace did. Since the age of ten, probably longer, the girl's life had been a series of car crashes. By the age of twelve she'd discovered that drugs could take her away from her reality and there wasn't a foster home in the county that could hold her.

She'd been picked up for solicitation, possession, theft, assault and dealing and that was just by the Guards. She was also a frequent flier for the ambulance service. Jerry himself had given her Naloxone on two occasions, bringing her back to her shitty old life. Both times she'd cried. Once when she was sixteen and again about two years ago. She'd been abused and neglected every day of her life and when someone else wasn't doing it, she did it to herself. But until the day that her misery finally ended, Jerry would never refuse Grace and Amber what little help he could give. They'd been denied it by so many throughout their lives.

'Fuck this,' he muttered, looking in his rear-view mirror at the car that was pressed against his back bumper. He inched his way left, ignoring the blast of car horns directed at him and pulled into a loading bay. He grabbed his raincoat off the back seat, zipped himself in and took himself for a walk.

The usual down-and-out faces sat in their usual spots, despite the weather. Jerry didn't allow himself to consider their personal circumstances. The paths that had led them to the bottom of their bottle or to the sharp end of a dirty needle. He couldn't. In order to do his job effectively, he could only see them for what they'd become. The Murphy sisters were proof of this.

'Hey, Rolo. How're tricks?'

The boy was in his mid-twenties and not dressed for the weather.

'Is your friend there all right?'

He looked at the old man slumped on the bench beside him. The older man let out a groan and swatted something that only existed in his mind.

'That's Roger... or Redmond; something like that.' Rolo spoke with a monotone and didn't look up at Jerry.

Actually his name was Roy and he usually hung out by The Lough. For some reason he'd ventured into town and Jerry kicked the sole of his boot. 'Hey, Roy!' he called loudly.

The man stirred and lifted his heavy head enough to throw Jerry a dirty look. 'What do you want out in this weather harassing innocent people, Hughes? Have you nothing better to be doing?'

'The pair of you will end up in the Lee before the night is

out if you stay here. Will you head over to Simon early and get in out of it?' He knew they wouldn't.

Roy rolled his eyes and then closed them again, while Rolo snorted out a laugh.

'Roy?' Jerry kicked his boot again.

Roy tutted and opened his eyes again. He was still slumped over in the same position, hardly moving a muscle as he looked up at Jerry again, conserving what little energy he had.

'When was the last time you saw Amber Murphy?'

'Amber?' Roy barked, half a laugh, half a gurgling cough. 'What did she do now?'

'Can you answer the question?'

'Who's Amber Murphy?' Rolo asked.

'Can't you leave the young one alone, Jerry? She bothers no one, only herself.'

Jerry was holding a photograph in front of Rolo's face.

'She's all right, isn't she?' he perked up.

Even after the drugs had taken a hold, through the scabs on her face, the sunken eyes, the dirty limp hair, Amber's beauty was still evident. Many still saw her and took what they wanted from her and Amber had all but given up fighting. Except for the time she smashed a vodka bottle off a guy's head and used the shards to slice open his face. The man had been ugly before he met Amber, but his face was now the reason why so many people avoided the Bishop Lucey Park in Cork city.

'She's not in any trouble,' Jerry said, looking pointedly at Rolo.

He looked back at Jerry for a minute. 'So why are the cops looking for her?'

'The cops aren't. *I* am.'

'Oh, I see.' Rolo grinned. 'Slumming it are ya?'

Roy straightened up now and kicked Rolo in the side of the ankle. Rolo glanced in Roy's direction, then straightened himself up and cleared his throat, spitting a brown glob onto the ground. 'I haven't seen her in weeks,' he finally said.

'Where was she, when you last saw her?'

'Fitzgerald's Park. But that was weeks ago. I doubt she's still out there.' He chuckled.

'I saw her just there,' Roy pointed towards the next bench up, 'but that was a good while ago too. I assumed she was in a hospital somewhere. Or maybe the morgue.'

Jerry put the photo back in his pocket and pulled his hood up tighter. 'Go find somewhere more sheltered than this, lads. The pair of you will be drowned before the night is out.' He shoved his hands deep into his pockets and walked on, all the way up the quays to St Patrick's Bridge. He spoke to six more of the quay's fixtures on the way. Those who could speak to him, did. They knew him. Knew he wasn't there to hassle them, but none of them had seen Amber. He walked up Patrick Street, through the Bishop Lucey Park and back down South Mall. Amber wasn't out and about in the city centre and according to those who were, she hadn't been for some time.

CHAPTER EIGHTEEN

'You scared the shit out of me!' Grace put her hands on Amber's shoulders to shake her awake, but she stopped herself. She could never hurt or frighten Amber.

Amber, for her part, didn't notice. She'd had her medicine and was sleeping soundly. Or at least, that's what Grace told herself. She'd never tried heroin, so she had no idea what kind of "sleep" a person had while it was in their system. But Amber always looked peaceful after she'd had a fix and it was the only time she did.

Grace gently lifted her sister's head and sat down beside her on the couch, resting her head back in her lap. She stroked her hair. 'I've got him, Amber.' She spoke softly. Almost in a whisper. 'He's paying for what he did to you. To *us*.'

She hadn't said that to Amber before; the *us* part. Amber didn't know anything about what went on in her sister's bedroom at night and that's how Grace wanted it. If Grace had been in her bedroom that day, where she was supposed to be, instead of stuffing her face with birthday cake in town, Amber would have been safe. He wouldn't have noticed her and she would never have had to stick a needle in her arm. Grace could handle it. But Amber was her baby sister. She was just a child.

If Amber heard her, she didn't reply. But Grace was certain that she saw a small smile play on her sister's dry, chapped lips.

'I've got him, my love.' She kissed the top of her sister's head and gently slipped out from under her. She removed the half-eaten chicken dinner from the folding table and scraped the remainder into the small kitchen bin. She removed the bag, tied a knot in the top and let herself quietly out the back door. She put the bag of rubbish in the wheelie bin and headed for home, with a dirty plate in her hand and a contented smile on her lips.

Grace's phone rang as she walked across the green towards her own house. She was drenched to the skin now, but she didn't mind. Her sister was home and safe and that knowledge kept her warm.

'Jerry! She's home. I should have called you back, but I wasn't thinking. I hope you didn't get too wet.'

Jerry exhaled on the other end of the line and Grace could have kicked herself. Jerry was as decent as they come, despite being a Garda. She should have remembered that she'd asked him to go out in this weather. She should have remembered that he'd be worried about Amber too.

'Well, that's good news,' he said.

Then they were silent for a bit. She didn't want to say the words out loud; to explain that she'd probably been out to see her dealer and Grace had overreacted, though he probably knew as much.

'I spoke to a few of her friends downtown and it seems none of them have seen her for a few weeks?'

'They're not her friends, Jerry. You know that as well as I do. None of them care about Amber.'

'You're not wrong there, Grace.' He paused, then, 'Still and all, she doesn't normally stay away for that long. Is everything all right with Amber, Gracie?'

'Amber is better than ever, Jerry. She's sleeping in her own home, instead of whatever shithole she falls over in. She's having hot dinners every day too.' Though she's hardly eating anything, but she didn't tell him that.

'That's great to hear.' He sounded genuinely pleased. He didn't ask if she was still using, because he knew the answer. Any and all attempts that were made over the years to clean the poison out of Amber's body, had failed from the off. She was too far gone and she had every right to be. But Grace knew that once she'd dealt with the man who ruined her life, Amber would *want* to get clean. To get her life back. She'd move in with her sister and Grace would get her a job at *Jake's*. She'd be happy. For the first time in Amber's life, she'd be happy. And Grace would make that happen even if it killed her.

CHAPTER NINETEEN

J erry was sitting alone, staring once more at the faces on the whiteboard. He kept them right there in front of him while he worked through their information. He needed to keep them fresh in his mind at all times. Not that they had many opportunities to venture elsewhere, but he had to hope that something, anything new might jump out at him. Or at someone else.

They were also there to remind the whole team that they were four individual men. They had four individual lives and four individual sets of circumstances. They needed to be investigated as such. Again, not altogether necessary, but what else was he going to do? Each picture was surrounded by each man's details; timelines of their last-known movements, CCTV images and anything else that might point to their whereabouts.

'It's Sunday. Don't you ever go home?' Stephanie Casey had popped her head into the small conference room.

He smiled at his old friend. 'All right, Steph. How are they all below in Midleton?'

Stephanie left the force six months after walking into Liz Murphy's house. Seventeen years as a Cork City Garda and that day was the one that finished her. It forced her to make a decision she hadn't realised she'd been debating over. Now she drove a taxi part-time and was the proud parent of a UCC graduate, her only daughter, Pennie, who was exactly fourteen days younger than Amber Murphy.

'Ah, you know yourself.'

He nodded. 'I suppose I do.'

Steph was carrying two cups of coffee from Spar. She often popped into the station unannounced and Jerry knew that she missed the place. The banter with the lads and the occasional action. He also suspected that she called to remind herself of all the reasons why she left.

'What do you think about these lads?' He took a steaming cup from her and gestured towards the board. Steph had a sharp eye and an even sharper mind and Jerry was always glad to see her. Everyone was. To this day, Steph was missed around the place by anyone who'd worked with her. She was a woman who could banter and put someone firmly in their box at the same time, without taking a breath or breaking a sweat. She also had an incredible eye for detail.

'Yeah, I was thinking about them.' She sat down beside him and removed the plastic lid from her cup. 'That fella there,' she pointed to Terry Reynold's photo, 'why do I think I know him?'

'You too?'

She looked at him. 'Have we come across him before?'

'Nope.' Jerry took a sip and burned his tongue.

'You have to admit, they all look a little bit alike, don't they?' This was the real reason why Steph was here today and she knew that Jerry would be too.

He looked at each of them again. It wasn't blatantly obvious, but there were certainly similarities. They all had different haircuts, but they all had a hint of ginger in their blondish hair. Alan Manning's head was tightly shaved, but the colour showed through in his goatee. They were all around the same height, around five ten and broadly built.

'They do a bit.' Jerry was drumming his fingers on the table now.

'Jerry?'

'You have a theory, Steph, and I'd love to hear it.'

'Not so much a theory, but *The Examiner* ran a feature about the missing men yesterday. They had a full page taken up with their photos, did you see it?'

Jerry shook his head. 'I'm leaving the tabloids alone at the minute. I can do without the conjecture.'

'Agreed. But you know the types of photos that always show up? The ones that paint a picture of an innocent and happy person enjoying their life? Well, one of the photos of Terry Reynolds, smiling like the cat who got the cream; it gave me a bit of a jolt.'

He turned to look at her now.

'I got a sudden flashback of a similar feature. The one about Philip Munroe. Do you remember that picture of him, laughing with his friends at a party?'

She said the name Philip Munroe, like the combination of syllables might summon the devil himself. He was the man who had destroyed Amber Murphy and no doubt, Grace too.

Jerry's eyes whipped back to the whiteboard and as if seeing the images for the first time, he knew where he knew those men from. Not *those* men specifically, but Steph was right. That's who they reminded him of. *That's* why they looked so familiar! They were all physical versions of Philip Munroe.

CHAPTER TWENTY

MAGGIE – 1977

'You're so beautiful, you know that, Mag?'

Maggie smiled up at him. Paddy Wilson was so far out of her league that lying there with her head in his lap, him playing with her hair, telling her that he loved her, was enough to make her giddy. He was a stunning man; a foot or so taller than her, broad with handsome green eyes. Paddy hadn't had it easy in life, but it wouldn't break him. Nothing could break this man.

'It won't be long now til I'm dancing you up the aisle, girl.'

She sat up and looked at him. Was he asking her to marry him?

'I can picture you now, in a flowing white dress, flowers in your hair and that smile.' He cupped her chin in his massive hands and kissed her tenderly.

'Really? You want to marry me?'

He laughed. 'Of course I want to marry you! I know I've been an idiot, Mag, but I've always loved you, you know that. But first, we have a few things to do like,' he looked around at the damp bedsit that had been his courtesy of Cork County

Council for over two years, 'upgrade our living conditions,' he said.

Maggie looked too at the black mould that crept down the walls where the green, floral wallpaper had peeled away. It might have bothered her once. It was, after all, a far cry from where she'd started out in life. But she'd been in a lot of other places since then and compared to most, this wasn't so bad. He'd only just moved her in and in all honesty, she didn't care what their room looked like. So long as Paddy was in it with her. 'It's not so bad, Pad.'

He sat back and looked at her appraisingly. 'You shouldn't settle, Mag. You deserve better than this. You deserve a house with three bedrooms, for all the kids we'll have together.'

Maggie looked at the mouldy wall again and tried not to think about the three kids she already had. The last two were taken off her and put in foster care within weeks of being born. She had no idea where they were now. And then there was her girl. Her and Paddy's. Twelve years she'd managed to hang on to her, but she saw so little of her that the social workers didn't seem to know she existed. Neither did Paddy, come to that. He panicked when Maggie said she was pregnant, then he came and went right up until their daughter was born. But as soon as Maggie went away to give birth, Paddy went another way. It broke her heart when he left her that time and she never forgave their little girl for it.

Of course, Paddy didn't know about the two that followed, but Maggie had to do what she had to do to survive when he left her. He'd been in and out of her life so much during those twelve years that all three might have been his for all she knew. But things were different this time. Things were good, so it was no time to start speculating. Now that Paddy was back, she would not lose him again.

'Did I say something wrong?' Paddy asked.

Maggie shook her head. 'Just thinking about our girl.' She sounded sheepish just mentioning her.

'That's right, yeah.' His fingers stopped stroking her. 'You went ahead and had that, didn't you? How old would she be now?'

'She'll be twelve.'

'Jeez, is she that age already?'

'Time doesn't be long going, does it, Pad?'

'True. And where is she?'

Maggie shrugged. 'My neighbour is minding her.'

Paddy looked confused. 'Your neighbour?'

She nodded, feeling her bottom lip start to tremble.

'Maggie, you were living in a tent two weeks ago. What neighbours did you have?'

There was a knock on the door before she had to answer him.

Paddy got to his feet and pulled her up with him. 'Remember, Maggie: you deserve better than this place and together, we can save enough money to get out of here, get that gorgeous white dress and dance our way to the top of the church.' He kissed her tenderly and then gently nudged her back onto the bed – his only item of furniture, while he went to answer the door.

Maggie craned her neck to see who it was. Not that she knew many of Paddy's friends. She hadn't met them yet, but this guy didn't look like someone that Paddy would associate with. He was old; at least sixty with a voice that sounded like he'd been chewing nails. Not that she could hear what he was saying, but he and Paddy exchanged a few quiet words, then they both looked her way. The man handed Paddy some money and then Paddy turned towards her and smiled tenderly. Then he winked and left. The other man did not.

CHAPTER TWENTY-ONE

MAGGIE – 1979

When Maggie opened her eyes, it wasn't bright anymore. It had been when she asked Paddy to stay home with her. To not let anyone else in. Why did she have to torment him all the time? Why couldn't she have kept her damn mouth shut?

She cried as she tried to sit up, partly because she'd been so bloody stupid. But mostly she cried from the pain in her ribs. What if he didn't come back? Or what if he did and he told her to leave? She was on the floor between the bed and the wall, with no idea how she'd gotten there. There was no space there. She shoved the bed, which moved easily enough and then used it to lever herself up. She reached the light switch on the wall and turned it on, which hurt her fingers. Three of them were swollen. A circular bruise encompassed her wrist and there were welts on both legs from his belt.

Poor Paddy. He'd never forgive himself for this and it was her fault for being so selfish and needy. Here he was trying to create a better life for them and she did nothing but complain. It broke his heart to see other men with her. He'd said it so many times before that he'd swap places with her if he could. She smiled, imagining Paddy being felt up by a randy docker. God love him, he wouldn't know what to do with himself. She hugged her ribs and limped towards the window. She sat on the cold, damp sill and waited, watching the road below for his return, all the while saying silent prayers that he would.

It took a few days, but eventually he did come home and as soon as the door opened, he fell into her arms.

'I couldn't face you, Mag.' He hugged her close and then cupped her face in his hands. Tears pricked his eyes as he examined the damage he'd done. 'Christ, I'm so sorry, Maggie. I love you, you know that.'

'I know.' She cupped his face in return and looked into those handsome eyes, wishing she could take away his pain. 'It's all right, Pad. It was my own fault. You were tired. You weren't able for my whining.'

'I just hate it so much that you have to do that. I hate that it's the only way for us to make enough money to get out of this life. I'd trade places with you in a heartbeat if I could, you know I would.'

'Don't worry, it won't be for long more. We must be nearly there now.'

He nodded. 'We would be, if this place didn't cost so fucking much. They're bleeding us dry with the rent and bills on this old kip, Mag.'

Maggie's heart sank. 'So, how long more do you think?' The words barely came out. She didn't want to make him feel like he wasn't working hard enough, or that he was failing her in any way. But she needed to know how many more men needed to come through her door, and her body, before she could just be with the one man that she actually loved.

'I've been thinking about that, Mag.' He took her by the

hand and led her to the bed. He sat beside her and took both of her hands in his. 'That girl of yours; how old is she now?'

Maggie pulled her hand away.

'I'm only asking because I thought, well, you two should be together. She's your daughter, Maggie. She could come and stay here.'

'She's yours too, Pad.'

'Ah yeah, but you know what I mean. She doesn't know me from Adam, but she's yours outright. You should have her with you.'

Maggie looked around again. The front door was three feet from the bed and ten feet from the sink, fridge and hotplate. There was no space for one person, let alone three.

'I know what you're thinking. This place is tiny. But I've done nothing for the past few days, only try to think of a way out of this, Maggie. Can I tell you what I came up with?'

Maggie nodded hesitantly.

'Well, I've been to see this fella I know. I used to work with him down the dock, only these days he's working on that new housing estate out by the shopping centre. If we can get another few grand in the bank, one of those houses can be ours he reckons. Have you seen them?'

She had seen them. Beautiful rows of brand-new red-brick homes with white, double-glazed windows and PVC front doors. She imagined the inside; fitted kitchens with a dining table and chairs against one wall and a cosy sitting room with an open fire and a three-piece suite. Television in the corner and a spare room for her girl to call her own.

She nodded. They'd never afford one of those, surely. Still, the dream was growing in her mind and if anyone could make that dream a reality, it was Paddy Wilson.

'If we keep going the way we're going, it could be ours in six or eight months,' he paused, 'assuming they're not all snatched up by then.'

Six or eight months. Maggie's heart sank and tears welled in her eyes.

'But,' Paddy continued, 'if your girl came to stay with us, we could be out of here and into our new home in less than two months. The three of us could be a family there, Mag.'

Maggie pulled back and shook her head, but Paddy caught her hands again.

'I know, Mag. It's the last thing either of us would want to do. But I promise, she wouldn't have to do it all. I mean, she could just use her hands. Hands only for her, nothing more.' He gently brushed her hair back from her face and tucked it behind her ear. 'You're the most beautiful woman I know, Maggie. And if your girl looks anything like you, then honestly, I think we could be in our house in a matter of weeks. Then none of us will ever have to look at this life again. What do you say?'

Maggie thought about it. Hands wouldn't be so bad, especially if it meant that they could finally get out of here and be a normal family. 'But there's no room here for another person.'

'I know. I've been thinking about that too. I'll sleep in my car. That way you ladies can have your own space.'

'You can't sleep in your car, Paddy. You'd freeze.'

'And I'd be happy to do it for you, my love. Is that a yes? Are you ready to say goodbye to this dump?'

She took a deep breath and nodded. 'Okay, Pad.'

He smiled and stroked her hair again. 'That's my girl.' Then he lowered her onto her back and showed her once more how much he loved her.

CHAPTER TWENTY-TWO

PRESENT DAY

'The strongest coffee you have please, Grace.' Jerry smiled as he stepped inside *Jake's*.

'Oh Christ, here come the fuzz. Will you want a few doughnuts with that, officer?' Maggie cackled.

Grace smiled. 'Don't mind her, Jerry. Have a seat and Maggie there will stop tormenting you, any minute now.'

'Gracie, the day Maggie Hayes stops tormenting me, is the day I'll truly worry about her,' he replied good-naturedly. Jerry was always kind to Maggie, if you could call their relationship a kind one. They bounced insults off each other whenever they met, but they did it with affection. Deep down, they liked each other. Grace could tell.

'And the day Garda Hughes solves a crime, is the day I'll hand myself in for all of mine.' She grinned.

'I know a really good dentist, Mag. Let me know if you need his number. He's also a trained vet should there be anything else you require.'

Maggie laughed out loud and then coughed for a full five minutes.

Grace brought Jerry his usual; an Americano with an extra

shot and four sugars. He really should cut down on the amount of sugar he consumed, but she'd told him that once before. It wasn't her place to harp on about it. Then again, Jerry didn't have anyone else to tell him these things. He'd never married and as far as she knew, he lived alone. That was sad. He was a good man and he deserved more. But it wasn't her place to say that either.

She used to fantasise that Jerry was her dad when she was younger. That he'd go off to work in the morning carrying a packed lunch that she'd made for him. And when he came home in the evening, himself, Grace and Amber would curl up together on the couch and watch television with their dinners on their laps. He'd tell her all about the bad guys he locked up that day and he'd kill anyone who even thought about hurting Grace or Amber.

But she was a child then and that was no more than a childish fantasy. In reality, she was glad that Jerry didn't have a wife and children. She worried that she might feel jealousy towards them and Grace prided herself on not feeling jealous of other people. She'd learned long ago that envying other people's lives only made your own life that bit more unbearable.

'You're a star, Grace.' Jerry hugged the cup, inhaled the aroma and then took a sip with a blissful smile on his face. Just like he always did.

'Do you know, it must be great to be a civil servant,' Maggie piped up again, now that she'd recovered her breath. 'Having bucketloads of cash thrown at you, while you sit on your arse drinking coffee and eating doughnuts all day long.'

'Actually, Mag, I'm thinking of asking for a pay cut,' Jerry replied. 'I just can't seem to spend all the money they pay me. My villa in Spain is paid for, my four houses here are too big to live in and the diamond-encrusted walls of my one-bedroom flat are too hard to keep clean. Too much money isn't all it's cracked up to be. It's a pain in the arse if I'm honest.'

Maggie cackled again and took a small sip of her tea. She liked to make it last.

'Where's Amber gone, Grace?' Jerry asked, and his question seemed to suck all the air out of the room. Both Maggie and Grace stopped what they were doing. There was silence for a second before Maggie spoke.

'Town, I think. I saw her heading for the bus earlier.'

Grace looked at her. 'Did you, Mag?'

Maggie nodded and took another, longer sup of tea.

'Why do you ask, Jerry?' Grace sprayed the counter and cleaned, while she waited for his reply.

'Well, I was all over town looking for her on the evening of the storm and no one's seen her for months. Most couldn't remember the last time they'd seen her, including her dealer. I just thought that was strange.'

'How many years have we been trying to get her away from them, Jerry? Now she finally is, and you're complaining about it!'

'I'm not complaining. I'd just like to know where she is? I'd like to see for myself that she's all right.'

'My word isn't good enough anymore?'

'Your word has always been good enough for me, Gracie, you know that. I just worry about Amber. I'd like to see her, that's all.'

Grace kept cleaning.

'Well, I'd imagine if her usual *friends* haven't seen her, then she's off somewhere kicking that bastard of a habit. That's not an easy thing to do, Garda Hughes.' Maggie again. 'It's even harder with the fuzz breathing down your neck, so give the girl some space, eh?'

Jerry didn't answer. He just kept smiling into his coffee with his eyes on Grace.

'Jerry doesn't breathe down our necks, Mag,' Grace retorted. 'I'll pop in to see her tonight, Jerry. I'll tell her to call you.'

'Do that, Grace. Thanks.'

Jerry finished his coffee and Grace smiled and waved as she watched him leave. She knew Jerry well enough to know that his body language didn't always match the words that came out of his mouth. Sometimes, it was less about what he said, and more about what he didn't say.

'Did you really see Amber getting on the bus, Mag?' Grace asked, as Jerry walked away from *Jake's* and back to the station.

'Gracie my love, I haven't seen your sister in so long, I'd hardly recognise her.'

She wanted to ask why she'd said it then, but Maggie sounded a bit down all of a sudden. Her natural instinct was to cover for people, even if she had no idea why she was covering for them. And of course, lying to cops came as naturally to her as breathing. 'It's all right, Mag. Amber isn't in any trouble. She hasn't a bad bone in her body, that girl.'

Maggie looked more sceptically at her now, but Grace ignored her. Of course Amber had committed the odd crime to feed her habit. But most of those crimes were against herself.

'Jerry just likes to keep tabs on us. He worries, that's all.'

Maggie nodded, her face softening. 'I know, Gracie. I know.'

CHAPTER TWENTY-THREE

'Here you go, Roy.' Jerry placed a triple-decker BLT and a large coffee on the man's lap and then took a seat on the bench beside him, with another coffee of his own. They were watching the swans gliding around The Lough, like they hadn't a care in the world. This was Roy Harris's home. It had been since the violent death of the Celtic Tiger put an end to his banking career and took his wife and two daughters away from him, along with his five-bedroom house in Douglas.

'Cheers, Jerry.' Roy removed the lid from the cup, wrapped his cold hands around it and sipped, before replacing the lid to keep in the heat.

Jerry knew that he had a window of just a few hours early in the day to speak to Roy. Reality became too much for him after that. 'I need to ask you about Amber Murphy, Roy.'

'What did she do?'

'Nothing that I know of.'

Roy nodded. 'That poor girl is her own fiercest enemy.'

'She is these days, that's for sure. But like everyone else out here, she had some help getting to where she is.'

'Ain't that the truth.'

'So when was the last time you saw her?'

Roy shrugged. 'It's been a while.'

'Can you be more specific?'

He grinned wryly. 'Jerry, there's not a whole lot that I can be specific about these days, except how much money I have in my boot, how much booze I'll be able to get my hands on today and which kitchen appliance boxes keep you dryer at night. The last memory I have of Amber, was over there.' He pointed to a lane beside a pair of houses. It led up and away from The Lough.

'The last time we spoke, you said it was on the bench near where you were sitting with Rolo on the quays?'

'I don't remember that, Jerry. But I do remember seeing Amber over there.'

'Who was she with?'

'Well, where there's Amber, there's usually Princess Poppy. He was there and about four others. I don't remember who they were.'

'And when was this?'

'Like I said, I'm not one for specifics these days, but it was a warm, bright afternoon. A bunch of small kids passed in school uniforms. They were very shiny-looking. Everything about them looked new. Brand-new-looking clothes and backpacks; no jackets. I remember all that because I actually thought about mugging one of them.'

Jerry lowered his coffee and looked at him.

'Relax, I didn't. Not many of us sink that low, Jer. They were just kids. Besides, Crayola products don't hold the kind of street value you might think they do.'

'So you're thinking it was probably around the end of August or early September? Back to school time.'

Roy shrugged.

'We're heading into March now. That's a good six months ago, Roy. Your mind is still sharper than you give it credit for.'

'I was as sharp as a fucking blade, Jerry. Once upon a time.'

Jerry nodded. He was. 'Where does Princess Poppy hang out these days? I haven't seen him in a while either.'

'Rumour has it, he cleaned himself up.'

'When?'

Roy shrugged again. 'No idea. I think something might have happened.'

'Like what?'

'Don't know. I don't tend to listen to those tales. You know yourself, Jerry; there's always drama on the streets. Someone's always getting a pasting or whatever. I can't listen to all that. It just makes things more depressing than they already are. Now,' he stood up, 'if you're done with me, I'll thank you for the sandwich and be on my way.'

'Where are you off to?'

'I need to check out for a while.'

'Why not check into somewhere instead?'

Roy smiled again, his humourless smile. 'See you around, Detective Hughes.'

'You take care, Roy.'

'Mike, can you get me a last known for Peter Delaney?' He held the phone to his ear as he watched Roy amble away. It was hard to imagine that he once would have gotten back in his shiny BMW to make his way through *his* city. Now he plodded along with holes in the soles of his boots and the gait of a man twice his age.

'Princess Poppy? What do you want with him?' Mike asked, but his tone was one of concentration, meaning that he was already searching for what Jerry needed.

'Ah, just passing the morning, Mike.'

'You never just passed a morning in your life, Jerry. But anyway, I just have his mother's place, up on Evergreen Road. Otherwise, there's the bedsit on Blarney Street, but I doubt he's still there. There were fifteen of them in that one room on my last visit and that was last year sometime. Need a hand with anything?'

'Nah. I'll just take a spin up to his mother and see if she knows where he might be.'

'You think he might know our missing boyos?'

'Probably not, Mike. But I have no other straws to grasp at for today.'

'Any chance of a chicken-fillet roll when you're coming back?'

CHAPTER TWENTY-FOUR

'Hello, Mrs Delaney.'

Aileen Delaney's eyes filled with tears and a panic came over her. A woman who was small in stature, made smaller still by the heartbreak brought on by her son.

'Jerry? What...?' She looked up and down the street as if she expected the world to come crashing down around them both.

'Aileen, I'm not here with any bad news,' Jerry said softly. Aileen had been a primary school teacher up until she took early retirement at the age of fifty. People said it was due to *her nerves*. Jerry knew that it was due to her son, Peter, who'd started smoking weed at the age of fifteen with his friends. He snorted coke for the first time at the age of sixteen, again with his friends. His friends probably still did that at weekends, but as far as Jerry knew, most of them went on to college and got decent enough jobs.

In their once close little group, Peter was the one who became tangled in the web of drugs that they'd all been experimenting with. His plans of going to art college were soon forgotten as the need for a stronger and longer lasting high became his number one priority. Aileen had coped as well as any mother could, and she lived hand-to-mouth thanks to her son's addiction.

'He didn't do anything!'

'I know he didn't. I just want to have a chat with him. That's all.'

'He's clean, Jerry. He's back under my roof, but if you're here to jump down his throat over something... he's done nothing.'

'He's not in any trouble, Aileen.'

'So why are you here?'

'Like I said, I just want to talk to him.'

She started to cry and stepped out of the house, pulling the door closed behind her. 'Do you have any idea what it's like to have a child and never know whether he's dead or alive? Or to never know what might be happening to him at any given time?'

'I know...'

'You don't. His sobriety is as fragile as cracked glass, Jerry, and I will claw the eyes out of anyone who messes with that. Do you hear me?'

Jerry was taken aback by the language used by the small woman in the floral apron. Aileen Delaney was a lady in the truest sense of the word. But Jerry understood her fear and her determination to protect her son. If anything, he admired her even more.

'I'm not here about Peter at all, Aileen. There's a girl gone missing. She was a friend of his...'

'Peter doesn't have any friends. Not one single true friend.'

'Mam, calm down.' Peter stepped out behind her. 'Who's missing?'

Jerry hardly recognised him. Peter was known on the streets as Princess Poppy, which was maybe to do with his pink mohawk or maybe because he was gay and had been very camp until he realised how dangerous that was for him on the street. As much as the world likes to think it's moved on, another world exists within it. A world of addiction, homelessness, and survival.

'I like the hair, Peter.' Jerry smiled at him. Back to his natural shade of brown, his hair was short and spiked quite stylishly. He looked like a different person, which was probably the point.

'I thought I might evade you lot if I blended in a bit better.' He half smiled.

'Can I talk to you for a minute?'

Aileen looked at her son and her shoulders sagged. 'Come in. I'll make some tea.'

Peter went back inside, followed by Jerry with Aileen close behind. The kitchen was small, but homely. There was a faint smell of burnt toast and some carrots were cut up on a chopping board, which Aileen moved off the table and replaced with three mugs, before filling the kettle. Once it boiled and tea was poured, she took a seat alongside Peter.

'Mam, can you give us a minute?'

Aileen shot a worried look at her son. Then a warning glare at Jerry.

Jerry said nothing. He just blew on his tea and took a sip. Eventually she nodded and got up. She hesitated again before leaving. 'Five minutes, okay?'

Jerry nodded and she left.

'Sorry about that. She's a bit on edge.'

'Can you blame her?'

'No.'

'I knew you could do it, you know.'

'Did you? Because I didn't. Still don't some days.'

They sat quietly for a minute, before Peter spoke again.

'Is it Amber who's missing?'

'Why do you say that?'

'You said it was a friend of mine. She's the only one in existence, so call it an educated guess.'

'Have you seen her lately?'

He shook his head, sadly.

Jerry nodded.

'I can't see her. She and I...'

'I get it. You're clean now and you want to stay that way. Good on you, Peter.'

'Yeah, but she... I,' his voice began to shake, 'she's the only one who knows what it's like to be out there.' He pulled up his sleeve and slapped the ugly track marks on his arm. 'And what that stuff makes you do. What it brings down upon you.' He yanked his sleeve back down and brought his hand to his head. 'No one else gets what this is like.' A tear rolled off the end of his chin.

Jerry reached out and placed his hand on Peter's arm. 'I get it, Peter. You two have been through the wringer together and addiction or not, she was a friend to you. But being here at your mother's kitchen table rather than out there on the street – that's you beating the bloody odds. We both want that for Amber too.'

He lowered his hand, sat up straighter and bravely pulled himself back together. 'Is she all right?'

'She may be. Her sister tells me she's working hard to get clean. Spending time at home and eating well, which is all good to hear.' Though Jerry wasn't sure how much of that he really believed.

Peter smiled a small smile.

'When did you last see her?'

His smile faded, then died.

'It's all right.'

Peter got up and went to the kitchen door, opened it a crack and looked out, checking that his mother wasn't listening. Then he came back to the table. 'The last time I saw Amber, was the night both of us hit *actual* rock bottom. And when you've seen as many rock bottoms as we have, that's saying something.'

CHAPTER TWENTY-FIVE

T he sound of the baby crying was affecting him as much as anything else this time. It had been playing for days and nights on end and he was visibly pained by it. And so he should be. It was a sound that transported Grace back to a time when it pained *her* to hear it, night after night when her baby sister gave the only indication she could that she was hungry. Night after night she cried for their mother. She'd heard her too, but instead of coming to sooth her baby girl, she left the house to get away from her. Sometimes she didn't even bother to tell four-year-old Grace to mind her. Not that Grace needed telling. She loved her sister and her sister loved her, even then. But Grace couldn't satisfy the baby's hunger any more than she could satisfy her own at that age.

'What did I do?' His words were slurred and he drooled when he spoke, which he tried to do, often. Not that he'd been saying anything of interest. Just different variations of *I didn't do it.*

She didn't usually do this; sit with him and give him an audience. But she'd tried ignoring him. She'd tried starving him, drugging him, purging his body of all that sustained him. She'd tried teaching him a lesson and she'd failed. It seemed men like him just couldn't be taught. Still, it angered her to hear him ask, as if he didn't remember. Like destroying the lives of Grace and her sister could just pale into insignificance.

'Please... tell me. What did I...'

She jumped to her feet before she had to hear another word and swung the wrought-iron poker at the side of his head. The flesh on his cheek opened immediately and let loose a steady flow of fresh blood, as his body jerked violently. His head lolled, to the side at first and then downwards, so that his chin came to rest on his chest. She stood over him for a minute, the poker held loosely by her side. She remembered the all-consuming fear that she'd felt as she stood over him all those years ago. Fear that they wouldn't believe her. Fear of what she had done and of the consequences it would bring. Fear that they would blame her. That they would blame Amber.

She felt no such fear now. There was nothing they could do to hurt her sister any more than she was hurting herself, and they'd already shown Grace their hand. Still, she held back on the beating that she desperately wanted to give him. He wasn't going home this time, but he *would* suffer. She dropped the poker and used two fingers to open the wound on his face a bit more, to draw more blood, and he cried out as she did. She'd already used the poker to open both of his shins. She'd possibly broken the bones there, which wasn't her intention but nor was it something she'd lose any sleep over. Blood pooled around his feet, along with the diarrhoea that she'd afflicted him with. He was a mess.

Perfect.

She took a rolled-up pair of black socks and stuffed them in his mouth. She secured them there with a roll of gaffer tape, which she wound round and round his head, taking care to avoid the cut on his cheek. She needed that to be exposed. She stood back and looked at him. Satisfied, she went and hunkered down against the wall facing him again and waited for his crying to stop. She wanted him to be aware of what was about to happen.

'I grew up in a house full of rats.' Grace spoke in a low voice that immediately grabbed his attention, because he fell into an abrupt silence. 'Most people might think that's a bad thing. But it's not.'

She paused for a while, to take in his reaction. To feel his fear, which was palpable now.

'People see a rat and they freak out. They think they're disgusting, smelly, disease-ridden blights on society. But, did you know,' she continued, 'that a rat will always take care of an injured or sick rat in their group? Rats care about each other, see? They'll do whatever needs to be done for their family. Chinese people know rats; they dedicated a whole year to them. They say that rats are creative, intelligent and honest. What do you think?'

He struggled to lift his head and look at her, but he didn't seem ready to offer an opinion. Not that he could with the gag in his mouth.

'Don't worry, I don't expect you to answer. I already know what you think of rats. You see one and your instinct is to step on it. Pin it down; torture it. But did you know that rats also have excellent memories. They never forget anything.' She stood up, walked slowly around him and picked up a small cardboard box that she'd placed in the corner of the room. 'Unlike you it seems. You have a very short memory, don't you?'

His eyes narrowed at first and then widened when she hunkered down against the wall facing him again. In her hand, a box containing four beautiful brown rats. 'I used to think you were a rat when I was small. But that was before I knew that even to think it was an insult to these incredible creatures.' She stood and walked over to him again. She bent down, so that her face was closer to his than she ever wanted it to be. But she wanted to make sure that he both heard and understood her. 'Rats are fucking survivors. We survived you. But can you survive us?'

She stepped back again and placed the box on the floor. She kicked it open and watched as the curious and hungry little creatures sniffed their new surroundings and began to explore their freedom. Then she headed for the door. She stood for a second watching while the rats grew in confidence. She stayed just long enough to see them sniff him out and then bolt for his open wounds. She smiled, knowing that they would feast on them like their lives depended on it, as she closed the door and snapped the lock back into place.

CHAPTER TWENTY-SIX

'She told me about you. That's why I never bolted when you came along.' Peter was wringing his hands on the table now. 'She said you were the first face she saw when she woke up in the hospital that time. She said that you were crying.'

Jerry was looking at his own hands now. He didn't want to hear this. He didn't need this trip down memory lane, but he suspected that Peter Delaney lived in a memory lane of his own which would make Jerry's seem like Disneyland in comparison. The least he could do was let the boy talk. That was why he was here, after all.

'She said she never knew men could cry until she saw you that day.' He half laughed then. 'Course then she met me and realised that men cry all the fucking time!'

Jerry smiled in return, though it took considerable effort.

'She didn't think she was a girl anymore after what he did to her. Not a human being, like.'

'She wasn't in his eyes.'

Peter nodded. 'But she was in yours.'

'She was. And she still is.'

'And me?'

'Have you asked that woman who threatened to gouge my eyes out if I upset you?' Jerry thumbed in the direction of the kitchen door. 'I'd safely say, you're held in very high regard there.'

Peter laughed quietly. 'Mothers don't count.'

'That's where you're wrong. Mothers count for everything.'

Peter silently drank his tea.

'Can you tell me about that night?'

He kept the mug up to his lips, but he was breathing heavily into it. 'How much of this will be repeated?'

'None of it.'

'How much will I have to repeat, *for the record*?'

'None.'

He put the cup down and roughly rubbed his face with both hands. 'When you talk about being human and all that... I think the last time I was human was the first night I went out to score without the lads.'

'The lads being?'

'The friends I grew up with. I'd been to pre-school, primary and secondary school with Gary and James. Played rugby with them, went out every weekend with them. They were the first people I came out to. Not that I needed to. They knew before I did. It was Gary who supplied our first spliffs. It was also him who managed to get his hands on cocaine back when I wouldn't have had the foggiest idea where to start looking for it. We all snorted whatever he supplied and we fucking loved it! But then after a while, every second or third weekend wasn't enough for me, and the lads didn't want it as often as I did. You know, probably the same old story you hear all the time.

'The two boys went on to college, Gary is married now from what I hear, and James is in Australia somewhere. Anyway, one night I went out by myself, found a gay bar, safe space and all that. I asked around and was sniffing powder off a toilet cistern five minutes later. I didn't notice the colour. It was heroin incidentally, but what a fucking high! Found a new boyfriend that night as well. The same guy who shared the cistern with me as it happens, so it was a win–win.

'Two weeks later he injected me and I've spent every night between that one and this in the goddamn gutter. There was nothing I wouldn't do for heroin. It was the love of my fucking life, and no matter how much I got, it was never enough. But I never got anywhere near that first high again. I became a degenerate, while my friends went on to live perfect lives.' He paused and then, 'Why did it have to grab me and not them? That's what I can't figure out.'

Jerry had heard versions of this story from many victims of heroin, where experimentation leads to addiction and where a person's body and their dignity become inconsequential. Still, it didn't make it easy to sit through and there was nothing Jerry could say to take away the boy's self-loathing. Still, he tried.

'None of that was you, Peter. You know that. Heroin is too powerful and this is what it does. The real Peter Delaney is the man sitting in front of me now.'

He sniffed and shook his head. 'But this isn't what you came to hear. You came to hear about the last time I saw Amber.'

Jerry knew that it was important for Peter to explain the time leading up to whatever he was about to say. 'You were a friend to her.'

He shrugged. 'As much of a friend as a heroin addict can be. But, yes. Like you said, she was my friend.'

'Why do you think no one has seen her for so long.'

'The last time I saw her, we were in Fitzgerald's Park and the pair of us were fucking crawling with the want of a fix. I mean, we were in a bad way, like. We went to the park because we knew we'd get something there, one way or another. You see the same faces in the same places, so you come to know where you need to be. You could set your watch by most of them and, where possible, we all kind of looked out for each other.

'But that night there was a different crowd there. Three lads with Dublin accents. Someone said they'd come down on the train that morning with a lorry load of gear. Whatever we needed, they had it, is what we were told. So myself and Amber made a beeline for them. Anyway, long story short, they massively short-changed us. What they supplied barely touched the sides, so we went back to them. The rest is a bit fuzzy, but I ended up tied to the back of a bench and Amber was pinned to the ground in front of me. They were vicious. One of them bit her until she bled, they used sticks, they kicked her, pissed on her, you name it.' He lowered his eyes and his voice. 'They used the same sticks on me and they filmed it all.'

Jerry forced himself to keep looking at the boy and not let his features change.

'It went on for hours. Every time we thought, *finally, it's over*, they came back and started again. Neither of us were strangers to having people take what they want from us. But this was different.' Tears rolled uninterrupted down his face. 'This was a contest between three *men* to see who could inflict the most damage upon us. Who could take us the furthest away from the human beings we once were.'

'Did Amber survive it?' Jerry asked, before he couldn't.

Peter nodded. 'If you could call it that. Someone untied me after what seemed like days. The Dubs were long gone by then and Amber was unconscious. Whoever it was that freed me said that an ambulance was on the way and then they took off.'

'Who was that?'

He shrugged. 'One of the park regulars. Don't know his name, but he'd probably seen it all and wisely kept himself hidden. He called for help and then took off. That's the done thing.'

Jerry didn't fill the silence that followed. He didn't have the words.

'I shit in a bag now, among other attractive things. But at least I'm clean.'

'I'm sorry, Peter.'

'Why? It's not your fault.'

'And Amber?'

'I heard her crying into the paramedic's shoulder while they worked on her and I asked about her at the hospital when I was able to. They told me she'd checked out, which I took to mean that she actually left the hospital. Or do you think they meant that she'd *checked out*?'

Jerry shook his head. 'I think they'd be more literal than that at a hospital. Was that Cork University Hospital?'

He nodded.

'And that was the last time you saw her?'

He nodded.

'Did you see the video, Peter?'

He shook his head. 'I don't want to see it.'

'We could possibly trace it. Find the men who did this to you?'

Peter shook his head more vehemently now. 'I'll deny that it was me. I don't ever want my name mentioned in association with that night, do you hear me? You can't investigate something if there is no victim, can you?'

Jerry wanted to scream that they needed to taken off the streets and if possible, off the planet. But Aileen was right. The boy was as fragile as glass, and Jerry sure as hell wasn't going to be the one to crack him. Still, he made a mental note for the near future to investigate it. 'No, Peter. I told you earlier that you won't have to repeat anything and nothing you say is for the record and I meant that. I just want you to know that I'm here if you ever want my help.' He took one of his cards from his pocket. On the back he wrote down a name and number and slid it across the table. 'When you're ready, you should call this number.'

Peter looked at it but didn't respond. Ken Wells was a councillor in the city, but Jerry first encountered him when Ken was foaming at the mouth, with a needle poking out from between his toes.

'I think you'll find that you're not alone in what you've been through and there is light at the end of the long, dark, shitty fucking tunnel that you've been living in. You just have to keep moving forward, Peter. Even when that feels impossible.'

The kitchen door opened and Peter's mother came back in, looking ten years older with bloodshot eyes, making Jerry suspect that she'd been listening in on their conversation from somewhere. Jerry got to his feet.

'Thanks for your time, Peter. If you do happen to see or hear from Amber, you might give me a call. You have my number there.' He indicated the card on the table. 'Or if there's anything else that you might need, you know where I am.'

CHAPTER TWENTY-SEVEN

Jerry had been sitting in the office of Dr Trevor O'Dea at Cork University Hospital for forty-five minutes. Or at least, he thought it was an office. He now suspected that it was a consultation room of sorts, used by his entire team and an unlimited number of medical students, judging by the number of people who had walked in on him since his arrival. Some trudged in with patients in tow, before looking at him confused and then ushering the patients back out again. One student actually tried to take the place of Trevor O'Dea, stating that, "Dr O'Dea is a bit busy" and was there anything that he, the student, could help Jerry with. Jerry was confident that the student in question wouldn't be back until long after Jerry was gone, but his patience with Dr O'Dea was seriously diminished.

'Detective Hughes, sorry to have kept you.'

Finally, he decided to grace Jerry with his presence. He came in and closed the door behind him without looking up from whatever he was reading. Jerry knew that it was him based on his profile, which he'd looked up on the hospital's website before coming in. The man himself looked too old for his skinny fit chinos and shirt but the entire male staff seemed to be wearing a variation of the same thing. Perhaps he was feeling the pressure to conform to this new doctor's uniform of sorts. Jerry also noted that he didn't look nearly as tired as the younger members of his team, but he guessed that's what came with age and experience in the medical game. Going only on his appearance and his monotone greeting, Jerry already had him pegged as someone who delegated a lot.

'For forty-five minutes, no less.' Jerry stood and held out his hand. He wanted to keep the man on side, for now. But he struggled to keep his irritation at bay.

The man finally looked up from the file in his hand, smiled and shook Jerry's hand. 'I am sorry. I've had a morning and a half. What can I do for you?'

'I'm investigating the whereabouts of one of your patients, Amber Murphy.'

'Yes, I got your message. She did come through A and E a while back, but I'm afraid I never met her. I can see from her file that she had a lot of narcotics in her system at the time of admission, she had been raped, sodomised, beaten. She had three broken ribs, some minor damage to her bowel, dislocated fingers and a dislocated jaw. And that's to name but a few of her injuries, none of which were helped by the withdrawal symptoms that closely followed her admission.'

'Was she treated for that?'

'She was treated for her physical injuries, yes. And with regard to her withdrawals – as much as we could. I prescribed Clonidine, but from what I gather, as soon as she could walk, which was a couple of days later, she left.'

'Just like that?'

'She's an adult, Detective. She's also an opioid addict.'

'Meaning what, that she doesn't warrant your time?'

He sat up straighter and his face became less friendly. 'Meaning, Detective Hughes, that self-care is further down on her list of priorities than yours or mine. Meaning that this is an acute hospital and not an addiction treatment facility. *Meaning* that if we were to spend our time trying to convince people with addiction issues to do what was best for them, our trolly crisis would be *far* worse than it is today. In fact, before you leave, why not take a walk through our emergency department and speak to some of our staff there. Just last Friday our clinical nurse manager had a syringe held to her throat while her patient demanded the keys to the controlled drugs cabinet. I believe she's working today. You may also meet the porter who had his nose broken while trying to stop a patient from tearing his own cannula out. I could go on and on about the rewarding job of caring for people who don't want our care, but perhaps you would be better to see it for yourself.'

So Jerry had misjudged Trevor O'Dea. It seemed he did care. Just not about heroin addicts.

Dr O'Dea let out a long sigh and rubbed the bridge of his nose. 'I apologise, Detective. Work in emergency medicine for as long as I have and your sympathies tend to flow in a different direction.'

'I can understand that.' And he could. He'd dealt with more situations in emergency departments than he cared to remember. It had just been a while since his uniform days.

'Honestly,' he shook his head, 'I would worry for her physical health. The bowel injury alone would have caused her significant problems within hours of leaving hospital and that's just the tip of the iceberg. She was brutalised in ways that not many would survive and still, she left. Such is the need to feed one's addiction.'

'And that was the last time she's been in?'

He looked again at the file and after a few minutes, he nodded. 'Six months, almost to the day. That's not to say that she didn't pass through the Mercy or another hospital and I hope for her sake that she has. Otherwise, I hate to say it, but I'm not sure she will have survived.'

Jerry nodded, then stood to go. The doc stood too and the pair shook hands again. As he walked out the main door of the Cork University Hospital, Jerry put a call in to Mike and asked him to ring around the other Cork hospitals. Though he had a terrible feeling that Amber wouldn't show on any of their records either. At least not within the last six months.

CHAPTER TWENTY-EIGHT

'What exactly is a barring order, Grace?' Mary-Assumpta had been exceptionally quiet since her arrival at *Jake's,* more than ten minutes before she finally asked this question.

Grace stopped what she was doing and looked to Maggie, who looked equally perplexed.

'Eh, what have you done, Mary-Assumpta?' Maggie asked. Grace's head wasn't in the game today and she wasn't sure she could take too much of Mary-Assumpta. Though she was interested to know what prompted this question.

'It's just something Nigel said. He's a bit more dramatic than I remembered.'

'Who's Nigel?'

'The lad she went to school with.' Grace supplied the answer. She had a good memory, even for things she had no interest in remembering. 'The one she found on Facebook.'

'Yeah, him,' Mary-Assumpta added. 'I was only trying to get onto him on Facebook, but like, he obviously thought I was someone else. I suppose I can see why when my profile picture is my three rugrats. I need to change that,' she added thoughtfully. 'Anyway, he blocked me because, you know, he thought I was someone else, so I had to try a few different ways to contact him. We used to have a right laugh in art class, so I know that if he knew it was me, he wouldn't have blocked me. Anyway, he came barrelling out of his house the other night, screaming that he was going to get a barring order, and...'

'Eh, what were you doing outside his house?' Maggie asked again, though she seemed to already have guessed the answer.

'I wasn't *doing* anything, Maggie.' Mary-Assumpta responded like Maggie was some kind of imbecile.

'How did you know where he lived?' Grace asked. But again, she could probably figure it out. Or at least, a version of it.

'Well it's not like I stalked him or anything.' She was becoming high-pitched and a bit indignant. 'I mean, he put it up on his Facebook that he worked in the Mercy and attended UCC. I happened to be near the Mercy one day and saw him coming out and I called him, but he didn't hear me. He was with some real nerdy-looking lads and probably felt like he had to seem interested in whatever they were rattling on about. But later on he headed out the Western Road, towards Wilton and I saw him going into a house there, so I...'

'So you bloody well did stalk him.' Maggie cackled and choked a bit.

'I did not! I was going that way anyway!'

Grace shook her head and continued to clean around the coffee machine.

'You? Just happened to be *walking* from the Mercy to Wilton at the exact time when this Nigel character was coming out of work and going home? How long did you spend standing outside the Mercy before you finally caught him on a day when he was working?'

'It was your man in reception. I know it was. He was right up his own arse when I asked if Nigel was working.' Mary-Assumpta seemed to be failing to see the problem in all this.

'How many times did you ask him?'

Grace was becoming more impressed by Maggie's line of questioning. She seemed to know exactly the right ones to ask.

Mary-Assumpta shrugged her shoulders. 'Not that many times.'

'So let me get this straight. You kept contacting him online and he kept blocking you. You turned up at his work, often enough to figure out his work schedule and then you followed him home. Then you returned to his home often enough for him to come barrelling out, threatening you with a barring order. Have I got that right?'

'You don't have to say it like that, Maggie, making me sound like some kind of weirdo. You can be really mean when you want to be, you know that?'

'And you can be really thick when you want to be, Mary-Assumpta. Do *you* know that?'

Mary-Assumpta looked at her feet but didn't respond for a while. Eventually, when she did speak, she sounded like a child, which in a way, she was. 'I just wanted him to know it was me. To remember me. He kissed me once, in a game of spin the bottle and it was really nice. I know he liked it.'

'Well, that probably didn't mean much to him, Mary-Assumpta,' Grace added. She didn't mean to sound so unsympathetic. But she couldn't understand how a girl got to the age of nineteen, had three kids to raise alone and *still* thought that men were worth their time. 'But, to answer your question,' Grace continued, 'a barring order is something that you don't really want your name on. So please, stay away from him. Take it that he's seen you now. He *knows* that it's you and he's still opting to be a prick about it. He's not interested and he's not worth any more of your time.'

Tears pricked Mary-Assumpta's eyes and Grace felt sorry for her. She didn't have an easy life and she oozed loneliness. Yet, she always had a smile and she was always overly enthusiastic about just about everything. What's more, despite it all, she was a good mother who cared for her children and for that alone, Grace didn't like seeing her crying.

'Here, have a muffin.' She held a fresh blueberry muffin over the top of the counter and waited until Mary-Assumpta came to claim it, which she knew she would.

'Thanks,' she mumbled, taking it and sitting back down.

'Speaking of the rugrats,' Maggie chirped, in an effort to ease the weirdness, 'where are they?'

'My mam has them.'

'Really?' Maggie couldn't hide her surprise. It was common knowledge that Mary-Assumpta's mother moved her mobile home so often, that they had little or no contact most of the time. It was also known that Mary-Assumpta didn't quite trust her mother with her children, for reasons only she knew.

Mary-Assumpta looked at her watch. 'She's had them for more than a half hour now. That's enough,' she said, getting to her feet. 'See ye tomorrow.' She sounded sadder than she ever had as she headed for the door.

'Hey,' Grace called to her, 'never mind any of them, Mary-Assumpta.' She gave the girl a smile and Mary-Assumpta returned it, which took effort on both their parts. Grace's mind was on the rats.

'So eh, what did Hughes want with Amber?' Maggie asked, less than a minute after Mary-Assumpta left and they were alone for the first time that day.

'What?' The question caught Grace by surprise.

'Jerry? He was in here the other day asking you all about her.'

'Oh. He's always asked about her. You know Jerry, he's all questions, all the time.'

'Yeah, but he seemed more interested than usual, don't you think?'

Grace thought back to the three-way conversation between Jerry, Grace and Maggie. She didn't think he'd sounded any more interested than usual. Maggie had a tendency to add two and two together and get five sometimes. Aside from Grace herself, no one cared more about Amber than Jerry did and she didn't want Maggie, or anyone else, speaking ill of him. 'I didn't notice.'

Maggie nodded, then shrugged. 'Maybe I'm feeling a bit paranoid, but you know, I'm sure someone was in my house while I was being held captive at the hospital.'

Grace stopped what she was doing now. 'Who would have been in your house?' she asked, after a beat.

Again, Maggie shrugged.

'What makes you think there was?'

'Two half-full coffee cups sitting on my kitchen table. I thought about warming them up and having a sup, but you wouldn't know what might be in them.'

Grace could feel Maggie's eyes on her, as she replenished the already well-stocked takeaway cups and lids beside the machine. The silence felt heavy until Grace finally said, 'You're probably right though, Mag. If you had squatters while you were away, those cups could have been spiked with piss for all you know.'

153

Maggie coughed loudly and then laughed, which was always a sign that her laugh wasn't genuine. Her *laugh* led to her *cough*. Not the other way round.

'Is that why you told Jerry that you saw Amber getting on the bus?' she asked, to change the subject. 'Or did you really see her?' Grace doubted it. Amber had been out of it that morning when Grace called on her way to work.

Maggie shook her head. 'It's just what you say when the cops are asking questions, isn't it?'

'Jerry's not the cops, Mag.'

'He's a detective inspector, Gracie love. Whatever else you think he might be, he's a copper first and foremost.'

'What I think he might be, Maggie, is the only person in this world who ever gave a damn about me or my sister. But I suppose you're right; he's also a cop.'

Maggie was quiet then. Or at least her mouth was. Grace could almost hear the rusty old cogs of her mind whirring. Eventually, she did say something.

'You're wearing a different scent these days, Grace.'

Grace stiffened. No one had referred to Grace and a smell in the same sentence in many years and Maggie's comment jolted her.

'Environmental,' Maggie added then, absent-mindedly. She was back to the harmless old woman again. 'Spend enough time in any environment and we start to smell like it. I probably smell like mink.'

'Hmm,' Grace replied. 'And I suppose I smell like coffee?'

'Hmm,' Maggie replied unconvincingly and for the rest of that day, Grace thought about nothing else. Not even the rats or what they were feeding on. Had she become so accustomed to the smell of a man's body decomposing while he still clung to life, that she'd begun to carry the scent with her?

The arrival of the school kids for their Coke and cakes was

most welcome. But despite the noise and clutter that they created for the next half hour, Maggie's eyes were like streams of lava, burning through Grace and for the first time she wondered, what exactly was going on inside the mind of Maggie Hayes.

CHAPTER TWENTY-NINE

'Amber?' Grace called from the empty sitting room later that evening. She wasn't going to go upstairs this time because she knew Amber wouldn't be there. 'Amber?' she called again, letting a bit more anger or frustration, or fear – whatever it was that had overcome her – into her voice. She needed to see her sister. To speak with her, properly. Not when Amber was in need of a fix or had just had one. She needed to speak with her actual sister. Something wasn't right.

'Hey, Grace. Everything all right?' Jerry sounded wary as he answered her call on the first ring.

'I don't know where she is, Jerry. I think she might be back on the gear, fully like.' She sounded unconvincing, even to herself, but Jerry didn't rub her face in that.

'When did you last see her?'

'Yesterday.'

'And where was she when you saw her?'

'Here, at home.'

He was quiet for a minute, but she could hear him breathing. 'Did you speak to her?'

Now it was Grace who was quiet.

'Just tell me, Gracie.'

'No.'

'Why not?'

She hesitated. 'She hasn't been as well as I've been letting on.'

'In what way?'

'I think something happened to her, Jerry. She hasn't been herself.'

Jerry didn't respond, but she knew he was listening.

'She's been more... inside herself, you know?'

Again, no response.

'Are you there? Are you listening to me?'

'I am, Grace. I'm here and I'm listening.'

'I'm worried about her. Everybody hurts her, Jerry. I don't know why, but they do! And Amber's not as strong as me.' Grace was crying now. It had been many years since Grace cried, but she couldn't help it. Being told that she smelled after all these years, and after all the effort she'd put into changing her life, had caused a darkness to descend upon her. She could see nothing but blackness.

'It's okay, Grace.' Jerry sounded as sad as she did. 'Has she said anything about where she's been spending her time recently? Do you have any idea where she might be now?'

Grace shook her head.

'Grace?'

'No,' she whispered. 'But I need her back. I need her to be okay.'

More silence on the line between two people in pain. Again, it was Jerry who eventually broke it.

'If you saw her yesterday, why are you so worried about her today?'

'Because she hasn't been right, I said! Something happened. I don't know *what* happened, but I know something did and she hasn't been right.' She was repeating herself. Grace had lost her calm and she didn't like how it felt. 'I have to go, Jerry.'

'Grace, hang on. I'll come up.'

'No. She's not here and I'm going out to find her.'

'Hang on, I'll—'

'I won't be here and neither will Amber. But please, Jerry. Find her.'

CHAPTER THIRTY

'What the fuck was that?' Mike asked, having heard both sides of the conversation.

Steph heard it too and was waiting quietly for Jerry's take on it. Steph had been in and out of the station as if she still worked there, ever since pointing out the similarities between the missing men and Philip Munroe. Jerry was glad to have her there. She stopped him from feeling like he might be going mad.

Jerry shook his head, looking worriedly at the phone. It had been a very long time since he'd heard fear in Grace Murphy's voice. 'I don't know, Mike. But what I really want to know is, where the hell is Amber Murphy?'

'Well, I'm afraid I'm not going to be much help with that today either. The South Infirmary have no record of Amber at all, but the Mercy have a good thick file. Amber was one of their frequent fliers, but nothing since an overdose nearly eight months ago. Did you know she was pulled from the river a month before that?'

Jerry nodded. He did know that. Amber had been pulled from the river three times during her life, that he knew of. Jerry got to his feet.

'Where are you off to?'

'Fitzgerald's Park.'

'For an ice cream or what?' Mike said, only half joking. Mike was always thinking about food in some shape or form.

'Someone witnessed the assault on Amber and Peter. They untied Peter and called for help. I want to know who. They're a close-knit community for the most part and someone knows what happened to her. Find Amber Murphy and it'll bring us a hell of a lot closer to finding our missing men. I just know it.'

'What are you really thinking, Jerry? About Amber I mean?' Steph asked.

Jerry let out a long sigh and stood facing the whiteboard. Then he looked at Steph, hoping that she came to the same conclusion without him having to say the words out loud. To do so felt like a sort of betrayal of the Murphy sisters. If he was wrong, which he hoped he was, then they did not need this added to their plates. Or their reputations. Mud sticks, it's true. But it doesn't just stick to the Murphy sisters. It seeps into their skin and becomes a part of their DNA.

'You think she knows where they might be?' Steph said, nodding towards the board, but keeping her eyes on Jerry.

Mike raised his eyebrows and looked sharply at the board, then back to Jerry. 'What did I miss?' he asked.

'Probably nothing, Mike,' Jerry replied, but he was looking at Steph now. Did she really think it too? 'Could Amber Murphy really have gotten it together enough to make these men vanish without a trace?'

Steph shrugged. 'Well, you did say that Peter Delaney was a new man following his ordeal. Clean as a whistle. Maybe Amber is too. Maybe her newly cleared mind started thinking about all the wrongs that had been done to her and this time, instead of running for the needle, she went after the man who launched her into her downward spiral?'

'She's too badly injured though, according to the doc.'

'But none of them are the man who launched her into anything... are they?' Mike asked, still sounding confused.

'No. But look closely at them, Mike. Do you see it?' Jerry produced a photo of Munroe, blown up to the same size as the missing men. He pinned it to the board alongside them. It was time to share the theory.

'Holy shit,' Mike mumbled. 'She does know a lot of dodgy people. Maybe she's getting help?'

Jerry bobbed his head from side to side, unsure. 'Common sense is telling me that she isn't capable of this, but...'

'It would be nice to talk to her,' Steph added.

'So, where oh where is Amber Murphy?' Mike asked.

CHAPTER THIRTY-ONE

MAGGIE – 1982

Maggie's head throbbed where clumps of her hair had been pulled out and she spat a tooth out onto the footpath. She was in pain, but the little tramp doing the damage would never see that. So Maggie ran at her again. A large crowd had gathered on the street outside the pub and they were hooting and howling like a pack of animals. Maggie drove her shoulder into the woman's ribs and the pair of them hit the ground with a hard thump. Still, the other woman got the upper hand and rolled Maggie so that she was beneath her once more. Jacinta was her name, apparently. She'd been taunting Maggie all night, when all she wanted was to have a quiet drink. Now for the second time in as many minutes, she was being straddled by Jacinta on the cold, wet ground.

As another clump of hair was pulled from her head and nails scraped her face simultaneously, Jacinta was pulled off her by the women she'd been drinking with. They were laughing as they dragged their friend away.

'Leave her, Jacinta!' one of them said with a happy howl. 'If she can't keep her man on a leash, that's her problem.'

'He's...' Maggie tried to retort, but blood spluttered from her mouth.

'He's, he's, he's what?' Jacinta taunted again. 'He's engaged to my sister! That's what he is and if you don't stay a million bloody miles away from him, I swear to God, I'll...'

'Ah well now, he didn't exactly give her a ring, Jacinta.' The same friend howled again. It seemed she didn't care who she was laughing at, once no one was laughing at her.

'Go home, you haggard old whore,' Jacinta spat, ignoring her so-called friend.

As soon as they walked away, the crowd began to disperse. She heard them all mumbling, passing Paddy's name back and forth between them. They too were delighting in their evening's entertainment. Maggie, meanwhile, didn't feel like she could pull herself up off the road, but somehow she did. Then she turned and headed for home. One heel had broken off her shoe, but she still marched away with as much dignity as she could muster, stopping at the off-licence on the way. She picked up the cheapest vodka they had and ignored the look on the man's face behind the counter. He didn't comment on the state of her because he knew Maggie by now. She was so often in a state, thanks to Paddy, or the men he sent her way, or the women who claimed he was theirs. Onc of these nights, if Maggie could be bothered, she'd ask him why he still looked at her like that. Like he was torn between calling the Guards or the paramedics. Or maybe the street sweepers to clean her away from his otherwise respectable street. The man had rarely seen her looking any better than she did right now.

After the girl came to stay, it only took Maggie a week to realise that Paddy wasn't sleeping in his car, like he said he would. When she asked, he told her that he was couch surfing, staying with this friend and that. But word on the street said otherwise and they saw less and less of him at the bedsit. When he did come around, it was to collect his money.

As she trudged up the stairs, clutching her vodka wrapped in brown paper, she met three laughing college boys on their way down. She knew where they were coming from. They looked like rich boys who were slumming it for the night and Maggie didn't greet them. Nor did she care that they fell silent as they passed her. They stared like she was a rare zoo animal, before bursting into even more animated conversation about their wild night on the wrong side of the tracks, as they headed out of the building and back to their real lives.

Assholes. But at least they were young. And clean. But of course, Maggie knew that clean clothes and clean faces, didn't make a *clean* man. They'd both had enough visits to the STD clinic to know that.

When she went inside the bedsit, she didn't say anything. She kicked off her broken shoes and dropped her bag and coat in the corner, on the floor. The girl was sitting on the edge of the bed, which they shared for the most part. Only because they had no other option. The girl hated her. That's why Maggie stayed quiet when she went inside, because she wouldn't get a response to anything else. At least not a civil one. She sat down wearily on the corner of the bed, as far away from her daughter as she could get, which wasn't very far. Then she looked ahead to the mirror on the wall. Her, with a scarecrow's head of hair and bloody face and scalp, beside the girl. She didn't have any bruises, but at sixteen years old, she looked far more broken than Maggie was and that said something.

'Fuck you, Paddy Wilson,' Maggie muttered.

The girl stood up, finished dressing and headed for the door. 'And fuck you too,' she said before leaving.

If Maggie had known that that would be the last time she'd be alone with her daughter, she would have thought of something more meaningful to say. She *saw* her around in the years that followed, with this boyfriend and that one, and she'd heard enough stories to know that Maggie had started her on a life of prostitution and all that came with it. Cork is, after all, a small place. But Maggie's daughter never acknowledged her again after that night.

The girl spent four years in that bedsit, but that night was her last. Maggie watched her go, but it wasn't until the door closed behind her that she finally said, 'Mind yourself, Liz.'

CHAPTER THIRTY-TWO

F at and seemingly happy, it didn't take much to get the rats back in the box and the sight of what they left behind, still tied to the upturned chair, was quite pleasing. His flesh was a mess and one of his eyeballs was missing. She never realised that four rats could do so much damage to a human body. She supposed the body was already quite damaged, thanks to her. Now though, she was conscious of the fact that his stink was clinging to her and this was far more distressing than anything in that room.

Grace showered every single day and she washed her hair too. Every. Single. Day. She washed her bedclothes once a week and only ever wore an item of clothing once, before sending it to the laundry. But maybe his stench had drifted towards her wardrobe and clung to the otherwise clean clothes that hung there. Maybe he permeated the air to the extent that he poured over her as she moved from the shower to her bedroom and from her bedroom to the stairs. Grace knew from experience, that when you lived with a smell for long enough, you ceased to smell it. Maggie had reminded her of this and she'd been hit with wave after wave of anxiety ever since. She needed to rid herself of it. She needed to rid her house and everything in it of the disgusting stench of that disgusting man. But first, she needed to rid herself of the actual man.

The sixteen-year-old Fiat Punto, which sat outside Grace's house, was bought at a time when the idea of owning something as extravagant as a car, and the knowledge that she had the required nine hundred of her very own euros to buy it with, combined to make its acquisition come about. The car itself was yellow, but it had one red door on the passenger side. Grace liked this feature. However, she soon discovered that she did not like driving. She was pulled over on her very first venture, which was only as far as Aldi, by a Garda who asked to see her licence. He was unimpressed by her confusion and went on to inform her that she could expect a summons for failing to have one. When she also failed to provide him with insurance or tax, he became really unhappy. It led to a whole hullabaloo where Jerry had to come along and sort out the summons situation.

Grace then had to discover the insane number of hoops she'd have to jump through just to get a licence, on account of her detention in the nuthouse and insurance would cost her more than a brand-new Mercedes. So now, Grace's Punto was purely ornamental. But she never considered selling it. She still liked to be able to say that she owned a car, and right now, she was glad that she did.

It was four in the morning when she dragged his stinking corpse, wrapped in thick industrial plastic, down the stairs and out to the car, but not before having a good look around the estate first. It was in darkness, and no one was around. It took considerable effort to get him into the back seat, once she realised that the tiny boot was not an option. She'd given some thought as to where she would take him, beginning with the Glen Valley, which was only a few miles away. But she decided that was a bit too close to home and was too popular with those people who walked without really going anywhere.

Then she thought about dumping him in the Lee, but there were cameras everywhere these days. Not that she particularly cared. Removing Philip Munroe from the planet was a public service. One that she would gladly do time for if she needed to. Peace of mind for her sister was worth any number of pills being forced down her throat. And any number of *and how did that make you feel* conversations. She usually knew the answer they wanted to hear anyway.

But until she was better, Amber still needed someone to look after her, and Grace couldn't do that from behind a locked door. She needed to be careful. She couldn't afford to drive around with no licence, no tax, no insurance and a half-eaten man on her back seat. Not that if she were pulled over before she dumped him, it probably wouldn't get to the part where they worried about her documentation. No. She would take the least number of risks possible. She'd simply drive through Blackpool and onto the Mallow Road. There shouldn't be much traffic around, so when she was far enough away from home, she'd just throw him in a ditch. Somewhere where only cars whizzed past and not pedestrians. Somewhere where days, maybe weeks could pass without him being found. All she needed was enough time to find Amber and tell her that he was gone. Tell her at a time when she can absorb the information and its implications, and after that, Amber will want nothing more than to get healthy and *live.*

It took several turns of the key and coughs from the engine before the Punto finally spluttered to life. It died again several times before leaving the estate. Grace never had mastered the use of the clutch and her Punto's clutch had problems of its own, Grace's feet notwithstanding. Eventually though, she did get going and onto the main road. She paid close attention to the many sets of traffic lights between her house, Blackpool and the Mallow Road because she didn't want to be pulled over for anything stupid. There could be any number of bored Gardaí out tonight having pulled the short straw. She needed to watch her driving and while she wasn't up to speed on the many rules of the road, she would at least obey the basic ones. Speed signs, traffic lights and lanes to a certain extent. Though there were times when they made no sense whatsoever.

As it happened, she didn't see any Gardaí, bored or otherwise. She didn't see many cars at all, aside from a few taxis and articulated lorries. Once she hit the Mallow Road, she drove for about thirty minutes, never going above fifty miles per hour. Then she pulled in on the hard shoulder. There were fields on both sides of the road, which she imagined was a busy stretch by day. But it didn't seem like a patch of road that was frequented by walkers. There seemed to be nothing of interest here and no houses. This was the place.

The road was straight ahead and behind her. She'd see any headlights before they saw her and right now there was nothing. She hopped out and hurried around to the passenger side, opened the back door and dragged him out. She'd been wearing thin black gloves that were almost like a second skin. They were running gloves. Not that she ran. But she knew that her prints wouldn't be found on the plastic, when eventually someone did find him. She wanted him to be found. She wanted to see him on the news. She wanted Amber to see it on the news. To hear the details of his death and how much he had suffered. If that didn't give her a whole new lease of life, Grace didn't know what would. But she didn't want that tonight.

She adopted a weightlifter's squat, gripped the thick plastic in both fists and heaved him up, bringing him to rest temporarily on her bent knees. She adjusted her grip and pulled him up to her chest, but the weight of him pulled her forward so they were both pressed against the ditch, him horizontal and her, just about vertical. On the other side of the ditch should be a field, or a gully, or something other than a main road, so she pressed him harder against it, steadied herself and then rolled him upwards until she could use her shoulders to shove him on top of the ditch. Panting hard now, she pushed him and waited for the thump of him hitting the ground on the other side. When it came, she didn't waste time congratulating herself. Instead, she got back in the car and started it up. It died and started, then died and started again before it finally spluttered and juddered back out onto the road.

There was a concrete divide between the two lanes headed away from Cork and the opposite lanes headed back, so she had to continue further on for now. She didn't know this road so she had no idea how long she'd have to keep driving or how far away from home it might take her. But before she could worry too much about that, she came to a sign telling her that she was in New Twopothouse, which made her wonder if she'd read it correctly. She'd never been a strong reader, but that really didn't look right. It was a barely there village, it seemed, and this made her wonder if she'd put him in the wrong place after all. Maybe people from the village walked this road all the time.

She was able to turn now and head citybound again, so she did. And she stopped worrying about the people of this strangely named place finding *him*. It was too late now. There was nothing she could do about it, so thinking about it wouldn't help. On the other side of the road was another sign, stating that the place was indeed called New Twopothouse. The sign was there to let her know that she was now leaving it. It was mildly amusing. In fact, Grace was feeling good. Happy even. Philip Munroe had had all the chances he was getting in this life and now she and her sister finally had a chance to get on with theirs.

She couldn't wait to finally tell Amber. And to tell her that there was such a place as New Twopothouse!

CHAPTER THIRTY-THREE

I t was almost six in the morning when Grace got home and she had to hurry if she was to make it to work on time. Which she would. Grace Murphy was never late, even in the most extreme of circumstances. If today was to be her first time, then that was one more thing to blame Philip Munroe for.

She parked the Punto in exactly the same spot it had been in for the past number of months. This was easily done, because the tarmac under her car was a different colour to the rest of the road. It was a relatively clean, dry patch of road in the shape of a Fiat Punto. A Fiat Punto with an oil leak. Once that was done, she hurried inside and removed her clothes right inside the door, leaving them in a pile at the bottom of the stairs. She took the stairs up two at a time. Outside the spare room was a bundle of cleaning supplies. A spray bottle of cleaning solution which guaranteed her that it would remove 99.9 per cent of, well everything. She had a bottle of bleach for the other 0.1 per cent. And of course, a bottle of Aldi's finest carpet and upholstery cleaner, several brushes, gloves, cloths and the hoover.

She still had one long roll of industrial plastic leaning against the wall, with loads left on it. Three more lay horizontal on the floor, but they'd have to stay a while longer. They were big, awkward things that came with the house. She had no idea who'd left them or for what, but she was grateful. Still, she would clean his scent off them.

She started by spraying the outside of the plastic rolls and wiping them down before bringing in the hoover and dragging it over and over the old but stain-free carpet. After that, she got on her knees, poured the carpet and upholstery cleaner on the floor and started scrubbing. By the time she'd scoured the small room, her knuckles were glowing red and she was sweating. And it was seven fifteen in the morning. She hurried with the spray bottle, spritzing the four walls and both sides of the door. She scrubbed quickly. There weren't many visible stains thanks to the care she'd taken and her placement of the plastic during his stay. But this deep clean wasn't about stains. It was about smell. She got back on her knees and scrubbed the skirting boards. Seven thirty-five.

The room smelled so strongly of cleaning products that the smell wafted through the rest of upstairs. But Grace was no longer naïve enough to think that might do the job, so she planned to do the rest of the house later that night, after work. She hurried to her wardrobe and grabbed as much as she could from in there, leaving hangers swinging on the rail behind her. Carrying everything in one bundle, she ran downstairs and dropped the pile on the floor beside the washing machine. She ran back up and jumped in the shower. She washed quickly, but thoroughly and without spending too much time drying off, she hurried back to the kitchen.

Seven fifty. She opened the washing machine and pulled the wet clothes out onto the floor. The clothes in the tumble dryer could have done with ten more minutes, but she pulled them out too and bundled them onto the kitchen table. She shoved the wet pile in and switched the dryer on. She was out of time. She needed to get dressed and get to work. From the table bundle, she picked out a jumper, some underwear and a pair of jeans, not her nicest ones, but more importantly, they smelled of only one thing; washing powder. Whatever *new scent* she'd been carrying to Maggie's nose, would not be on her today, or ever again. She quickly put on a new pair of Marigold gloves and shoved the pile of clothes from her wardrobe into the machine, followed by a scoop of powder. The dial was set to forty degrees but she upped it to sixty and set the wash going. Then with her wet hair and wrinkled clothes, she hurried out the door.

It was four minutes past eight when she arrived to open up and because anything under five minutes didn't count, she was happy to say that she was on time. But her pride was short-lived. She struggled to think about the list of jobs that she worked through every day at *Jake's,* because she had an even longer list of jobs that urgently needed to be done in her own home that night. If she had her way, that's where she'd be right now. Removing all traces of the Munroe stench from her house and from her person. But she'd never faked an illness before and she wasn't about to start now. Munroe would not make a liar out of Grace. She was not her mother. But she swore that before her head hit the pillow that night, all traces of him would be gone and tomorrow, Grace and Amber could finally put Philip Munroe out of their minds and out of their lives for ever.

CHAPTER THIRTY-FOUR

'You said you hadn't seen her.' Jerry managed to keep his tone light. Friendly even, as he spoke to Rolo again. 'Actually,' he shook his head and grinned, like this was bordering on being funny, 'you commented on her looks, like you'd never seen her before. Why didn't you tell me that you saw her being assaulted – tortured even, along with Peter Delaney?'

'Jerry, I didn't know whether I was looking at an average Saturday night in the park, or the makings of a snuff film. And another thing, I was bombed off my fucking nut! They could have been shagging Santa Claus and his elves for all I knew. Now if you want to arrest me for any of the above, please do. I could do with a few hot meals and all the gear I can get into my veins in the comfort of my cosy cell.'

'But you untied Peter and called for help.' Jerry ignored his dig at the prison system, which was probably an accurate assessment. But he wasn't going to reward Rolo for this.

'I untied one of them I think, yes. Despite popular opinion, we are actual human beings you know. But again, he could have been anyone. To me they were just two junkies having a shit night. I called the ambulance from his phone and then I nicked that phone and swapped it for what I needed.' He held out his hands, wrists together.

'You're quite the hero.'

Rolo shrugged. 'I'm a junkie, Jerry. I'm not pretending any different. I need what I need and I can't afford to pass up any opportunities. There's nothing I can do about any of that and you know it.'

'Have you ever tried to do something about it?'

'Once.'

'And?'

'I'm here, aren't I?'

'So try again.'

'I'll be at the bottom of the Lee, or maybe tied to a bench somewhere myself before I get anywhere near the top of that waiting list. No one gives a damn about me.'

'Hang on,' Jerry rooted in his pockets, 'I'm sure I have a violin in here somewhere.' The public system was a revolving door for people like him, assuming of course, that they could get anywhere near that door in the first place. But Jerry was all out of pity today.

Rolo looked self-pitying all of a sudden. 'So what, you only give a toss about the good-looking, *female* addicts, is that it?'

'I give a toss about Amber Murphy. And if you showed any signs that you might like to help yourself, I might give a toss about you too.'

'Did you come all the way here to lecture me, or make me feel like shit, or whatever it is you're trying to do? Or did you actually want to ask me something?'

'Okay, so now you know that it was Amber, what can you tell me?'

He shrugged again. 'Truth is, Jerry, I just wanted them to

finish what they were doing so that I could get the fuck out of there and get what I needed. I was dying for a fix.'

'So why didn't you just go?'

'I couldn't have gotten out of where I was without them seeing me. Yes, I was dying. But I wasn't about to have my ass tied up beside them and go out the same way. Or at least, I assumed they were on their way out. If you say they survived that,' he shook his head, 'I wouldn't want to be what's left of them. If that was Amber Murphy, then maybe you should start checking the morgues or maybe the bottom of the Lee. If they didn't kill her that night, then without a doubt, she topped herself.'

Jerry thought about what he was saying. He'd been waiting for the call telling him that Amber was dead for many years now. He didn't *want* to get it, but he wouldn't have been surprised by it. Rolo could have been right. Except, according to Grace, Amber had been at home.

Either Grace was lying, but why would she? Or Amber had somehow gotten it together and was out there now, killing any man who reminded her of the one who ultimately put her in this park, at the mercy of the three dealers from Dublin.

As if reading his mind, Rolo added, 'Either way, Jerry. Have you seen the state of my body?'

'Can't say I'm looking, Rolo,' Jerry replied in a droll voice.

'From what I gather, Amber's been out here a lot longer than I have. But as it stands, my body feels like it's being eaten from the inside out by parasites. Given how long she's been on this scene and what I saw happen to her that night... if she is still out there somewhere, she won't be winning any prizes for health and fitness or whatever.'

Which is exactly what Jerry had been thinking. Yes, Peter was doing well and he looked like a fully functioning member of the human race. But as he'd said himself, he was shitting in a bag now. Jerry had no idea what that entailed, but he guessed Peter wouldn't be overpowering any healthy males any time soon. Best-case scenario, Amber had somehow managed to clean up her act. Her body was ravaged from years of drug use and abuse, her latest assault notwithstanding. Could she really overpower one, let alone four men? Or did anyone care enough about Amber Murphy to do it for her?

Grace certainly did. She loved Amber enough to do absolutely anything for her and she had. But Grace knew that Munroe was dead because she'd done the time for killing him. So why would she start killing anyone who looked like him now? Amber on the other hand, hadn't had much of a chance to process the fact that he was dead. Grace and Amber Murphy were the only ones who made sense for these disappearances. But the realities of that made no sense whatsoever.

Jerry walked away from Rolo, headed for one of the many benches in the otherwise beautiful Fitzgerald's Park.

'Bye so, Rolo. Thanks for all your help,' Rolo called sarcastically after him.

'Bye so, Rolo. Thanks for all your help,' Jerry responded.

CHAPTER THIRTY-FIVE

'Hello, Maggie.' Jerry pulled the unmarked squad car up to the kerb and crawled alongside the woman. He'd been waiting for her. It was almost four in the afternoon and Jerry knew Maggie's routine almost as well as she did. She'd hang around *Jake's* for as long as she could, place a bet that she couldn't afford to place at the bookies, buy some tinned food at the Spar and then trundle home.

Maggie glanced sideways at him and rolled her eyes. She was pulling her shopping trolly behind her, which would contain nothing more than some baked beans and maybe some bread. 'What do *you* want?' She didn't stop walking.

'It's going to lash down with rain. Jump in, I'll drop you home?'

'Rain doesn't bother me.'

'Maggie?'

She stopped walking and gave another even more dramatic roll of her eyes. 'What?'

He smiled and gestured to his passenger seat.

'Well, what about my trolly?'

Jerry stopped the car and got out. He gently took the trolly from her and carried it to the back of the car. He opened the boot and put it in. 'Will that do?'

'Am I being arrested or something? Is that what this is?'

'Just offering you a lift home, Mag.'

'Offering? It seems more like you're telling me to get in the car, Jerry.'

'Get in the car, Maggie,' he replied, still with a soft smile on his face.

She grumbled and struggled into the passenger seat, then she coughed violently as she wrestled with her seatbelt.

Jerry started driving and at the first opportunity, he did a U-turn and drove Maggie even further away from home. Maggie threw him another sideways glance but continued with her coughing fit. When it finally passed, she propped her elbow against the door and rested her chin in her closed fist. She stared out the window, like a petulant child ignoring her dad. She refused to give him the satisfaction of asking where he was taking her because she knew that he wouldn't tell her.

Likewise, Jerry stayed quiet as he drove down towards the Jack Lynch Tunnel. She glanced suspiciously at him as they entered the tunnel and she sat up straight in her seat as they took the exit for Douglas and Rochestown.

The Rochestown Road was funny in that, one side of it was considered to be very affluent, while the opposite side of the road, while also very nice, was populated with ordinary housing estates. Still not a cheap place to live by any means, because nowhere in this suburb was. But those homes weren't quite as high value as their opposing neighbours. Jerry pulled the car into the gated entrance of one of the *well-to-do* homes on the good side of the road and killed the engine. The gate was electric, naturally enough, and the house itself was barely visible beyond the treelined driveway, which led to its front door.

'Drive the car, Jerry.'

'I need a break, Maggie. I've been driving all day. Let's just sit here and talk for a minute.'

She turned to face him, her face filled with rage. 'What do you want from me?'

'Electric gates. They weren't there before.' He made a show of being curious about the property beyond the gates.

'I don't want to be here. Unless I'm under arrest, take me home now.'

'You are home.' He gestured to the grand old home which was built more than seventy years ago by a family who wanted the world to know that they were upper class.

Maggie opened the door and made a halting attempt to get out of the car, but was nearly wiped out by a double-decker bus as it flew past, headed for Douglas village.

'Not really a safe road to be walking on with a trolly, Mag. Sit back in. I'll take you home in a minute.'

Maggie fell back into her seat, resigned.

'You okay?'

'I'm bloody marvellous. Now what the hell do you want? Spit it out, Jerry and get me the fuck out of here.'

'Do you ever think about it? The life you could have had. The life your family could have had?'

'You're a bastard,' Maggie mumbled, her bottom lip trembling.

'I'm not trying to be.'

'No?' She looked accusingly at him now. 'So why would you bring me here then?'

'I think better when I can visualise things, that's all.'

'And what exactly is it that you're thinking about?'

'The family who used to live here, back in the day.'

Maggie didn't respond. Instead, she went back to staring out the opposite window, perhaps trying to figure out how she could make her own way back to Heatherhill.

'He worked in import/export as far as I know, the fella who built this place. Met a girl from a wealthy background and moved in here after they were married. From what I hear, he built this house as a wedding gift to her.'

They sat in silence for a minute. Even Maggie's breathing, which usually made a sound like she was being strangled, was still now.

'A nice place to raise a family,' he said thoughtfully. 'If the story is right though, they weren't to be blessed with a child of their own. Common problem I suppose.' He turned to look at her with a soft smile. 'Look at me for example. I always thought I'd have a family too. But it wasn't to be. Although in my case, it's because I couldn't in good conscience inflict myself upon a decent woman.'

'A decent woman wouldn't bloody have ya,' Maggie muttered at her window.

'You're right there, Maggie.' He grinned and nodded. They concentrated on their own windows for another bit before Jerry spoke again. 'How old were you when they adopted you?'

Maggie opened the door and struggled out, huffing and puffing as she did.

'Get back in, Mag. You'll be killed on this road with those legs.'

'Fuck you, Jerry.'

As soon as she got outside, she bent over and started coughing again. A car screeched to a halt and three more behind it. She hobbled across the road, giving the finger to the drivers, who to be fair, hadn't honked their horns at her. Only an asshole would, but there were plenty of those on today's roads.

She trundled in the direction of Douglas village, as quickly as she could. Which wasn't very quickly at all. Jerry watched her go and waited until she was far enough away that she wouldn't want to go too much further. As she approached the point where he could pull in at the next gated entrance opposite her, he drove slowly, but still got there ahead of her. He waited for her to catch up.

'What's your plan here, Maggie? You gonna walk all the way back to Heatherhill? Because if you are, I'll need to follow you anyway. I couldn't in good conscience let you go it alone when I'm trained in first aid. And you know you'll need it.'

'There's these things called buses, Jerry. Ever hear of them?' she called across the road. Then she had an all-consuming fit of coughing. It was so bad, Jerry had to kill the engine, get out of the car and hurry over to her.

He wrapped an arm around her shoulders as she heaved and gasped for breath. He patted the pockets of her fur coat, but they were empty. He turned and hurried back to the car, as Maggie fell against someone's hedge. Jerry opened the boot and pulled Maggie's trolly out onto the road. He quickly went through it, until he found an inhaler. He ran back to Maggie, pulled her upright and wrapped his arm around her again. He held the inhaler to her lips and instructed her to breath in, as he pressed the inhaler and listened for the puff. Maggie wrapped her two hands around his and he pressed again. Maggie pressed it a third time, still gripping his hands in hers. Eventually her breathing started to quieten down and level out, but she looked even closer to death than usual and that said something.

'You okay, old girl?'

Maggie shoved him with what little strength she had, but then pulled him back to support her again.

'Come on.' Jerry led her gently across the road. The fancy road where Maggie Hayes had spent her childhood. The road that could have shaped the old crock in his arms into a woman of substance. Right now, Maggie looked like she wanted to die. She often looked that way. But Jerry knew that she had one reason, and one reason only, to live.

CHAPTER THIRTY-SIX

Grace's stomach sank into her shoes when she arrived at Amber's house that night. It was late by the time she got there because she'd spent hours scrubbing every corner of her own house with the same ferocity as she'd scrubbed the spare bedroom that morning. She raced home from work to get it done and now layers of skin were gone from her knuckles and both her hands and knees were raw. Her body ached, but she was sure that no trace of a smell remained, other than cleanliness.

Amber wasn't home again. And there were no signs that she'd been back since yesterday. Grace had been excited to see her. She desperately wanted to tell her their news. But that excitement was mixed with something else. Amber's behaviour of late was unsettling. She'd been unpredictable for years, but that almost made her predictable. She'd go missing for weeks at a time, always. But then she'd come home out of the blue and she and Grace would cuddle on the couch for a few hours and talk. Amber would tell Grace how she was going to get clean and where in the world she'd like to go, and Grace would tell her that she would get her a job at *Jake's* and she could save up and they'd both travel the world together. Neither of them really expected any of that to happen of course, but they both enjoyed pretending. They relished their closeness during those few hours, until Amber's skin started to crawl once more. Then Grace would go to the bathroom or fall asleep, and Amber would disappear with whatever money was in the USA biscuit tin. And that would be that for another few weeks. But that was their routine.

This new routine was throwing her. Her being there night after night, albeit still passed out from heroin, but safe and warm in her own home. Then gone and then back again. It had been months since they'd cuddled on the couch between fixes and months since they'd had anything resembling a proper conversation. Something had brought Amber in off the street and *something* had made her want to stay oblivious to the world around her. This worried Grace. With everything she'd already endured, what could have triggered this change?

She couldn't bring herself to clean Amber's house tonight. She was exhausted from cleaning. Not that there was anything more than a light layer of dust since she'd cleaned Amber's place last. That was how she knew she hadn't been home. Not that Amber used the facilities of her home much, but still. There was no trace of her at all today. Grace flopped onto the couch and turned on the television, deciding to wait in the hope that her sister would come back. That tonight would be the night when they would cuddle on the couch. The night that they would make plans, for real. For however long it took, Grace would wait. She had nothing to race across the green for tonight and despite the makings of a chicken casserole resting in her fridge, she didn't have much of an appetite.

Grace didn't own a television, so she didn't recognise the programme that came on. A bunch of Americans; three men, three women, all beautiful and perfect, sitting on a couch in a coffee shop. One of the men had had a spray tan and it had gone horribly wrong. Canned laughter rang out on some sort of loop. As she watched, she wondered briefly if people like that actually existed in the real world and if so, what kind of lives did they lead? They seemed so carefree. Did they have to get up and go to work, so that they could afford to sit around drinking coffee and having spray tans? Or were they made rich by someone else in their family, like their parents? Did they have the kind of parents who worked hard all the time so their children could grow up and never have to worry about anything, ever? Grace decided she didn't like this show, so she changed the channel. She put on the news instead.

Sharon Tobin came on. She remembered her from Dublin. There was a woman in the hospital at the same time as Grace, who was fully convinced that she *was* Sharon Tobin. She'd sit in the lounge and read the news at midday and six o'clock in the evening, every day. Grace had no idea if the news that she was reporting was real or not, because they weren't allowed to watch the actual news. But she was very convincing. Now though, looking at the real Sharon Tobin, it was clear that she was no relation to Grace's ward mate. She was white for one thing. Though her voice was remarkably similar.

'*And in news just in, a body has been discovered in a garden near New Twopothouse in County Cork this evening. The grim discovery was made when the owner of the property was bringing washing in from a clothesline at the top of her garden, which is separated from the main Cork to Limerick road by a hedge row. Our Southern Correspondent, Paschal Sheehy has more.*'

Grace sat up straight as Paschal Sheehy came on screen, looking frozen with the cold. He was standing outside a house that didn't look in any way familiar to Grace. It had to be a different body. She'd dumped hers in a field, not in someone's garden. But what were the chances of two bodies being dumped in a place as random as New Twopothouse?

'Yes indeed,' Paschal began. 'At around four o'clock this afternoon, the owner of the house here in New Twopothouse returned from work. You can see behind me, that the driveway wraps around the house, so she exited the car on the opposite side to where the remains were discovered. She went inside briefly and then went back out and around to the other side of the house, into the garden where her washing had been on the line since yesterday. What she noticed first was what she thought was rubbish having been fly-tipped over her hedge from the main road, which runs just alongside the property. However, when she went to investigate, what she found instead was human remains wrapped in clear plastic. It's not believed that the victim was known to the family. Gardaí were called to the scene and got here at around four thirty. The scene has been cordoned off awaiting technical examination.'

Sharon Tobin from the newsroom.

'And do we know yet if the body is that of a man or a woman? Do we know anything else about the circumstances surrounding the death or indeed, where the body has come from?'

Back to Paschal. He nods for a bit while he waits for his audio to catch up.

'We don't yet know the gender of the remains or indeed the circumstances of their death. The woman who discovered the remains was quick to think that rubbish had been tipped over their hedge from a passing car, which locals say is a regular occurrence in these parts, with the main Cork to Limerick road running through the village. The remains appear to have been wrapped in plastic, which would indicate that the cause of death was suspicious, but Gardaí have yet to comment on that.'

Back to Sharon.

'Do we know when the technical examination is due to take place?'

Paschal, nodding.

'*Forensics are due to arrive imminently, in fact...*' a Garda SUV drives slowly past as Paschal steps out of its way, '*this is them now. They'll begin examining the scene immediately and the State Pathologist has been notified as well. Gardaí are questioning the family as we speak and we hope to have more information as the evening progresses.*'

Sharon, back in the studio.

'*Thank you, Paschal.*' She turns her back on Paschal, who tries hard to pretend he's not dying with the cold on a big screen beside her. '*And we'll bring you those details as they emerge.*'

More than two hours passed before Grace could bring herself to move. She sat there, staring at the screen, waiting to hear that the body they found was someone else. She didn't get that information from any of the *Nationwide* people who talked incessantly about farming, pollen and some weird lotion being mixed in someone's shed. *Fair City* was equally uninformative and by the time that eventually ended, Grace had started to forget about the news and was instead staring at the chair where Amber usually slept. She still wasn't home.

CHAPTER THIRTY-SEVEN

'If that's one of our missing lads in there, then where the hell are the others?' Paul Jenson stuffed his hands deep into the pockets of his parka jacket, wishing he'd brought gloves with him. It was bloody well freezing.

'We don't know who that is yet,' Jerry mumbled, without taking his eyes off the tent that had been erected by the forensic team.

Paul nodded.

Forensics got there before them, so they hadn't had a chance to look yet. But the description given by the woman who'd found him certainly didn't tally with any of the smiling men who were stuck to the whiteboard back at the station. According to her, the body was that of a man who looked like he'd visited at least two out of the nine levels of hell before landing in her garden. She also informed them that she herself would never be the same again.

'Who fly-tips a dead body?' Jerry mumbled.

'Someone whose wheelie bin can only take three grown men?'

Jerry didn't respond to Paul's dark humour.

'But if fly-tipping is their thing, then the other three could quite literally be anywhere,' Paul added.

Jerry answered his ringing phone. 'Mike, what have you got?'

'The little shop, slash, post office pretty much *is* the village of New Twopothouse. It's the bungalow-type building on the side of the main road, but it's built kind of sideways so it's not actually facing the road as such. It has just the one camera, but it's only covering the front of the building itself. It does take in a little bit of the road, but not enough to be of any use. He's pulling up the footage for the past forty-eight hours now, just in case our killer stopped to post a letter or buy some Tic Tacs. I'll let you know if there's anything, but I wouldn't hold my breath.'

'Look through that footage as if your life depends on finding something, Mike. If you tell yourself there's nothing there, then that's exactly what you'll see. I don't want to hear *Don't hold your breath*, okay? Take it that I'm holding my fucking breath.'

'Sorry. Okay.'

Jerry hung up as Leanne Byrne came out of the tent. She stood for a minute, looking off into the distance. Jerry had known Leanne for more than six years and he knew not to interrupt her at this time. She always took a minute to herself when she walked out of a crime scene and Jerry fully understood why she needed it. When she was ready, she turned and walked towards him. She blew out a long breath and shook her head.

'I honestly thought I'd seen it all.'

Jerry didn't say anything. She'd tell him when she was ready.

'It's impossible to say if that's one of your guys, but what I *can* tell you is that he did not meet with a pleasant end.' Leanne gestured for them to move further away from the scene and from the crowd that had gathered on both sides of the hedge and all around the property. Everyone from police to reporters to looky-loos had come in their droves. Jerry and Paul followed her and she lowered her voice again. 'Obviously all of this will need to be confirmed by the pathologist after the autopsy, but what we do have is ligature marks around the wrists and ankles. Plenty of cuts and bruises...'

'Caused by what?' Paul interrupted.

Leanne threw him a withering glare. 'Well, I'm not sure yet. My guess would be cable ties, but they were removed prior to him being landed here. This is a secondary location, as you might well guess. He certainly wasn't killed here. The bits that *don't* appear to have been gnawed at by an animal are covered with a variety of excretions which, again will need to be confirmed, but looks to me like blood, vomit and bowel. Oh, and he's missing an eye. It appears to have been clawed or possibly chewed out of his head.'

Jerry and Paul looked at her in silence. Paul seemed a little unsure whether she was saying all this by way of punishing him for interrupting her, but Jerry knew that she wasn't.

'And before you ask, no I can't confirm the *being eaten by an animal* part, but it sure looks that way. He was naked except for heavily soiled underwear and we've managed to collect a few hairs, which didn't look like they belonged to him.'

'What colour was his hair?' Jerry asked.

'Somewhere between light brown and ginger I'd say, but it might appear different in daylight.'

'Like most of our lads,' Paul mumbled.

'That's about all I have for you for now,' Leanne said, walking away slowly.

'Leanne?' Jerry asked.

She turned back wearily to face them.

'The bit about the animal? Any chance he's been here for

longer than we think? Could the animals have gotten to him after he was dumped?'

She shook her head. 'He was fairly well wrapped in industrial strength plastic. Whatever it was that got at him, would have had to eat its way through that first and there's no signs that it did. And like I said, we collected a lot of hair from his body.'

'And you think that might be animal hair, or human?'

'Some of both would be nice, but we'll see. There is a lot of plastic there too. We can hope to collect a few useable pieces of evidence from that. A big fat fingerprint, maybe.'

It'd make sense that that could happen. Even the most careful of criminals could easily leave a print or one of their own hairs in all that plastic. And yet Leanne sounded utterly unconvinced that this would be the case.

CHAPTER THIRTY-EIGHT

Shane and Maureen Lowry were somewhere in their fifties by Jerry's estimation, but they both looked older. Farming life, he guessed. Hard work and no time for impracticalities, like hairdos and face creams. They were a weather-beaten couple, but their home was warm and cosy and it smelled like baking. Though there didn't seem to be anything in, or recently removed from, the oven. Perhaps it was one of those country kitchens that saw so much home cooking that the smell had attached itself to the room.

Maureen was sipping whiskey at the kitchen table. Her hands were shaking and her face looked deathly grey. She'd been crying on and off, but now she was just staring into her glass, not knowing what else to do with herself. Her husband Shane seemed more unsettled by his wife's emotional state than the dead body at the bottom of his garden. He'd reach a hand across the table towards her, then slide it awkwardly back before they connected. Then he'd glance up at her from under his serious, hooded eyes, then look down again. Jerry wondered briefly if it was love or circumstances that brought these two together and if now, they were together purely out of habit.

This was his impression after just sixty seconds in their company.

'Hello, Mister and Missus Lowry, I'm Detective Inspector Jerry Hughes. I understand that this is very difficult, and you've had quite a shock.'

Maureen glanced up at him, her eyes rimmed red. She attempted a quivery smile before her face collapsed again. Shane sat up straight, cleared his throat and nodded stoically. He seemed relieved to have someone else to focus on.

'I know you've been over this with my colleagues, but I just want to make sure that nothing gets overlooked here, so is it okay if I ask you a few more questions?'

They both nodded, Maureen again providing him with the same grimacing smile.

'Maureen, what time did you leave the house today?'

She swirled the whiskey in her glass and Shane hurriedly topped it up from the bottle, even though the glass tumbler was three quarters full. Maybe it was the only thing he felt he could do for her. 'I went down to check on the cattle at around six. Then I came back inside and had a cup of tea and a bit of toast. I left for work at around seven, like I always do.'

'And where were you, Mister Lowry?'

'I was down the yard since about half five.'

'Do you always start your day that early?'

'Pretty much. Cattle generally aren't late sleepers.'

Jerry nodded. 'And which door did you go out?'

He pointed to an open door which led to a utility room. The house was north facing, meaning that the gable end of it faced the main road and the part of the garden where the body was found. The garden wrapped around the back of the house and met up with the driveway on the far side. Both their cars were parked at the side of the house, rather than out front. In a lot of Irish farmhouses, the front door is more or less just for visitors, while the rest of the family traipsed their mud and mess in through the utility room. It seemed this house was no different. The driveway became a dirt path which Jerry guessed led down to the farmyard.

'And you went directly down the yard? You didn't see or hear anything out of the ordinary? You didn't go around the other side of the house for any reason?'

'Sure why would I? I had enough work to be doing in the other direction.'

'And what time did you come back to the house?'

'About half three.'

'You were down the yard from five thirty in the morning until half three in the afternoon?'

'Well, things are busy at the moment. We have a heap of calves and a few problem ones. I had to walk the paddocks to check growth, sort the fodder and Seamus is away in hospital with the past three weeks and Peggy isn't able for the place herself, so I had his cows to sort out as well. He was never the same since the thing with the bull last year. I don't know what they'll do with the place, but...'

'So you didn't come back to the house at all before three thirty?' Jerry cut him off, sensing that Mr Lowry was about to hit his stride in a one-way conversation about land and farming.

'No. No, I didn't.'

'Do you take a lunch break?'

'Indeed I do, but I was up at Seamus' place at that time so Peggy, bless her, gave me a feed of bacon and cabbage. She does the whole lot in one pot, boiled for about four hours, spuds and all. It's a bit like eating baby food, but it filled a gap.'

'And did you see or hear anything unusual throughout the day? Would you have a view of the house or garden from where you were working?'

'Ah, no. I heard nothing and saw nothing and this is all very unnatural altogether.'

'And where is Seamus and Peggy's farm?'

'Over yonder about two miles is where you'll find the homeplace.' He gestured over his shoulder, again in the direction leading away from the main road. 'And another couple of fields past that, is as far as I went today.'

'And Maureen, did you see or hear anything unusual as you went between the house and the yard?'

She shook her head, her lip trembling.

'So when you left for work, was that through the front door?'

Another shake of the head. 'We hardly ever use that door. Only the census people use that. Or Jehovah's Witnesses.'

'And where do you work, Maureen?'

'I'm a home help. I call to one lady over the road about three miles. And the rest are all back in Mallow.'

'Did you notice any cars pulled in anywhere, broken down, lost-looking or otherwise out of place while you drove today?'

'Outside our place, you mean? No.'

'And anywhere else?'

She appeared to be thinking. 'No, I don't think so.'

'And when was the last time either of you went around the other side of the house, or down that patch of garden?'

Shane looked quizzically at Maureen. 'Well, I suppose the last time I was over there was the last time I rode the lawnmower over it. Sure that was probably the end of September, or October. Tis in need of a cut now all right, but there wasn't much growth between then and now.'

'And Maureen?'

'Yesterday morning. I hung out a load of washing.'

Jerry nodded. 'And would you have looked towards the hedge at all at that time? Would you have noticed if the remains were there when you were hanging out those clothes?'

She frowned and tilted her head. 'I don't know if I looked. But today I saw it out the side of my eye. It drew my attention like, so I think I would have seen it if it was there yesterday.'

'And was it just the washing that took you around the other side of the house when you came home from work today?'

She nodded, seeming embarrassed all of a sudden. 'I don't normally leave my washing out for two days, but like Shane said, it's been very busy around here and sure didn't I completely forget about it. I only thought of it at all because Mrs O'Leary, God love her, had a bit of an accident and so my uniform was soiled. I always bring a change of clothes, so that was fine. But I was down to one clean uniform. I remembered the other two were on the line.'

'And who is Mrs O'Leary?'

'One of the ladies I look after back in Mallow. Bless her, she can't help it.'

Jerry nodded again.

'So you were bringing in the washing?'

She nodded. 'And just as I took the last few bits off, I saw this big lump of plastic at the end of the garden, beside the hedge. Says I, *for fuck's sake*,' then she stoically added, 'pardon my French, but you have no idea how much rubbish gets fired into the ditch along this road. I swear, people go out driving late at night for no reason other than to get rid of their household waste. And tis we end up paying for it!'

'And what did you do?' He cut her off before she got too sidetracked.

She looked down at her glass again and her chin began to quiver. 'I went stomping over to see what kind of rubbish it was. I'd have no bother going through it, to see if I could find something with a name or address on it. I've done that before. I'd find something I could pass on to the authorities and get a fine put in the post to the louts.' She took a deep breath that sounded like it might end in projectile vomiting. 'It was only when I was nearly on top of it that I saw what it was.'

'What did you see?'

'His face. It was squashed up against the inside of the plastic. It looked like he'd been smothered in it. His eyes were wide open, only one of them was gone. Just a black hole looking up at me.' She brought her hand to her mouth and started to cry. Shane squirmed in his seat and Jerry guessed that it had little to do with a corpse and a missing eyeball.

'I'm so sorry that you had to see that.' Jerry tried to keep her going. 'Did anything else stand out to you about what you saw?'

'You mean other than a fella with half his face gone?' Shane asked abruptly, coming to his wife's aid finally.

'The top of the hedge was battered-looking,' Maureen said.

Jerry waited for her to elaborate.

'I noticed that when I walked away from the clothesline. It really annoyed me because it's taken years to get that hedge right. I thought someone made a right mess of it trying to get their rubbish out of sight, instead of just tipping it out on the side of the road, which is what most of them do.'

Jerry nodded and made a few notes.

'Do you have any dogs?'

'Only Rory.'

'Rory?'

At the mention of his name, an almost bald chihuahua came dancing into the room. Shane looked at him and rolled his eyes.

'Oh. Not your usual farm dog, is he?' Jerry attempted a smile.

'Ray only went to sleep last month.'

'Ray?'

'The sheepdog. Now that was a dog,' said Shane wistfully.

'I see. And was Rory inside or outside last night?'

'Oh, Rory doesn't go outside at all really,' Maureen

answered, sweeping him up into the crook of her arm and kissing him on the head.

'And did he seem in any way unsettled last night?'

Shane and Maureen looked at each other, as if both jumping to the same conclusion at the same time.

'Yes!' they said in unison.

'In what way?'

'Around half four this morning, he started yapping,' Shane began, Maureen nodding furiously beside him. 'He yapped and yapped until I finally went down to let him out. Course it was too late by the time I got there. He was after doing his business all over the blasted kitchen.'

'Did you let him out anyway?'

'No point by then. I threw him into the utility room there, where his bed is, and closed the door on him. But that didn't quieten him either. He was clawing away at the back door.'

'Did you check to see what was bothering him?'

A dawning look crossed Shane's face and he brought his hand to his forehead. 'I did look out the back door all right. Sure, you'd always hear a bit of traffic out there. We're on the side of the main road and the traffic never stops these days. I thought I heard a car spluttering a bit. Like maybe it was about to conk out, but then it spluttered another bit and took off again. Plenty revving too.' He looked down at the table and shook his head. 'Lord Jesus. Do you think that was him?'

'I don't know, Mister Lowry. Did you see anything when you looked outside?'

Shane shook his head. 'No, but I was looking out the other side of the house, towards the yard. When I heard the spluttering, I was going to throw on my boots all right, thinking maybe someone was in a spot of bother out on the road, but then I heard it taking off so I didn't bother. I went back up and got dressed. There was no point in going back to bed at that hour, so

I had breakfast and went to work. Didn't think anything of it since.'

'Jesus. That was probably him,' Maureen said, in an exasperated whisper. 'Was that him, do you think?'

Jerry made a gesture with his hands to indicate, maybe, maybe not.

'And you have no cameras on the property?'

They both shook their heads.

Jerry took a card out of his pocket and slid it across the table. 'We might be in touch again over the coming days, but in the meantime, if you think of anything, no matter how insignificant you think it might be, please do call me.'

They both reached for the card, but it was Maureen who got there first. 'We will.'

'And eh, when do you think they'll take him out of the garden?' Shane asked, sounding embarrassed by his own insensitivity, even though it was a reasonable question.

'Well, the pathologist is with him now and forensics are just about done, so he should be removed before long. These things just take as long as they take.'

'Of course.' He nodded vigorously. 'Of course they do.'

CHAPTER THIRTY-NINE

Grace wandered aimlessly around the English Market. It was Sunday, her day off, but she didn't know what she actually wanted in there. She wanted to cook something really special for Amber. Something like a fillet steak with peppered sauce and chunky chips, and on the side, some of those giant mushrooms and roasted cherry tomatoes on the vine. The kind of meal that they'd never let their younger imaginations stretch to. But steak had to be eaten immediately. It wouldn't keep. The microwave would utterly destroy it and she wouldn't do that to Amber. She could only cook that meal when Amber was sitting at Grace's kitchen table, waiting for it with her mouth watering. But what if Amber didn't turn up again tonight? What if Jerry couldn't find her?

'Hello again!'

Grace jumped at the sudden intrusion into her thoughts. It was Kevin, the butcher.

'Hello, Kevin.'

He was smiling brightly at her. He rubbed his hands together and looked like he couldn't wait to hear what she was having for dinner today. 'What are we having?'

'Er...' Grace glanced over the display.

'Looking for inspiration, eh?'

'I think that's exactly what I'm looking for. I need something for a special occasion, but it needs to still be special when it's reheated.'

Kevin furrowed his brows momentarily, but soon straightened his face back into its usual enthusiastic smile. 'Well, some would argue that cottage pie or even a lasagne actually taste better on the second day.' He gestured towards his beef display. 'Or maybe a curry, depending on the sauce?'

Lasagne! Amber loved lasagne and she could do garlic bread and some of those creamy sliced potatoes. She smiled back at him. 'I think you're right, Kevin. Lasagne it is.'

He looked pleased. She liked Kevin.

He applied a glove and scooped up a beautiful cut of round steak. He held it towards her for approval and she smiled and nodded. As per Kevin, he sang loudly while he minced. Grace rocked on her heels while she waited and looked around the market, still smiling. Until she saw Maggie, standing beneath the Farmgate with her trolly by her side.

The way she was stood there staring at her made Grace wonder if she was real, or an apparition. Grace's smile faded and she tilted her head in question. Maggie never ventured into town and Grace did wonder if she really was looking at the woman's ghost. Was she lying dead and undiscovered somewhere and was this her spirit coming to summon Grace? Not that Grace believed in any of that. But then Maggie's cough rattled through the indoor space, drawing looks of thinly veiled disgust from all around. Even Kevin stopped mid-song and grimaced at the mincing machine. He was too polite to stare at the shambling old woman in the five-euro fur, but he did seem to lose track of what anthem he was singing.

Grace turned away from Maggie again and looked to Kevin,

who was bagging up her mince. As he weighed it and added a sticker to the bag, she glanced again out the side of her eye, half expecting Maggie to have disappeared. But she hadn't. Her coughing had ceased, but she was still standing there, staring at Grace.

'Just four euro and sixty cents to you, love.' Kevin handed her the bag.

Grace handed him a fiver and took the beef. She put it in her bag and looked again at Maggie. This time she raised her eyebrows at her, by way of asking what she was doing. Maggie just continued to stare. Grace rolled her eyes and walked away from the butcher towards her.

'You look like you're haunting the place, Maggie.'

'Maybe I am.'

Grace had no idea if or when she'd last seen Maggie anywhere other than *Jake's* and was unsettled by the sudden break in their routine.

'So... are you buying something?'

'I need to talk to you.'

'You talk to me every day. What's so urgent?'

Maggie walked away towards the Princes Street exit. Clearly she expected Grace to follow, and she did.

'Where are we going?'

'Your house?'

'I have things to do, Maggie. I'm not going home yet and when I do, I'm going to be busy making lasagne. So whatever's eating you up, you'll need to spit it out here.'

They stepped out onto Princes Street, a part of which had become a hub for outdoor dining in recent years. It was quiet this morning and Maggie headed towards the outdoor tables and then gestured towards the nearest one, which was surrounded by many others, all empty for now. 'Buy me a cuppa then, Gracie?'

Grace exhaled loudly. She didn't want to drink tea with Maggie on her day off. She liked to keep her working life and her private life separate, and she'd never had to worry about the two colliding until now.

'What is it that you want, Maggie?' Grace walked ahead of her and sat down begrudgingly. She didn't want to seem inhospitable. Not when Maggie had always been good to her, but she really didn't have time for this today. Well she did. But she didn't *want* to spend her time with her. She felt a small twinge of guilt about this, but she wanted today to be all about her and Amber. This could be the biggest turning point in their lives and she didn't want Maggie's drama to be a part of it.

'Tea and a full Irish,' Maggie said, before the young waiter had a chance to ask. 'And she'll have the same.'

'Just an Americano, please,' Grace countered. She didn't appreciate the assumption that Grace would pay for a full meal for Maggie. She had the money, but that wasn't the point. *She* liked to be the one who decided where she spent it and on what.

The waiter gave a tight smile and walked away.

'Is there anything else you'd like me to buy for you, Maggie?'

'It's just an auld sausage, Grace, it won't break you. Anyway, after we have this talk, we might never sit down together again so... might as well make it count.'

CHAPTER FORTY

'Are you dying or something, Maggie?' Grace asked, but Maggie didn't respond. She just sat there, looking at Grace, looking all around her and looking in the door of the café. Grace couldn't tell if she was expecting someone to pounce on her, or if she was just really hungry waiting for her breakfast. She did her best to be patient with Maggie because she really didn't want to fall out with her. But she also needed to get home. She needed to find Amber and tell her their big news before she burst. She did *not* need to be a part of whatever situation Maggie seemed intent on creating.

Finally, Maggie's fry and Grace's coffee came. Grace watched as she attacked her food in the same way that Grace and Amber had attacked a pizza once upon a time and for a minute Grace worried that Maggie didn't have enough to eat. She rarely ate anything in *Jake's* and Grace made a mental note to stow away some leftovers for her in future. She didn't voice her concerns, knowing how awful it felt to be pitied. But she no longer minded that she was buying her breakfast.

'You look like you have ants in your pants, Maggie,' she said instead. 'If you're dying, please tell me. Otherwise, can this wait until we're both back in *Jake's* tomorrow? I have stuff to do today and I need to cook a lasagne for Amber.'

Maggie filled her mouth with a combination of bacon, sausage and fried egg and then slowly and deliberately she lowered her utensils. It took an age for her to chew it up and Grace couldn't imagine what had her so tied up in knots. Maggie had never been backwards in coming forwards. She always said exactly what she wanted to say, which was one of the things that made Grace feel like she could trust her.

'Maggie!'

'Okay!' She swallowed. 'This isn't easy for me, all right?'

'What isn't? What's this about? It's dramatic even for you, Mag.'

'You know how I asked you before, if you remember the first time we met?'

Grace nodded.

'Well, you've always known me as *this*.' She gestured to herself, pulling at her fur coat. 'You and the rest of Cork city. People's memories only go back so far, and I suppose this is the real me now.'

Grace raised her eyebrows but didn't speak. She had no idea where this was headed but she suspected it wouldn't get there any time soon. Not at this rate.

'I'm going to tell you a story, Grace. It's not a very nice one and I once swore I'd never tell it to anyone, but...'

'You don't have to tell me anything,' Grace said, cutting her off. She of all people knew how important it was to keep certain stories to yourself and she couldn't understand why Maggie felt the sudden need to share. Unless she really was dying, which seemed more and more likely.

'I do, Grace.' She took a visibly deep breath and exhaled a

stream of stale air across the table. Grace unintentionally filled her lungs with the same air and quickly coughed it back out. 'And I'm asking you to please not interrupt me when I start, because I honestly don't know if I'll get through it.'

Grace's mind was too full for this. Not with thoughts of the man she'd thrown over the hedge in New Twopothouse. She didn't care about him. But she did want to tell Amber that she needn't worry about him anymore and she needed to think, *really think* about where Amber might be. Plus, having put every piece of fabric in her house through the washing machine, she had a lot of drying to do. She'd left the Shake n' Vac down on the carpets too. It made sense that giving the scented powder more time to work its magic would eliminate any offensive odours that might be lingering. That all needed to be hoovered up and then there was dinner...

'Grace?'

'Yeah? Okay, tell me.'

'Right, well when I was a few months old, I was adopted by my parents. I don't know much about my *actual* parents, but the couple who adopted me were Jennifer and Eugene Loughnane. They were the only parents I ever knew and believe it or not, we lived on the posh side of the Rochestown Road.'

Grace arched one eyebrow sceptically. This seemed far-fetched even for Maggie, but she said nothing. Though she did glance subtly at her watch.

Maggie smiled ruefully. 'I know what you're thinking. *She's finally lost her marbles.* But I assure you, it's true.'

Even hearing words like, *I assure you* coming out of Maggie's mouth seemed all wrong.

'I lived in a big house and got driven to school in a BMW most days.' She paused again and this time it dragged on so long that Grace wasn't sure if Maggie expected a response, despite specifically asking her not to give any.

'They were very strict. My life revolved around school, homework, badminton, piano lessons and swimming lessons. I felt like I had no freedom whatsoever and they had my life planned out to a tee. I was to finish school, go to UCC, study business and finance and then go work for my father. He worked in import and export.'

Grace blew out a long breath to distract herself from speaking. She wasn't believing a word of this, but Maggie had never lied to her before today. At least not that she knew of, so she wondered what this was really about. 'Maggie...'

She held up her hand. 'Please, Grace?'

Grace raised her hands in surrender and gestured for Maggie to carry on.

'I thought I had it so tough. The worst life imaginable!' She shook her head and laughed, incredulous. 'What a bloody eejit, eh?'

Grace kept her mouth shut but looked pointedly at her watch this time. Maggie either didn't notice or pretended not to.

'There was a girl in my glass called Janet Greene. Her father worked in banking. Anyway, we were in second year so I suppose we were about fourteen years old. Old enough, we decided, to be out on the town. So one night Janet told her parents that she was staying in my place and I told mine that I was staying in hers, and off we went into Krojak's.'

'Krojak's?'

Maggie nodded. 'Best nightclub in the city back in them days. We left from Janet's house, got changed in a public toilet and hit the town. It was over eighteens, but we were dressed to the nines, and they never questioned us.' She looked down at the table. 'I wish to God sometimes that they had.'

Grace waited. She was becoming interested now. If this was a tall tale, which she still suspected it was, then it was a very detailed one. Grace was curious to know where it was headed, conscious still of all she had to do today, including walking some of Amber's usual haunts in the city. She needed to find her.

'That was the night I met Paddy Wilson.'

Another long pause.

'He was a stunning sight, Grace; tall with these big, powerful shoulders and a pair of eyes that could cut right through you. It's embarrassing to think I was that stupid. A silly little girl who thought good looks were some indication of the type of man behind them. But you know at that time, even if he were puck ugly, he still would have gotten me. It was his swagger, you see. That's what would have gotten Paddy any girl in that room. Do you know what I mean, Grace?'

Grace shook her head, no. She'd never been attracted to a man. Except maybe Jerry, but that wasn't the kind of attraction that Maggie was talking about. Grace had been attracted to Jerry and sometimes to the wife he didn't have. She fantasised that they would adopt her and Amber and the four of them would live happily ever after. But she couldn't care less about his looks or his swagger. Grace had never been attracted to anyone in that way, meaning that so far she couldn't relate to any part of Maggie's fairy tale.

'By Christ, he had swagger. The ugliest bastard in the world can walk into a room and attract anyone they like if they have that kind of confidence. But he was handsome on top of it all and by God he knew it. The cherry on the cake was that he didn't even glance at Janet and she was gorgeous. He just made a beeline for me and I was his from the second he opened his mouth to say hello.'

She started in on the fry again and Grace waited. But as minutes passed, she began to think the conversation might be over and felt a little frustrated. Eventually she asked, 'Is that it, Mag?'

'Well I went from the Rochestown Road, to this.' Again, she pulled at her coat. 'So what do you think?'

'I don't know, Maggie. It's not my story, is it?'

Maggie froze with the fork halfway to her mouth. Just a brief but noticeable pause before the food slowly continued its journey. 'Actually, Gracie, it kind of is your story.'

CHAPTER FORTY-ONE

The atmosphere at the station was charged and excitement buzzed like static in the air. Most of the cops around the table in the conference room had never worked a murder case before and cases like this were exactly what they had in mind when they joined the force.

'Quieten down.' Jerry dropped a file heavily on the table at the top of the room and they all fell silent. Detective Sergeant Paul Jenson sat to his right and around the table were Garda Martin Flemming, Garda Mike Duggan, Garda Linda Foley, Garda Toby Myers and Garda Luke Maguire. Steph Casey came through the door on Jerry's heels and was propped against a wall at the back of the room. Steph was a civilian and as such, she wouldn't normally be invited into a case conference. But her mind was on these men too, and that mind was one of the sharpest Jerry knew. He wanted her there and as SIO of this case, no one was going to instruct him otherwise.

'It's been confirmed that the body is that of Alan Manning, one of our four missing men.'

There was an intake of breath and a low mumble that died down again almost immediately.

'Mister Manning was the fourth man to go missing, which means the other three are either in grave danger, or they're already dead. Either way, we need to find them. He was wrapped in industrial plastic and SOCO took a number of samples from the scene. They were hopeful that they'd find more, but you know yourself. All we need is one finger to point us in the direction of our killer. We've put a rush on forensics but we're not waiting around. We have three more potential victims, so we need to find the person responsible for this ASAP. You can consider your lives on hold until we do. Mike, where are we with the CCTV?'

Mike straightened up and reddened significantly. 'Well, there wasn't any really. Only the post office, but the camera was angled towards the door of the building. I've passed it over to Mac for further examination.' He glanced towards Luke Maguire.

'Luke?' Jerry asked their tech guy.

Luke shrugged and shook his head. 'You *could* say there wasn't a lot to be gleaned from it really. But if I could just move you aside for a second, there *was* one thing.'

Jerry stepped aside and turned to look at the screen behind him, which suddenly came to life. Paul shuffled his chair further out from the table, to give everyone a good view.

Luke pointed a small remote and did his thing. A dark, pixilated scene filled the screen. 'It's dark and grainy, so not the best of cameras, but coming up now, at 4.53am, you'll see some headlights. The building is on the side of a main road, so headlights won't be unusual. But watch for a minute.'

They all stared silently at the screen, until eventually there was a faint light, clearly from headlights in the distance. But then those lights arced, then filled the screen, jumping and bouncing before swerving out of view on the opposite side of the road.

'It would appear that a car did a U-turn here. It's the only break in the road barrier, so it's the only place to turn back between there and where the body was dumped.'

Mike spoke up again. 'Not much on its own, but Mister Lowry said that he heard a car spluttering around outside their property not long before that. He thought it was someone with car trouble and he was about to go out, but then they took off, engine revving.' Luke rewound the recording to show the headlights again and Mike continued. 'As the headlights arc around, they're bouncing and shuddering a bit. It's possible that this is the same car that was outside the Lowry property moments earlier. Possibly a bit of an old crock, or a bad driver. Or maybe a combination of the two. Either way, it might make him easier to spot on camera closer to the city.'

'Good work. Mike, round up CCTV from—'

'Already on it. We have footage from Mallow Fire Station, two Supermacs premises, one on the Limerick Road and one in Mallow, Keary's garage in Mallow and as far back as the Commons Inn, just in case.'

'I'm going through it today,' Luke added.

'Good. While you're at it, we need to dig deeper into the backrounds of all four of our missing men, Mac. I know we've looked, but we need to look harder. Any digital footprint they've left behind. Clearly they all crossed paths with our killer. But how? Where? Did our killer contact them online? By phone? Check their calendars. Did they arrange to meet them? Or did they randomly bump into each other? Did they all work in the same place, once upon a time? Did they go to the same bloody pre-school? I don't care how tenuous it seems. I want to know how they were chosen and how they were incapacitated by this person. I want everything. Get some uniforms to trawl through the CCTV. Take any help you need, but get me those answers.'

Luke nodded.

'Linda and Toby, go back to the families of all four men and spread it out to their circle of friends. Find a connection. Alan Manning's boyfriend is in the hospital at CUH. He didn't take the news well. Had some kind of breakdown.'

Jerry's phone was on silent, but it buzzed loudly against the table. He glanced at the screen. A message from Leanne Byrne popped up.

We need to talk.

'Okay, get to work.'

The uniformed Gardaí got to their feet and buzzed out of the room leaving Jerry, Paul and Steph, who'd stayed silent throughout. She wasn't here to get involved in anything that was discussed before now. She was here to run through the unlikely scenario that these victims were somehow connected to the Murphy sisters. There was nothing to suggest that their paths had ever crossed. They'd have no reason to. The slight physical resemblance to someone from their past was the only reason Steph was here at all and to anyone else, that was a very thin thread. She was there to help investigate a niggling hunch that both she and Jerry shared. Though for once, neither of them wanted their hunch to be right.

'A spluttery old car?' Steph mumbled, as soon as the others left.

Jerry glanced at her. 'There's a lot of them in the country.'

'True.' Steph nodded.

'Grace Murphy's piece of shit Punto. Is that what you're trying so hard not to say?' Paul asked without looking up.

'I honestly don't think that thing even runs. It had two flat tyres last time I looked at it and it's rusted all over.' Jerry picked up his phone and opened Leanne's message fully, but it contained no further information. Just the announcement that they needed to talk.

He texted back:

> Where and when?

> I'm on my way back to Cork. I'll be there by two.

> Costa, Blackpool?

She replied with a thumbs-up emoji.

CHAPTER FORTY-TWO

'Hughes!' Superintendent Carl O'Connell barked in the door and immediately turned and walked away.

Steph and Paul both took on the same look of surprise; eyebrows raised, mouths slightly agape. Jerry for his part managed to keep his features neutral, but whatever bee had landed in the Super's bonnet was not a good one. Carl never bothered Jerry. As far as bosses went, he was one of the best. He trusted his team and allowed them to get on with their jobs until such time as one of them fucked up. When that happened, he was known to go nuclear. His bark made it seem very much like that was about to happen.

'I think he wants you to follow him,' Steph said in a stage whisper.

'What did you do?' asked Paul in the same manner.

Jerry didn't respond to either of them. He picked up his file and followed Superintendent O'Connell to his office. The door was slightly ajar when he got there so he knocked and poked his head around. 'Everything all right?'

'No, everything is *not* fucking all right, Jerry. Close the bastarding door and sit your arse in that chair there.' If his finger were a blade he would have made ribbons of the chair opposite his own. He himself did not sit down. He paced, and that wasn't good.

Jerry did as he was told and sat down.

'Are you comfortable, Jerry? You look comfortable. You look like a man who's ready for some reminiscing. A nice trip down memory lane.'

Jerry frowned.

'I wondered at first how they got there, but then I remembered the kids.'

Jerry rubbed his forehead. He didn't have time for whatever this was, but he kept his mouth shut because Carl looked like he might blow.

'You remember the kids, Jerry? Fourth class at St Vincent's, I think they were. All dressed in high-vis Garda jackets, crowded around you while you smudged their fingers in ink and then, using your own smudged fingers, you showed them how you input fingerprints on the system to track the baddies. Wasn't that it?'

Jerry didn't answer. Not even to point out that his prints were in the system since his first homicide when he was still in uniform. He was printed for elimination purposes when he was first on the scene, but he kept his mouth shut. This was Carl getting ready to go into orbit, but Jerry had no idea why.

'Little did we know at the time, eh?' He squeezed the bridge of his nose and a bitter-sounding laugh escaped him. 'But enough about that. Maybe now you wouldn't mind telling me,' he clenched his teeth and growled out the rest of the sentence, 'how in the name of sweet fucking Jesus those same fingerprints turned up a match to the ones found on the plastic that our dead guy was wrapped in?'

Probably because he didn't want this news to travel through the station and around Cork city at the speed of light, Carl didn't scream, nor did he shout. And yet his breath still dampened Jerry's face. Had he been able to think, he would have picked up on the chicken chow mein that Carl had for lunch. But Jerry hadn't heard a single word that followed the revelation that *his* fingerprints were among the samples collected from a body dump.

'Give me something, for Christ's sake, Jerry?'

A dense fog descended on Jerry's brain.

'I needn't tell you that you're done as far as this case goes. And unless you can come up with a damn good explanation, you'll be done in far more ways than just that one.'

When Jerry failed to answer, Carl stormed out of his own office, leaving Jerry sitting there alone, staring unblinking at the wall.

'Christ, the Super looks like he's having a stroke!' Paul peered in the door and stage-whispered at him again, but it was enough to snap Jerry out of whatever state he'd been in. He blinked rapidly and got to his feet. He tried to speak but his throat had dried up. 'Jesus, Jerry, you don't look so hot either. What's going on? What's happened?'

A glass containing a murky brown liquid sat on O'Connell's desk. Jerry floored it and grimaced. Red Bull. He hated Red Bull. He cleared his throat again and handed the file that was still in his hand over to Paul. 'You're SIO as of now.'

'What?'

'I'm off the case.'

'Wh...'

Jerry didn't offer any further explanation as he left the office, leaving Paul staring after him. Out on the street he met Steph, who was leaning against the bonnet of her car.

'Hey, I was just heading away. I figured you...'

'I'm glad you're still here,' he walked towards her, 'saves me having to ring you to come back. Come on. Let's go.' He sat, uninvited into her car.

She turned and looked at him through the windscreen for a few seconds, but he busied himself tying up his seatbelt and fixing his jumper. Eventually she shook her head and got in beside him.

'Are you going to tell me what just happened, or will I start guessing.'

'Drive, Steph. We don't have long.'

CHAPTER FORTY-THREE

'I'm sorry, Maggie, but I have to go.' Grace looked at her watch and stood up. 'You can tell me the rest tomorrow. I just really need to find Amber.'

'You know exactly where Amber is, Grace, now sit back down,' Maggie barked. She sounded nothing like the kind, eccentric woman that Grace knew. This was a different side to her and Grace was intrigued enough that she did sit back down. 'I killed him, Grace. That's what I'm trying to tell you.'

Grace stared at her, not sure she'd heard her right.

'He started gaslighting me the very night we met and I was so desperate for a bit of excitement, that I made it so bloody easy for him. From that night on, I kept running away from home and by the time I had my first child at sixteen, I was addicted to drugs and alcohol and my parents finally gave up. I disgraced them, over and over again until they finally turned their backs. Liz was Paddy's child of course, but he always referred to her as *your girl.*'

'Liz?' Grace sat up straighter.

'*How old is your girl now?* That's what he'd asked me and that's when I *should* have killed him. But I didn't. Not that it mattered. By the time I went and brought Liz to be pimped out right alongside me, the world had already put her through the ringer. It was too late even by then.' She was staring into the middle distance now with a resigned look on her face. 'Paddy had women all over the city and was earning a pretty penny off their backs and mine. And Liz's. I could have grown up with a decent family and made a decent life for myself. I *could* have had my daughter with a decent man and given her a decent life. And my grand-daughters might not have gone on to lead the lives that they have. You weren't even the first of her children, you know that? You were just the ones who got stuck with her.'

Grace stood up so abruptly that she sent both her chair and the table flying. Their plate and cups smashed onto the road beneath them and other patrons jumped with fright. They all turned to look at them, but neither of them cared and as Grace walked away, Maggie followed her, doing even more damage with her trolly.

'Don't you see, Grace?' Maggie continued to talk to Grace's back as she trotted to keep up with her. 'I killed the man who hurt me and someone that I loved. And you did the same thing. It's in your blood and that's my fault.'

Grace picked up the pace and Maggie started coughing violently behind her. The sound got further away after Maggie stopped trying to keep up and Grace didn't look back.

She half ran, half walked towards St Patrick's Street. She needed to go straight home. She'd get the lasagne started and look for Amber after. As she crossed St Patrick's Bridge and onto Bridge Street, she started jogging. MacCurtain Street was packed as always with people thinking they were in the South of France, dining outdoors all along the suddenly trendy Victorian Quarter of Cork city. Grace wasn't a runner and was out of breath as she rushed past them all and when a car pulled in alongside her, she almost prayed that it was a taxi.

'Hop in, Grace.' It was Jerry. And a woman who looked vaguely familiar, but Grace couldn't place her.

'I'm fine, thanks,' she replied. She didn't like this. Everything about today was wrong.

'Grace, get in the car.' Jerry sounded more forceful now. Everyone was acting out of character and Grace's skin started to itch. It hadn't done that in years. It had itched constantly from the time she was stretchered out of her house on her fourteenth birthday, up until a few months before she was released from the CMH. But suddenly the creepy-crawlies were back and as she ran her nails up along her arms, she realised that her hands were free. She'd left all the ingredients for Amber's lasagne under the table on Princes Street.

'Shit!' She turned and hurried off in the opposite direction, back towards Bridge Street. 'Shit!'

Suddenly Jerry was beside her on foot. He caught her by the elbow and she yanked it away from him. 'I need to get my ingredients. I left my bag behind. I need...'

'Grace, you *need* to come with me, right now.' His grip tightened on her and he steered her roughly back towards the idling car that was now causing a traffic obstruction, though Jerry and the woman didn't seem to care.

Grace didn't feel right all of a sudden. She felt dizzy and her arms were burning as she tore at the skin. Jerry made a brief attempt to stop her, but his priority was to deposit her in the back seat of the car and once he'd done that, he jumped into the passenger seat again and the woman took off. Jerry was out of breath and looked close to a medical emergency, but Grace didn't notice as her vision blackened around the edges.

CHAPTER FORTY-FOUR

There was a symphony of car horns as Steph pulled out into traffic, but she didn't bat an eyelid. An ex-cop who now drove taxis in the city centre was not easily intimidated. They drove towards Kent Station and Steph pulled into the car park at the back.

'What are we doing?' Jerry asked, still not breathing as steadily as he should be.

'This is as far as we go until you tell me what the hell is going on,' Steph said, then she turned in her seat to face Grace, 'and why are you so quiet all of a sudden?'

Grace was staring straight ahead. She wasn't blinking. She hardly seemed to be breathing and her features were completely impassive.

Jerry turned in his seat now too. 'Grace?' He snapped his fingers in front of her face, but she didn't respond. 'Shit. Grace?' He clapped his hands loudly this time, just inches from her nose. No response. Jerry groaned and rubbed his hand across his face.

'What's wrong with her?'

Jerry shook his head. 'I've seen her like this once and so have you.'

Step looked at him and then back at Grace. 'Yeah, but she was catatonic then. She'd just...' she glanced at Grace again, 'she was in shock. Jerry, what's going on?'

Jerry brought his other hand to his face now and dragged both palms roughly around, pulling the bags under his eyes closer to his chin. 'Fingerprints found on the plastic turned up a match,' he said into his hands.

'The plastic? You mean what he was wrapped in? Were they hers?'

He took his hands away and looked her in the eye for the first time since leaving the station. 'They were mine.'

Steph turned more deliberately in her seat and was facing him full on now. She shook her head. 'What?'

He glanced at Grace. She was completely tuned out and this saddened him, despite the circumstances. Everything about this was breaking his heart. He turned back to Steph. 'She needed some help when she got out. I tried everything I could to get her a house in any other part of the city but Heatherhill. She was offered a couple but she turned them all down. Despite everything she endured there, it's still the only place she's ever felt at home. And of course there was Amber. So finally I convinced the council to release the house she's in now. It was boarded up at the time and a complete shambles on the inside, but with some persuasion, they got the basics sorted out – kitchen, bathrooms, windows and doors and the rest we sorted out with elbow grease.

'There was a huge roll of industrial plastic in the back garden. The garden was so overgrown that we didn't see it at first, but it had been dumped there. I offered to get rid of it, but Grace was never one for waste. We ended up using it to cover the floors while we painted, sanded or any other job that created a bit of a mess, and even then she didn't want to throw out the bits we'd used. There was more plastic on one of those rolls than a normal person could ever use. It was the size and shape of a roll of carpet. But when we finished each job, she made me take each room-sized piece I'd cut off and roll it back around the main roll. Just in case it would come in handy again. To the best of my knowledge that was the only industrial strength plastic that could possibly have my fingerprints on it. As soon as I saw Alan Manning rolled in plastic at the bottom of the Lowrys' garden, I thought of Grace Murphy's garden and the roll of plastic there.'

Steph continued to look at Jerry until she was sure that he'd finished. Then she turned to look at Grace. If she'd heard any of what he'd said, she didn't show it. Her features hadn't changed at all.

'Grace?' Steph said softly. Her old professional tone. 'Did you hear that, Grace?'

No sign of anything from Grace.

Jerry took out his phone. It took him a second to find the contact he needed, but when he did, the call was answered on the third ring.

'Hello... Jerry Hughes, is that you?'

'Hello, Doctor Williams.'

'Miriam was fine the last time we spoke and it's still fine today, Jerry. But the fact that you're calling me at all means that something is wrong.'

'Can you come to Heatherhill Station?'

'When?'

'Now?'

'Er... hang on.'

He could hear her tapping on a keyboard. 'I could be there in an hour.'

'As soon as you can.'

'Give me a heads-up here, Jerry. What am I about to walk into?'

'Grace Murphy is in trouble. She's with me now and she appears to be catatonic.'

'Then she can't possibly be interviewed or put under any form of pressure.'

'She's in serious trouble, Miriam. I won't be able to hold back the flood for long.'

More keys were tapped on the other end of the line. Miriam blocked the speaker while she spoke to someone else. Jerry could hear her asking for something to be rescheduled. There was a rustling sound before she returned to him. 'I'm on my way. But I won't meet you at the station. I'll meet you at the CUH. Head for the AMUH and ask for Doctor Cian Bradford. I'll let him know you're on your way. Anyone who needs to speak with Grace, will need to do so under medical supervision and only when it's deemed safe for Grace. Is that clear?'

Grace had been in the Acute Mental Health Unit, or AMUH of the Cork University Hospital for a short time following her committal in Dublin and Jerry sincerely hoped she would never have to return there. But right now, it seemed to be her best option and while he didn't know this Doctor Cian Bradford, he both knew and trusted Miriam Williams. 'I'll see you there.'

There were no beds to spare in the AMUH, but thanks to Miriam, Grace had a trolly in a room that was possibly once an office. Jerry had sat with Miriam and her colleague and let them know about the wave of trouble that was about to come Grace's way. He told them about the similarities between the victims and Philip Munroe and Doctor Bradford seemed to already know who that was. He seemed very well briefed on Grace Murphy and Jerry wondered if it was because he and Miriam were in a relationship. Their body language was telling him nothing, but then Grace had made national and international headlines when she'd killed Munroe. Her case was probably a case study for medical students by now, but Jerry was glad. It meant he didn't have to keep explaining her history.

Grace hadn't responded to anything they'd tried since they'd gotten there, but Miriam gave her a sedative anyway.

'If Grace did kill Alan Manning, then it's logical to think that she knows something about our other three missing men. In which case, she will have to be questioned. They may be alive somewhere and in need of emergency care.'

'I understand.' Miriam nodded. 'But no one is getting anything out of her in her current state. I will help you here, Detective. But for the next number of hours at least, you need to continue your investigation without her.'

Again, Jerry pulled his increasingly saggy skin in all directions around his face. Miriam was right and he knew it. But that didn't make it any less frustrating.

When they'd settled Grace and both doctors were in the room along with Steph, Jerry stepped outside and took his phone out of his pocket. It had been silently buzzing incessantly and he had a total of seventeen missed calls. Most were from Paul, three from Carl and the rest were from the team who probably didn't yet know that they had a new SIO at the time of their calls to him. No doubt they knew now. There were notifications of four voice messages and a slew of text messages. He ignored them all and was about to dial Carl on his mobile.

'Hey?' Steph caught him by the elbow. 'I need to get home. Pennie is there.'

Jerry patted her on the arm and nodded.

'Call me as soon as you know anything. Or if you need me,' she added.

'Thanks, Steph.' He brought his phone to his ear as Steph walked away towards the exit. Jerry hadn't even heard it ring when Carl answered.

'Where the fuck have you been? You're lucky I don't have a warrant out for your arrest. But if I don't see you in here with a damn good explanation in the next ten minutes, then I will send lights and sirens your way and don't for one goddamn minute think that I won't.'

'Send Paul, boss. But send him to AMUH minus the lights and sirens.'

O'Connell was silent. He was processing, though he wasn't sure what exactly he needed to process. 'Are you taking the mental health route or something?'

'You no more think I killed Alan Manning than I do, sir. I'm leaving here now, but I'll give Paul a call to fill him in. Meanwhile, can you send Mike to meet me in Heatherhill?'

'What part of *you're off the case* didn't sink in, Hughes? Because the way you're throwing out the orders, anyone would think *you* were in charge here.'

'Give me the next couple of hours, sir. After that, you can do whatever you think needs to be done with me. But please, send Paul here and send Mike to meet me.'

'Where in Heatherhill?'

'Amber Murphy's house.'

CHAPTER FORTY-FIVE

'I don't like this house, Jerry,' Mike mumbled as he stepped out of his car and went to stand alongside Jerry, who stood at the garden gate. He was looking straight ahead at the Murphy house. 'Martin Flemming was gone like the clappers when the Super mentioned meeting you here.'

Martin was just out of Templemore when he walked into the Murphy house that day and Jerry didn't think he ever got over it. He'd been back there a handful of times over the years. They all had, but Martin only ever went when forced. In truth, Jerry hated this house too. And yet, he had his own key to the front door, given to him by Grace when she returned to live in the estate.

'Why are we here?' Mike asked. 'And why are you putting off going inside?'

Jerry didn't answer either question. He didn't know what he expected to find inside the house, but his gut was telling him that it wouldn't be anything good. 'Have you your body cam on?'

Mike checked the device. 'Yeah.'

'Good.' Jerry rooted his small bunch of keys out of his

pocket. He busied himself finding the right one as they walked up the short garden path to the front door.

'Christ, can you smell that?' Mike made a face and looked around the overgrown patch of garden. It was getting dark now, so they couldn't see much. 'What the fuck are they dumping in here?'

Jerry didn't answer. He smelled it too, but it wasn't rubbish. His jaw tightened and emotion crawled up inside him, but none of this was evident to Mike. He stood at the door twisting the key in his hand. 'Mike, if you want to hang back here for a minute, you can.'

Mike stopped looking around the garden and faced Jerry. Realisation dawned on him and he removed his cap. He ran his hands through his hair and exhaled loudly. 'Shit, Jer,' he mumbled.

Jerry brought the key up to meet the lock and as they slowly pushed the door open, they were slammed face first into the unmistakable stench of death. Mike gagged and turned to retch onto the path behind him. Jerry coughed and covered his mouth. He too could feel his stomach contents loosen. 'You don't have to come in but call SOCO.'

Mike straightened up but looked ashen, his lips wet with saliva. He put a hand on Jerry's shoulder. 'Wait.' He pulled his phone from his pocket and walked towards the car with it held to his ear.

Jerry didn't wait. He forced himself to walk through the door and he leaned against the wall in the hall, just beside the open sitting-room door. He tried to prepare himself for what he was about to see, before leaning forward and glancing into the room. He squeezed his eyes shut, but he'd already been branded with the image.

Amber Murphy was sitting in the armchair. Or at least, he assumed it was Amber. The body was so badly decomposed that its size, shape and hair were the identifying factors for Jerry. He covered his mouth again and released a shaky breath. Then he vomited onto the hall floor.

'Oh Christ.' Mike appeared at the sitting-room door and disappeared from it just as quickly. He paced back outside and down the garden path, before turning back. He stopped at the front door, took a breath and pulled himself together as much as he could. Then he returned to Jerry's side, just as he walked into the room.

Beside Amber was a small table. Her heroin kit was neatly stored away in its little case, with the rubber tube rolled up beside it. On the coffee table in front of her was a plate of shepherd's pie that looked to be a couple of days old, at most.

'Oh Grace,' Jerry whispered, his heart breaking once more for the lives that were wasted in this house.

———

SOCO arrived within thirty minutes and once again, Leanne Byrne led the team. Jerry and Mike stood leaning against Mike's car. Neither of them spoke and when they had time to think back on tonight, Jerry would be grateful to Mike for going through the door with him. Not that he wanted anyone else to have to live with what they'd seen for the rest of their lives and if it were a random stranger's house, Jerry would have insisted he stay out.

'You okay?' Mike asked.

Jerry nodded. He was standing with his back to the house now and was looking across the green towards Grace's house. 'You should have stayed outside.'

'Who are you telling?' Mike injected false humour into his tone, but his voice shook slightly. 'So you think Grace was in and out of there, cooking for her even though...'

'I don't know, Mike. But it looks that way.'

Leanne came out and took her moment to look up at the stars. Then she walked towards Jerry and Mike. 'Well, that's not something you see every day.'

'Which part?' Mike asked. Jerry just waited.

'Well, she's been there for months by the looks of things. Again we'll have a proper timeline once the pathologist is done, but the food is relatively fresh and there's evidence that someone's been cleaning the house. At least the downstairs section. Upstairs is like a creepy mausoleum. It looks like it hasn't been visited in years, but damn is it bleak. Everything has a layer of dust on it and none of the beds look slept in. But downstairs, there are streaks of what looks like furniture polish on the surfaces, there's a washing-up bowl in the sink with water in it. Dishes in the drying rack. The kitchen bin has junk mail in it, including a buy-one-get-one-free that's only valid for this week. Someone's been coming here. They've been cooking and cleaning and all the time there's been a decomposing body in the sitting room.'

Mike exhaled loudly towards his boots. Jerry continued to look towards Grace's house.

'Jerry?' Leanne asked. 'You know why I wanted to meet for coffee?'

'My prints?'

She nodded.

'I know.' He pushed himself off the car and walked towards the green.

'Where are you going?' Mike asked, but Jerry didn't answer. He just kept walking.

CHAPTER FORTY-SIX

Eventually, Mike went after him and by the time he caught up, Jerry was standing in the more pristine but equally tiny front garden of Grace's home. The same smell of death and decay permeated the air directly outside the front door.

'Get Leanne over here,' said Jerry.

Mike turned and moved away from the house. As he ran back towards the Murphys' childhood home, he brought his phone to his ear once more, without breaking stride.

'What have you done, Gracie?' Jerry whispered.

The last thing in the world he wanted to do was step inside this house and find something awful. But he reminded himself that there were three missing men. The smell was unmistakable to anyone who's smelled death before, but if there was even the slightest chance that any of those men were alive, then Jerry had to get to them. Even as this thought occurred to him, he still couldn't get his head around the idea that Grace had somehow overpowered four men and killed them. How could she have done that and continued to serve him coffee over at *Jake's*? How could she have done that, full stop?

He pulled his keys from his pocket again. Grace had given

him front door keys to both homes, just in case and again, he was overcome by guilt and grief. He opened the front door and shoved it with his foot. From where he stood on the doorstep, he reached inside and turned on the light. The smell was violent and Jerry doubted if it would ever leave him. Even the clothes that he wore would need incineration after tonight. He could see through to the kitchen where a large bundle of clothing or perhaps curtains lay on the ground beside the washing machine. There was a white powder covering the entire floor from the front door, through to the sitting room and from what he could tell, the kitchen lino too.

'I know you weren't going to go in there without me, Jerry.' Leanne was behind him now, breathing hard. She was carrying a large holdall and had removed the protective clothing she'd been wearing across the road. 'Here.' She pulled another white papery boiler suit wrapped in plastic out of her bag and handed it to him. She took out another for herself. They both got dressed up in the garden. As Jerry put on his shoe covers, Leanne reached over and tucked his hair into his hood.

Two more squad cars pulled up outside just in time to deal with the small crowd that had started to gather on the green. They were looking from one house to the other, not wanting to miss a thing. Speculation would be rife now about what the notorious Murphys had done this time.

When they were fully covered, Leanne led the way into Grace's house, with Jerry close behind. They closed but didn't lock the door behind them. The smell was a physical force that they almost had to wade through, but the source of the smell did not seem obvious on the ground floor.

'Look how clean this place is,' Leanne muttered. 'She picked up a cushion off the couch and brought it close to her masked face. 'It's still damp.' She walked to the kitchen, stood and looked around. Pots and pans hung beside Grace's cooker. They were all well used but were far better quality than Leanne's. There was a display of cookbooks on a shelf beside the cookware. 'She likes to cook,' Leanne said, more to herself than to Jerry, but he answered anyway.

'Food is important to Grace because she grew up without ever having enough of it. Not everyone can take basic human rights for granted.'

Leanne glanced at him but didn't comment. She could at any moment tell him that he was too close to all of this and kick him out the same way he'd come in. But she didn't. She knelt to feel the bundle of clothing on the floor. 'She's washed everything. I'd imagine if the smell of death weren't so overpowering, this place would smell of washing powder, bleach and,' she touched the powder on the floor and brought her gloved fingers close to her nose, 'Shake n' Vac.' She gestured towards the stairs. 'Shall we?'

Jerry walked ahead of her. The smell grew even stronger the higher they climbed. Before he'd even reached the top of the stairs, he saw the padlock and bolts on the outside of the door leading to the box room. The padlock was hanging open and the door was slightly ajar.

'What the...?' Leanne saw it too. 'Mike?' she called down the stairs.

The front door opened slightly and Mike popped his head into the hall. 'Yeah?'

'Get on the phone and get another SOCO unit up here.'

'Ah Christ,' Mike responded, punching his phone back to life again.

'No one else gets in here,' Leanne called back, as he pulled the front door shut again.

Jerry used the tip of his gloved finger to push open the bedroom door. The carpeted floor was clean and there was a foldable chair and TV dinner table in the centre of the room. A tall roll of industrial plastic leaned vertically against the wall in the corner.

'Jesus,' Leanne whispered, looking at the three rolls of plastic which lay horizontal on the floor beneath the blacked-out window. Three bodies, wrapped in exactly the same way as Alan Manning. 'I think we might have found your missing men.'

CHAPTER FORTY-SEVEN

J erry stared at the three faces looking back at him, each in a
slightly different stage of decomposition and distorted by
the plastic that encased them. Leanne was talking but her
voice was a far-away, muffled sound. Without responding to her,
he turned and walked calmly out of the room, along the short
landing and down the stairs. He wrenched the front door
opened and staggered as he stepped outside, but righted himself
quickly enough that only the keenest observer in the now
enormous crowd would have noticed.

'I'm pretty sure they've come from all over Cork,' Mike said,
nodding towards the green. There was a line of uniformed
Gardaí out on the footpath and the same on the other side of the
estate. 'What did you find?'

Mike didn't sound like he really wanted to know, and Jerry
didn't want to elaborate. But Mike needed to know. 'Our
missing men. Not a word until it's confirmed.' He stripped off
the protective clothing and walked down the garden path and
over to one of the uniforms. 'Who's driving?' He indicated the
squad cars of which there were two on this side of the green.

'That'll be me.'

'Darren, right?' Jerry knew the lad to see. He was based in town.

'That's right, Detective. Need a spin somewhere?'

'CUH.' Jerry walked around to the passenger seat and got in. Darren was buckling up in the driver's seat by the time he got there.

They drove out of the estate as if they were in no hurry at all and going nowhere important and Darren waited until they were on the busier road into the city before putting on the blue lights. But at Jerry's request, he didn't add the siren. Still, what traffic was on the road parted to let them through and they reached the hospital with no hold-ups. Jerry jumped out near the AMUH and left Darren to abandon the car somewhere less intrusive than the front step.

Inside, Jerry knew where he was going so he didn't stop to speak with anyone, nor did he wait for the lift. He half ran, half walked until he reached Grace's room. He pushed open the door, but the trolly was empty. The sheet and blanket were pushed back and the indentation of Grace's head was still on the pillow. Jerry looked around. There was no bathroom in the room, which he still suspected was intended to be an office. Still, they'd used it to accommodate Grace when she desperately needed it and so he couldn't complain. He breathed his pain and frustration out through his nose like a dragon breathing fire and shoved his way back out. He met a nurse in the corridor coming out of a nearby room.

'Where's Grace Murphy?'

'Who?' the nurse asked.

Jerry thumbed over his shoulder towards the room he'd just come out of.

'Sorry.' The nurse pulled a sheet of paper from his pocket and unfolded it. It was a list of names beside room numbers. 'I'm agency, so I've only been here for a few hours. I don't know anyone.' He smiled, not sensing Jerry's impending explosion.

'Where's Doctor Williams?'

The man sheepishly shook his head and lifted his shoulders. 'Again, sorry. I know there's a Doctor Meade around tonight if he's any good to you? I haven't met Dr Williams yet, but that's not to say she's not in the building.'

Jerry couldn't listen to him anymore. He turned and stomped down the corridor, stopping at a door with a toilet sign on it. He shoved it open without knocking, but there was no one in there.

'I'm sorry, sir, can I ask who you are and what your business is here?'

'I'm Detective Inspector Jerry Hughes and the woman in *that* room,' he stabbed his finger towards the office/bedroom door, 'needs to be found immediately!' He'd begun shouting, something he rarely did, but had no control over now. 'You have lockdown protocols here. Initiate them, right now! Or don't you know how to do that either?'

Before the nurse had a chance to release the indignation he was feeling, a young doctor in a Tommy Hilfiger tracksuit appeared behind him. 'Is there a problem here? Our patients are trying to sleep.'

'Clearly not all of them.' Again Jerry shoved his finger towards Grace's room, while pulling out his badge with the other hand. 'Lock this building down immediately. I want every square inch of it searched and I want Grace Murphy found, right now!'

The doctor hurried past Jerry towards a nurses' station and picked up the phone. He spat something short and sharp into the receiver and hung up again. Automatic doors started to close and before long, staff began to appear. Some even came running. Still at the nurses' station, the doctor held Grace's open file and pointed to her photo, which was clipped to the top corner. He moved it around so all the staff could see and then they began moving off again in different directions. It seemed like a well-practised routine and Jerry was grateful for that much. Still, he had an uneasy feeling in the pit of his stomach. It almost took from the fact that his heart was breaking in two.

CHAPTER FORTY-EIGHT

'Gracie, my love. This is a surprise.' Maggie was somewhere between shocked, frightened and embarrassed about the fact that Grace was at her door, though she suspected it wasn't the first time she'd seen the conditions she lived in. She was carrying two takeaway cups.

'Can I come in, Mag?'

Maggie had taken an age to open the door. She never answered when anyone knocked, because it was never anyone who actually wanted to see her. It was either kids looking for a chase, or kids trying to scare her. It was never a visitor. Only when she heard Grace's voice calling her name did she open up and even at that, she very nearly didn't. She opened the door wider and stepped back. 'Course you can. I'm sorry it's not very...' Her voice trailed off and Grace didn't respond. Nor did she look around her when she came inside. She just went straight towards the kitchen table and sat down and Maggie knew that she'd definitely been here before. Maggie joined her and Grace slid one of the cups towards her.

'Something to warm you up. It's freezing in here, Mag.'

Maggie took the cup and nodded. Grace took a sup from her

own and Maggie could smell coffee. She sniffed her own. It was tea. She took a sup and remembered the two cups that she found there when she came back from the hospital. Same cups. Same table. She wondered who Grace had drank with in Maggie's house that time.

'How did you let it happen, Mag?'

Maggie didn't look at her. She kept her eyes on the cup. Grace couldn't get away fast enough from Princes Street earlier. Maggie half expected that she'd never speak to her again. The other half of her expected this. Maybe worse.

'I mean,' Grace continued, 'you had a charmed life. And you gave it all up so that you could be pimped out by your boyfriend. You then *allowed* him to do the same thing to his daughter. *Your* daughter. My mother...'

'I'm not proud, Grace.'

'...who in turn, did the same thing to us.'

Maggie lowered her head again and drank from her tea. She didn't want it. She almost choked on it, but she needed something to do. Something other than look Grace Murphy in the eye.

'You're my grandmother.'

Maggie took another drink.

'You're Amber's grandmother.'

Maggie's hands shook.

'When I look back now, as a grown-up, I realise that *everyone* knew what was going on inside our house. *Everyone* knew that our mother left us alone for days on end. *Everyone* knew that we were hungry. That we were neglected. God knows they commented on it often enough. The good old Murphy Stench, isn't that right, Mag? They all knew. Why else would they lie to social services day in and day out?'

'They lied to keep you and Amber together.'

'Really? You don't think they lied to keep my mother out of trouble?'

Maggie shook her head. 'No one liked your mother, Gracie.'

'Why? Because they knew she was abusing her children? Because they knew she was allowing others to do it?'

Maggie's whole body was shaking now. She took another drink, a longer one this time.

'I remember you from back then. You were always there in the background. Now I know why.'

'Keeping an eye on you, Gracie.' She looked up now, hopeful.

Grace nodded and swirled her coffee in its paper cup. 'Keeping an eye on me,' she whispered. 'And what did that eye see, Mag?'

Maggie gripped the cup in both hands to steady them.

'You certainly saw me being carted out the door on a stretcher, behind the mangled body of my baby sister, I know that much. But I mean, what did you see before that? Did you see anything that might lead you to think, *Hmm, maybe I could help my grandchildren?*'

'Grace, please understand that by then, there was nothing I could have done. Liz hadn't spoken to me in years. She wouldn't let me anywhere near you, or her. She passed me on the street like I was invisible. I couldn't have...'

'It's okay, Maggie.'

Maggie finally started to cry. 'It isn't okay, Grace. I know that.'

Grace nodded. 'Anyway, there's nothing any of us can do about it now, is there?'

Maggie's shoulders shook.

'Where's our mother?'

'I don't know.' Maggie breathed out the words between sobs.

'You know it wasn't okay, Mag. Now I'm here asking you for

the only thing I've *ever* asked you for. It *wasn't* okay, but I can forgive you. Lie to me now and I never will.'

Maggie looked to the bulging ceiling and blew out a shaky breath. 'She lives on Connolly Road. About halfway along, there's a house painted pink. You can't miss it. Your mam is living next door to that. She has a yellow front door.'

'Who's she living there with?'

Maggie shrugged. 'Some poor bastard who lived with his mother up until she died. Liz has infiltrated the woman's home and has been claiming it as her own for some years now. Your mother is a cuckoo, Grace. A parasite.' She drank again, then twisted the cup in her hands. 'You asked me what I saw.' Her voice was no more than a croaky whisper.

'And?'

'I know what you've been doing.'

'Finish your tea, Maggie. It's freezing in here.' She took another drink of her almost cold coffee. 'Bet you wished you were tucked up in that house on the Rochestown Road now, eh? I know I do.' Maggie took the lid off her cup and drank, her shoulders shaking as she did. Grace stood up. 'I don't think we can be friends anymore, Maggie. But I do hope you rot in hell.'

CHAPTER FORTY-NINE

G race walked into town and had intended to continue on towards Anglesea Street, out to Turners Cross and up Connolly Road. She didn't mind the walk. A part of her felt she needed it. However, just as she was passing Merchant's Quay shopping centre, the 209 bus pulled up. The sun had come up and the bus services had started. She'd lost all track of time and she imagined that Jerry was somewhere having a fit over her disappearance by now. Knowing him, he could pull up alongside her any second and she wasn't ready for that yet. Anyway, she didn't want to think too much about Jerry now. She loved him, she really did. She'd loved him for most of her life, so the idea that he might have known all this and kept it from her was something she just couldn't think about. Not yet.

Had he known that Maggie was her grandmother? Had he known that she and Amber had great-grandparents living on the Rochestown Road? People who might have been able to rescue them all those years ago. Who might have *wanted* them. They could have saved them from all those years of hunger, fear and pain. How much had Jerry known? She didn't want to be angry with him and again she thought about him pulling up to the kerb alongside her. She jumped on the bus which would take her all the way to Connolly Road and the house with the yellow door. She knew Connolly Road. A long row of nice, warm, cosy houses. If her mother was indeed living there then she was living well. Without a care in the world.

As the bus ambled through the city, her thoughts flipped involuntarily back to Jerry. The *old* Jerry. The man who stood behind the desk in the Bridewell Garda Station all those years ago when she'd first walked through the door looking for her mother. The man who'd sent her away with enough money to feed herself and her sister for two days. She wondered at what point he might have looked into her family. Of course he knew who her mother was. Every Garda in the city knew Liz Murphy and as a result, most of them at least knew *of* Grace and Amber.

But at what point did Jerry delve into the resources that he had at his fingertips to see what relatives they might have had? He knew the conditions they lived in. He'd called social services several times himself, she knew he had. So why did he never follow-up? Why did he never look further, beyond Liz Murphy, or at the very least, why had he never given Grace the opportunity to do it for herself? Jerry was about the only human being on this Earth that Grace trusted. She'd trusted him for as long as she could remember. But had he, like everyone else, been conspiring to keep the lives of two little girls confined to the carpet under which they'd been swept?

By the time the bus shuddered to a stop on Connolly Road, Grace's insides bubbled like a boiling kettle. She stepped off and watched as it pulled away again. Then she stood there for a minute more while she got her bearings. Maggie had said the house was somewhere near the middle of the very long row and

Grace estimated that if she turned left, she might be on the right track. As she walked, she looked to both sides of the street for a pink house beside a yellow front door. It took a while, but eventually she saw it up ahead, on the other side of the road.

She crossed over but didn't speed up. As she approached the pink house, the yellow front door opened and a man came out. He was short and round, with a pink complexion. He looked like he might be close to a heart attack, but he didn't seem aware of it. He looked quite contented in fact. The off-white collars of an old shirt poked out of the neck of his brown V-neck jumper. He wore an equally drab tie. He seemed like the type of man who lived his life in brown and beige and Grace wondered if Maggie was lying about where her mother lived. She just couldn't picture this man with a woman like Liz.

'Hello,' he said to Grace, as she stopped beside him.

'Hi,' Grace responded, hesitantly.

'Not a bad old morning,' he said jovially, as he continued past her and let himself into a six-year-old Ford Fiesta that was parked at the kerb outside his house.

'Not bad at all,' Grace responded. Then she continued walking, past the pink house and the house with the yellow door. The Fiesta's engine fired up and the car revved a couple of times before it pulled out onto the road. It swung a wide U-turn and drove off in the opposite direction, towards town. Seconds later the car was out of sight and Grace turned back. She walked up to the yellow front door and knocked. Unlike when she'd knocked at Maggie's front door, she didn't have to wait long for a response here.

Liz was smiling when she opened up, but her face fell when she saw Grace standing on her doorstep. Grace for her part was somewhat taken aback too by how well her mother looked. Somehow, she looked years younger than she had when Grace was a child. The heavy make-up that she'd once worn was gone and was replaced with something much more subtle. Or else the woman's life and appearance had improved so much that she managed to look something close to normal, some might even say attractive, without wearing any make-up at all.

'Grace?' She began to look older again all of a sudden. It was as if Grace herself was her mother's kryptonite. She closed the door a little, so that only her head was visible. Clearly she didn't want to invite her firstborn child inside. But actually Grace wasn't her firstborn, was she? Maggie indicated there were several before her, but she and Amber were the ones who'd been stuck with her. The thought made Grace's mouth twitch, but she didn't launch into those questions just yet.

'Hi, Mam,' she said instead and gently shoved the door open.

Liz's strength seemed to evaporate, leaving Grace to walk right in. As she suspected, the house was both warm and homely. The brown floral carpet on the floor was probably put there in the old woman's time, but it was clean and still held some bounce. The magnolia walls reflected the man of the house in the sense that everything about him seemed beige. Far too boring for the woman she remembered. Grace could smell toast in the air.

She led herself along the short hall, past the closed sitting-room door and into a kitchen that had all the signs of being well used for its intended purpose. A full cup of tea sat on the table beside a plate holding two slices of hot toast with marmalade. On the opposite side was another cup, the tea having already been drunk. His plate was also still on the table, covered in crumbs. In the centre of the table was a fresh crusty loaf on a cutting board, with a breadknife resting beside it. There was *real* butter in a dish and an open pot of top-shelf marmalade. Not the generic one that Grace usually bought because she didn't believe there was a difference. Oranges were oranges after all. Grace sat down with the empty plate in front of her. 'Are you surprised to see me?'

Liz didn't say anything. She looked shook. *Small* even. She was nothing like the giant of a woman that Grace remembered. The woman who'd struck fear into their hearts as children and prided herself on doing so.

'You've become a breakfast eater?' Grace half smiled and nodded towards the plate of toast.

Liz glanced at it. 'Would you like some?'

Even her voice was smaller. Grace shook her head. 'No thanks. I just never remembered you sitting at a table, eating breakfast. It looks strange, that's all.'

'We never really had the makings of it, I suppose,' she said, moving forward suddenly and sitting down opposite Grace. She had a hopeful lilt to her voice. Like maybe she was about to reason away the hunger that she'd inflicted upon them.

'Well, *we* never did anyway. You're right about that.'

'Grace...'

'Yes, Mam?'

'I heard about your sister.' A tear rolled down her cheek.

'Did you? Which part did you hear? Eat your toast. It'll only get cold.'

Liz glanced at the toast again and shoved the plate away from her.

'That's a waste.'

'You were better off without me, Grace. You both were.'

Grace nodded. 'Well, we were certainly used to being without you, that's for sure.'

'I know you think I'm a... a terrible mother...'

Grace laughed involuntarily. 'You're wrong. You were the only mother we knew. All we wanted was to see more of you. We wouldn't have wanted that if we thought you were a terrible mother, would we? We would have loved to see you before school for breakfast and when we popped home on our lunch break. Maybe even at dinner time. We would have loved to splash about together in the bath with you washing our hair. We would have loved to have you tuck us into bed at night and kiss us on the cheeks.'

'Grace, I...'

'*You!* We would have loved *you* to tuck us in at night.'

Liz dropped her head into her shaking hands. Then she shoved her chair back violently from the table and it crashed to the floor. 'Who do you think you are, coming here uninvited and judging *me*?' she shouted. 'You think my mother was any better to me?'

'Oh, it *is* you? For a minute there I thought I had the wrong house.'

'Fuck you, Grace.'

'Why not. Everyone else did. How much did you charge them? Did you get more for me than for yourself? How much did he pay for Amber? What was her life worth to you?'

Liz's breathing became loud and heavy and then she screamed, picked up a sugar bowl and smashed it on the floor. She looked at it for a second and then reached for a sweeping brush and began cleaning it up. Grace didn't flinch.

'Cleaning? This is new.'

'Is this why you came here?' Liz snarled, without looking up from the task at hand.

'Did you know that we originally came from the Rochestown Road?'

This time it was Liz who laughed, though there was no humour in it. 'Oh. You've been speaking with your loving grandmother then, have you?'

'It was a shock to discover that I have one.'

'And did she tell you about *my* childhood? About what she did *to me*? She left me with so many people that for the first few years, I had no idea which one of them was actually my mother. She used to forget where she left me sometimes and so I wouldn't see her for weeks! Did she tell you that? Did she tell you that when she finally did stop dropping me on people's doorsteps, it was only so she could bring me into the family business? Not only that, but she was stupid enough to let someone else collect the money, so everything I went through was for nothing because neither of us saw a penny! Did she tell you any of that?'

'She did,' Grace replied calmly, 'and it all sounded so familiar. That's the bit that I can't get my head around. Having had the kind of childhood that we lived through, I could never watch another child go through the same thing. I can't imagine recreating that world for a child of my own. A child that I loved. Even for a child that I hated. I couldn't do it. But you didn't think twice.'

'What would you know, Grace, huh? What would you know about rearing children? Everything I did was to put food in your mouths.'

Grace shook her head. 'Well, that's not true, is it? No one put food in our mouths, Mam. Except me. Any food that made its way to our mouths, was put there by *me*.'

Liz exhaled a shaky breath.

'But I didn't come here to fight about all that. What would be the point? There's nothing we can do about the past now, is there? It's too late for all of us.'

Liz put the dustpan, full of broken glass and sugar, on top of the shiny chrome kitchen bin and she sat down opposite her daughter. 'It's not too late, Grace. I don't drink anymore. I don't... go out anymore. Not really. I don't *do* any of the things I used to do before. I have John now. He's kind. He looks after me.'

'I'm happy for you, Mam. Does he know that you have two daughters? Actually, how many children *do* you have?'

Liz looked stricken momentarily but recovered herself quickly. 'My point is, Grace, it's not too late. We can put everything behind us and move on with our new lives. Forget about the past.'

'That sounds nice.' Grace bobbed her head, as if agreeing. 'But what about Amber?'

Again, Liz brought her hands to her head and this time she clutched two fists full of hair.

'It's nice that you're able to forget about her. About *us* and move on with your new life. And you never answered my question; how many children did you forget, because I know I wasn't your first.'

Liz looked up at her briefly, but returned her eyes to the table, her knuckles white now as she tightened her grip on her hair.

'It doesn't matter. I only have one baby sister and I know I'd have trouble forgetting about her. Not that I've ever tried, I suppose. But I just can't see it coming that easily to me. Not like it has to you.'

'You think this has been easy?' she growled. 'You think *anything* about my life has been easy?'

'Maybe life's not meant to be easy.' Grace picked up the breadknife and ran her finger gently along the jagged edge.

'Why did you come here, Grace?'

'You say you heard about Amber?'

Liz glared at her, some of her old defiance visible now. She nodded once.

'But have you heard about me?'

CHAPTER FIFTY

'Leanne?' Jerry answered the call on the first ring. The search for Grace had concluded at the hospital and staff there were busy covering their arses. They were quick to point out that it was a hospital and not a prison and that, while they were aware of Grace's problems, everyone in their care had problems. If Grace was a threat, then why wasn't she under arrest *or* under Garda supervision? They were right. They shoved the blame back onto Jerry where it belonged, which made it all the more frustrating. Jerry fucked up when he walked out without telling anyone to stay there with her. He fucked up when he assumed that they would. This was on him.

'Jerry, this is...' Leanne blew out a long breath, which sounded loud and mechanical as it whooshed in his ear.

'I presume she hasn't turned up there?'

'Still no sign of her?'

Jerry shook his head but didn't respond verbally.

'Jerry, Grace Murphy is a dangerous bloody woman. She needs to be found.'

'How did they die?'

'Badly.'

He stayed quiet. A part of him didn't really want to know because it would reflect the fact that Grace's cracks had become canyons without him, or anyone else, noticing.

'These men are emaciated. There are signs of torture and the bodies are covered in their own excrement.'

'Like Amber was,' he whispered.

Now it was Leanne who was quiet. When she did speak again, it was much more softly. 'How did she do this, Jerry? How did she continue to pour coffee and look you in the eye, while these men were here, dying in her home?'

Silence.

'I'm sorry. I didn't mean... you know what I mean.'

He did. And she was right. Grace had somehow lured four men to her house and slowly killed them. And she'd done it right under his nose. 'Give me a call if she turns up there.'

'I will. Find her, Jerry.'

He hung up and lowered his head until it touched the steering wheel and he stayed like that for longer than was comfortable. He couldn't think about the families of the four dead men. He couldn't think about the lives that had been cut short and the trail of devastation that their murders would leave in their wake. He could only think about two starving and neglected little girls, with dirty hair, dirty clothes and cheeky smiles. The joy on little Grace's face as she blew out a row of candles on a Swiss roll that was bought at a discounted price of one euro, fifty cents because it was only a day off its best before date. *Everything* was best before that day and every day since had led them here, to a pile of corpses.

His phone rang again. It was Paul. 'Yeah?'

'I thought you'd want to know, ARU are on the way. It's turned into a full-scale manhunt.'

'Shit.' Jerry pulled his seatbelt on. He had a problem with the armed response unit. He felt that all Gardaí should be armed, but they weren't. Instead, they had the ARU who saw themselves as elite. Many of its members were chomping at the bit, waiting for their moment to shine. Waiting to be heroes.

'If they find her first, Jerry...'

'We don't want any heroes today,' Jerry responded.

'My thoughts exactly. I was also thinking, we don't know what state Gracie is in by now.'

Jerry nodded, as he pulled the car into traffic along the quays, switching Paul to Bluetooth.

'The pathologist is here. She's estimating that Amber's been dead for about six months. Now I'm no psychologist, but if I had to hazard a guess as to what might have happened here, I'd say finding her dead after everything they've been through... Gracie just snapped, Jer. It all coincides with the time our first lad, William Jones went missing.'

'Only she didn't see William Jones. She saw Philip Munroe.'

'They'll have to take that into account, won't they?'

'The ARU won't give a shit about any of that, Paul.'

'Where are you?'

'Off the case, remember? You'll get a bollocking for calling me.'

'Well, if it were any other case, then I might pay heed to that. But if Grace is going to respond to anyone, it'll be you. This case doesn't end well if you're not on it, so physically, where are you?'

'On the quays. I'm going to head up St Patrick's Street and through the city. I'll take a walk though Bishop Lucey Park and a few more of Amber's old haunts. Grace has been bringing dinners to her dead sister for six months. It's like sometimes she sees her sitting there in the chair and other times she doesn't. Then she calls me to tell me she's missing. As of my last conversation with Grace, she was still looking for Amber...'

'I'll head out to Fitzgerald's Park. Do you think we should check in with Maggie Hayes? She keeps a pretty close eye on Grace. She might have some idea.'

'Grace likes Maggie, but she wouldn't voluntarily spend time with her. She doesn't voluntarily spend time with anyone. Wherever she is, she'll be there alone.'

'Okay. Keep me posted.'

Jerry hung up, wiped his eyes and drove on through town.

CHAPTER FIFTY-ONE

He walked quickly through Bishop Lucey Park, the need to find Grace intensifying with each step. The park was pretty much deserted. She wasn't there and neither were any of her ilk. As he hurried back the way he came, Jerry thought about what Paul had said. He was right. He brought his phone to his ear again. This time he called Garda Toby Myers.

'Boss?'

'I'm not the boss anymore. Detective Jenson is. Take Linda and head out to Maggie Hayes' house. She's Grace and Amber's maternal grandmother and she's been watching Grace like a hawk for years now. Find out when she last saw Grace, what they talked about, how much time she spent *watching* Grace, any of the places she might have followed her to and what she might have observed. I want to know how much Maggie Hayes knew about these men. I want to know if she helped in any way. And most of all, I want to know where Grace Murphy is. Go. And call me back with answers.'

'Yes, boss.'

Jerry didn't hear him because he'd already hung up. He

walked out of the park, across the street and in through the Grand Parade entrance to the English Market. As someone who spent the first half of her life hungry, food had become one of Grace's top priorities when she was released from the Central Mental Hospital. The fresh produce sold in the English Market drew her in like a magnet.

It was still early, so it was quiet enough. There were too many vendors and Jerry didn't have time to waste, but he remembered Grace mentioning that she always tried to buy her meat there, so he headed for the butchers first. Two had no idea who he was talking about and when he showed them a photo from his phone, their curiosity led to a string of questions about what she'd done, but no, they didn't know her. He moved on to a man who was singing loudly as he sliced chicken fillets behind the counter. He was creating some sort of ready-to-go stir-fry mix.

'Excuse me,' Jerry called.

He stopped singing, removed his gloves, grabbed a fresh pair and came to the counter with a smile. 'Yes, sir, what can I get you?'

'Do you know this woman?' He held up his phone with Grace's half-smiling face filling the screen.

'Who's asking?' he enquired, still smiling but not quite as humorous.

'Detective Inspector Jerry Hughes.'

'Is she okay?'

'I hope so. How do you know her?'

'I don't really. I call her "the girl with the lucky sister". She comes in here once a week and tells me what she's cooking for her sister. She's a fan of shepherd's pie and beef in general.'

'You sounded a little defensive when I asked if you knew her.'

He shook his head. 'I don't know. She seems like a vulnerable sort, and you seem a bit angry.'

'Fair enough. When did you last see her?'

'Yesterday. She was here looking for ideas for a special occasion dinner.'

'Did she say what the special occasion was?'

'No, but she did say that the food still needed to taste special when reheated. We settled on lasagne.'

'Did you see where she went when she finished with you?'

'I did as it happens. There was a very strange-looking older woman in a terrible fur coat. She was standing over there, just looking at... what's her name?'

'Grace.'

He nodded. 'She was just looking at Grace. Grace seemed to know her and, if anything, she seemed a little bit fed up when she spotted her. But she did go over and the two of them headed that way.' He thumbed in the direction of the Princes Street exit. 'It could have been her mother, or nan or something.'

'You seem to take notice of your customers. Did you notice anything different about Grace yesterday?'

'I notice my regulars I suppose and in her case,' he shrugged, 'like I said, there's something about her. She seems lonely or something and she seems like someone who takes pride in her food. She's quite animated about dinner and people like that kind of stick in your mind. She was the very same yesterday, talking about cooking for her sister and this special occasion that they had. A pleasant girl, always. I like her.'

'And you're Kevin?'

'I am.'

'Thanks for your time.' Jerry pulled a card from his pocket. 'If you think of anything else or if you happen to see Grace again, please call me.'

Kevin took the card and looked at it, frowning. 'Is she okay?'

'I hope so. Please do call me, so I can make sure of it.'

Kevin nodded and Jerry walked away and out on to Princes Street.

CHAPTER FIFTY-TWO

AMBER MURPHY – SIX MONTHS EARLIER

Standing on shaking legs on the road outside the Cork University Hospital, Amber hugged herself tightly as she looked up and down the busy road. The pain that she was in was excruciating. It always was when she went too long without a fix, but there was more pain added to that now. Her insides felt like they'd been shredded and between her legs burned all the way up to her chest with every step she tried to take. Whatever they'd given her for the pain wasn't worth a damn and she knew that they'd probably denied her the good stuff because of who she was. If she didn't get something soon, she knew for a fact that she was going to die in agony.

She hugged herself tighter and doubled over. She sobbed loudly. She wanted her sister. She needed Grace to wrap her arms around her and tell her that everything would be all right. She wanted to curl up beside her and fall asleep on her shoulder. She needed peace and Grace was the only one who could ever give her that. Her mind flashed briefly back to the last time she'd scored in the park, and the three Dubliners who supplied her and Peter. She could see herself lying on the ground being beaten and abused by them, but her starving demons screamed to be fed and forced her to dismiss everything else.

She no longer had a phone and she guessed that Peter was dead. She'd seen what they were doing to him, but her only thought on the matter was, who was going to help her now? Who was going to give her what she needed? She tried to flag down one of the many passing cars, but none of them would stop. Amber had no idea what she looked like anymore, nor did it enter her head to check. Her ravaged skin and rotten teeth didn't bother her as much as they would someone else. Someone who could survive on fresh air, water and food. Someone who didn't have a larger-than-life, snarling black dog chasing them through their waking hours.

She turned and started walking. Fitzgerald's Park was only a few kilometres away, but she might as well have been standing at the foot of Mount Everest. Pain of every sort was overcoming her. Her bowel threatened to destroy her at any second and if it chose to do so, there would be nothing she could do to stop it. Nor would she care. She only cared about getting to the park and finding someone to help her, whatever the cost. The sun would set soon and so the happy families would be vacating the area. This was all she could hope for in life right now. She just needed to get there.

She cried as she struggled along the never-ending Wilton Road, using garden walls to support herself. Her bowel gave up and what little her body had left to purge was running down the inside of her already dirty tracksuit pants.

'Grace,' she cried. 'Grace, Grace, Grace... I'm sorry, Grace.'

'Hey!'

She hardly registered the voice and it sounded in no way familiar to her. It was the blast of a car horn that caused her to look. Even the act of slightly turning her head felt like an insurmountable task. An old black car with badly applied flames up the side was stopped on the other side of the road causing an obstruction. The guy leaning out the window was smiling at her, like he knew her. She didn't care if he knew her or not. All she cared about was whether or not he could provide her with heroin. The fact that he'd stopped his car and was smiling and calling to her, told her that he could. There would be no other reason or incentive for someone to stop at the sight of someone like Amber Murphy.

She staggered across the road.

'Jesus Christ, what happened to you?' he asked, still smiling like he really didn't care what the answer was. Except that maybe it would make a good story to pass on to whoever he met next.

'What have you got?' Amber asked in the window, not caring that she was in the middle of a still-busy lane of traffic.

'Jesus wept! You stink, Amber!'

She pulled a purse out of the sleeve of her jumper. She'd lifted it out of a handbag that someone had stupidly left under their trolly at the hospital. They deserved to have it stolen for being so thick. She opened it to find a bundle of fifty-euro notes. Five of them at least.

The man lifted his chin to look inside. 'Ah. You gotta love pension day.'

'Give me what you have and take me home. Then it's all yours.' She dragged herself around the front of the car and opened the passenger door.

'Woah, hold on!' he shouted, leaning across the seats, holding out his hand. 'You're after shitting yourself, girl. You're not getting into my car.'

She shoved herself in and his seatbelt saw to it that he couldn't stop her.

'For fuck's sake, Amber.' He groaned.

She couldn't respond or even really hear him, such was the

pain she was in. Her bowel gave out again and her body started to shake. Cockroaches ran up her arms and legs, underneath her skin. She clasped the purse to her stomach and leaned forward in the seat, but only one thing would ease the cramps. 'Take me home and fix me up. I'll give you everything.'

'Well that money is mine whatever way you look at it and you're in no shape to stop me.' He sat for a second looking at her. He wasn't concerned for her in any way. He wasn't even very annoyed. But he was inconvenienced. Like this was just another hazard of his job. He groaned and rubbed his shaved head, then he pulled out into traffic again without so much as a glance in his wing mirror, setting off another loud blast of car horns.

He talked non-stop while he drove from the city to Heatherhill. He knew where she lived so clearly he'd been there before, which again meant nothing because he was a dealer and she was an addict. He didn't pretend to care about the agony that she was in or about the medical attention that she so clearly needed, but none of that mattered to Amber. She wanted heroin and she wanted to be at home. He was a means to both.

'...I look at you now,' he said, continuing his one-sided conversation, 'and I thank fuck that I only ever dabbled in the merchandise. I mean I'm clearing a grand a day in the hand, for myself while you're absolutely fucking crawling, girl. You would have been a right lasher if you kept control of it. I mean I remember you from kids. You always stank, but you weren't bad-looking. Now you haven't a tooth in your head, there's shit running down your legs and you hardly even notice, let alone care. I wouldn't shag you now if my life depended on it.'

'Let me out,' she finally responded, as they approached her estate.

'Gladly. You're rotten, Amber.' He reached across and opened the glove box. He pulled out a black pouch with a zip. It was bulging at the seams. He opened it in his lap and pulled out a small bundle of her brown saviour wrapped in clingfilm.

Amber reached over and took three more. He grabbed her by the wrist and with her free hand, she dropped the purse with its bundle of fifties, into his lap. He let go of her. 'Where are you hoping to go with that lot, to the moon?'

She ignored him and struggled out of the car.

'There's enough there to make sure you don't come back,' he said, as she shoved the door closed and staggered towards home.

CHAPTER FIFTY-THREE

Amber stood with her back to the door, in the hall of her childhood home. This house had been her prison. Even with the front door open wide, she could never escape it. She hated everything about it, but she could never bring herself to leave. Not for long at any rate. As she stood there, she looked through the hall towards the kitchen and she could hear her mother's voice, telling Grace that she was a useless bitch. She could hear the slap of her hand across her sister's cheek, but Grace was never afraid. She'd simply wait for their mother to finish threatening her, or beating her and then she'd ask for food, for Amber. Never for herself.

She held on to the banister and on shaky legs, she climbed the stairs. She too, knew the many creaks and groans that the old steps recited, but there was one that turned her heart to ice. And it wasn't on the stairs at all. It was outside Grace's bedroom door. It creaked when you stood on it, but what Amber hated most was the tune that it played when someone stood on it and stayed standing there. It made a slightly different sound each time their weight shifted. This tune always played in the minutes before Grace's sobs seeped through her bedroom wall.

Her cries were muffled, but the grunts which sounded like a massive animal feeding at a trough, never were. Back then, Amber had no idea what was happening to her sister, but she knew that something bad was. She knew that someone was hurting her beloved Grace and she was too afraid to help. She didn't know how to.

Amber stood on the squeaky board and let the tune play out. She did this every time she came home. Her mind was gone now and the only way to bring it back was to force it to remember. She cried again and hugged herself tightly, imagining that they were Grace's arms wrapped around her. She could hear her whisper in her ear. *It's okay, Amber. Go to sleep.*

Amber nodded and tears ran down her cheeks. She never went beyond that point upstairs. She hadn't ventured towards her own bedroom door since the day she was carried out through it. Not that she remembered being carried. She remembered very little of that day, but she'd been crushed under the weight of it ever since. She turned and walked back to the stairs, but her legs gave way on the fourth step and she thumped the rest of the way down to the hall. The old carpet peeled a layer of skin off her back, and her coccyx screamed out along with the rest of her body. She was unable to stand up fully after she reached the bottom, so she half walked, half crawled into the kitchen. There was a note stuck to the door of the fridge. She pulled herself to her knees to read it. She'd never been good at reading but Grace made big, clear words that she could usually understand. Or at least, get the gist of.

THERE'S CHICKEN CURRY WITH RICE INSIDE. I'LL MAKE A ROAST WITH MASH AND

GRAVY TOMORROW IF YOU CAN COME OVER?
LOVE U
    GRACE
    XOXO

Amber put her hand against the note and heaved a loud sob. 'I love you too.' She cried. A tiny part of her wished that she could sit and have mash and gravy with her big sister. But what her body needed wasn't food. Not anymore and not for a long time. She had very few memories of food and what the different types of food tasted like. For the most part, it was just something that she rammed down her throat as fast as she possibly could, while trying not to get caught in the act. Though she distinctly remembered what ham and pineapple pizza tasted like. She'd eaten it once and never again. But sometimes she tasted it just as the heroin was entering her bloodstream. That little taste of heaven before being ushered back to hell.

She crawled away from the fridge and out of the kitchen. She struggled into the sitting room and climbed into her armchair. She took the bundles of heroin out of her pocket. Her kit was set neatly on the table beside her. She continued to cry as she prepared far more brown than she should. The sweet smell made all the bugs that crawled under her skin scramble to the surface and scratch and claw to get out.

She pulled the rubber tube tight around her arm and gripped it between her teeth, where tears, mucus and spit poured onto it, soaking it. Amber's arms were destroyed and most of her veins collapsed. But she found a sweet spot and watched as blood was pushed back into the brown liquid. Then she plunged the whole lot in.

Grace's face appeared before her. She enveloped Amber in her strong arms and she was smiling. Grace. Her Herculean big sister. Amber's heart, head and lungs filled with love and warmth. Grace was here. She was safe.

Sshhh, it's okay, my love. Close your eyes.

Amber always listened to her sister. And now for the last time, she did exactly what she told her to do.

CHAPTER FIFTY-FOUR

Grace sat on the railing of the flyover which stretched across all four lanes of the N40 near Mahon. Her legs dangled over the traffic below, which had come to a major standstill. The tailback was reaching as far as she could see in all directions thanks to the squad cars which were parked across the lanes with their blue lights flashing. They were making sure no one got past and Grace imagined a lot of angry people cursing them for delaying their journey home.

Someone had shouted at her earlier and now a whole bunch of Guards were down there, all looking up at her. One was on their phone. There was also a pair of Guards on either side of the flyover. They were diverting traffic away and watching her nervously. One of them was on the phone as well. Probably to the fella below. She gave a small wave because she was sure she recognised one of them as Jerry's friend, Mike. But she was quite high up and he didn't wave back, so she wasn't completely sure. She could hear sirens and when she looked behind her, she could see even more flashing blue lights coming out of the Jack Lynch Tunnel. The Guards were busy today.

She picked her phone up off the railing beside her. She

redialled Amber's number for the twenty-seventh time that day. She listened again to the voice message, that Grace had helped her to record a few years ago, when she'd bought her that phone. She could count on one hand the number of times Amber actually answered one of Grace's calls, but at least when it rang, she knew that Amber had recently had the presence of mind to charge it up, and that was good to know. Plus, it was nice hearing her voice and the hint of humour when she said *I'm too busy to talk to you right now, so shag off.* The pair of them could be heard chuckling before the message cuts off. Grace didn't leave a message, but she did redial one more time.

Jerry was becoming frustrated in his car when his phone lit up again and he answered before the first ring.

'Get your arse out to the Mahon exit off the N40.' No pleasantries out of Paul.

He was on the N40 when he got the call, stuck in the tailback. But not for long. Blues and twos parted the traffic and he got there minutes later. 'Shit,' he muttered as he approached. The ARU had gotten there before him and he could see Grace, perched far too high up for comfort. He found her name easily on his Bluetooth screen and dialled.

'Jerry? Are you okay?' Grace asked. He could see her talking on the phone.

'I'm okay, Gracie. Are you?'

'Ah, you know me. I'm always okay.'

'I know you are. Listen, is that you I can see sitting on top of that flyover?'

'You can see me?'

He could see that she was looking around her now and she leaned forward to look down on the road below as he approached. 'I can and you're doing nothing for my nerves, girl. Aren't you worried you might fall? Because I sure as hell am.'

'Are you down there?' She leaned further forward. 'Oh hang on, is that you just pulling up?'

'That's me. Listen, I'm going to come up, all right?'

'Okay.'

She hung up. Jerry jumped from his car and hurried over to the ARU who had shoved Mike and Martin out of the way. They were now on either end of the divide on traffic management.

'Jerry?' Mike called to him before he reached the ARU.

'Not now, Mike,' Jerry replied.

'Trust me, Jerry. Yes now.'

Jerry changed direction but failed to hide his irritation. *This better be good and those cowboys better not make a move.* 'What?'

'Myers and Foley went out to Maggie Hayes' house. There was no answer, so they went around the property, looking in windows...'

Jerry rolled his hand impatiently, indicating that Mike needed to get to the point.

'They saw her in there, sitting in a chair. She wasn't responding to their calls, so they broke a window and went inside.'

'And?'

'She was dead, Jerry.'

Jerry stared at him. 'How?'

'Looked like maybe natural causes, but there were two takeaway coffee cups on the table. SOCO are still out there, so I suppose we'll have to wait on them and for the pathologist to get there before we know for sure.'

Jerry nodded, his stomach turning another notch, as he jogged over to the ARU. 'I'm going up to her.'

'You're not,' one of them replied evenly.

'You can shoot me, or you can get out of my way. Either way I'm going up there.'

'You're Hughes, right?'

'And I've known that girl her whole life. Now unless you want the body of a very troubled woman on the bonnet of your nice shiny Audi, then I'm going up.'

The man exhaled. 'I was told you'd be a pain in the arse. Look, fine. But take this.' He handed Jerry a small body cam. When Jerry looked impatiently at it, the man took it back and quickly fitted it to Jerry's jacket.

'Has she communicated with you at all?'

'She waved a couple of times. She's very relaxed, all things considered.'

Jerry had no idea what Grace's intentions were, but the ARU were busy putting a plan in place that didn't take her intentions into account. He took the quickest way to get to her, which was to run up the slip road. When he got to the top, he was gasping for breath. But when he saw Grace, he lost what little air was left in his lungs. She was covered in blood. How had he not seen that from the road? She turned to look at him and then she smiled and waved.

'I hate heights, Grace,' he said, trying not to sound so shocked. 'Come over here to me, will you? I'm bloody light-headed just looking at you, dangling over the edge like that.'

'It's lovely over here, Jerry. You can see the whole city. Come on, I'll mind you.' She patted the railing beside her.

Jerry, still caught for breath, stood for a moment looking at her side profile. She wasn't going to come to him. He'd have to go to her.

'Fine. But if you give me a heart attack, I swear I'm coming back to haunt you, so no sudden moves, okay? For my sake.' He moved slowly and carefully until he was standing alongside her.

He looked down at the road below. 'I'm not happy here, Grace. Just so you know.' He tried to keep his tone light and level. Like he always had with her.

Grace glanced at him and smiled. 'I promise, Jerry, if you fall, I'll go after you.'

He ignored what sounded like a veiled threat. 'Grace, you have a lot of blood on you. Are you hurt?'

Grace looked down at herself and then lifted her hands to look at them. She was frowning, like she had no idea what she was seeing. Blood was smeared up her arms and neck. There were splatters across her face too and her clothes were covered.

'Did something happen? Are you all right?'

'I'm all right, Jerry. You'll have to stop asking me that.'

'Okay. Well, then what's going on? *Jake's* is falling apart without you today. Why are we here?'

'I don't know if I'll be going back to *Jake's*, Jerry. I think it might be time to move on.'

'Oh yeah? Where to?'

Grace shrugged and the two stayed quiet for a few minutes. Jerry trying all the time to gauge her.

'Did I ever tell you about my eleventh birthday, Jerry?'

Jerry looked at her again. 'No.'

'I wasn't thinking about the fact that it was my birthday. I was only thinking that we were hungry. So I was down town trying to get some dinner for Amber and me. My plan was to do the town first and then head over to see you,' she looked at him with a smile, 'you were always an easy touch, Jerry.'

Jerry smiled and nodded.

'Anyway, this fella was standing near the bus station and he had a black bum bag on. I saw him but I kept going. I tried never to rob anyone who looked faster than me.'

'That seems wise.'

'I was having no luck around the place. Everywhere I went,

staff were following me around and people seemed to clutch their bags tighter when they saw me coming. So by the time I came back around by the bus station, your man was still there, but he was arguing with this girl. Next thing she started clattering him across the face and shoving him and kicking him. The bum bag fell off and he didn't notice, because now he was shoving her back and they were roaring at each other. So I just kind of swooped,' she made a diving motion with her hand, 'grabbed the bag and legged it.'

'Did he catch you?'

She nodded.

'What happened?'

'Nothing. Maggie appeared out of nowhere and dragged me away from him. She handed him some money and shoved me away up the street.'

They were quiet for a few more minutes. Jerry didn't want to mention that Maggie was dead while there was so much free air beneath Grace's feet.

'I just remembered that now. She told me I'd just tried to rob a dealer's stash and I'm lucky he didn't kill me.' She leaned forward to look down again, making Jerry's heart thump a little louder. 'I didn't know her then. And even after she started coming to *Jake's* I never registered that it was the same woman. I don't think she was wearing the fur coat that time. I would have remembered that.' She grinned. 'I don't think I'd recognise her even now without it.'

'It was good of her to help you.'

'The more I think about it, the more I think Maggie might have been following me that day.'

'Why would she have been following you?'

Grace looked at him and her features hardened momentarily, before returning to her signature look of mild contentment. 'Turns out that Maggie was my grandmother,

Jerry. Me and Amber had an actual, living, breathing grandmother.' She turned and looked pointedly at him. 'Can you imagine that?'

Jerry leaned heavily on his elbows and hung his head over the railing, while Grace continued to look straight at him. 'You can tell me now. You already knew that, right?'

'I did,' he answered.

'And you didn't think a grandparent was something that Amber and I could have done with?'

'You and Amber deserved a hell of a lot more than either of you got out of life, Grace.'

'And yet, people only ever *pretended* to help us. If you cared as much as you say you do, then you would have told me that I had somewhere else to go. Somewhere to take my sister. Somewhere safe.'

'Grace,' he kept his voice low and calm, 'can we move away from here. Just come down off the railing. Stand here beside me, where they can't all see us, and I'll tell you everything.'

'I'm comfortable here.'

'Okay.'

'So? What's *everything*? What other secrets have you been keeping from me?'

He looked down again at the gathering of Gardaí below. They'd become impatient soon. But he hoped the fact that they had eyes on them and could see that Grace was calm, would be enough to keep *them* calm too. Not that the appearance of calm was telling of anything where Grace Murphy was concerned. He'd only just come to realise this himself. She'd managed to keep various men prisoner in her home and torture them herself, while still smiling and chatting with her *Jake's* customers. And with him. Jerry wasn't a religious man. Not by any means. But he said a silent prayer that he wasn't about to push Grace over the edge. Or that she wouldn't push him.

CHAPTER FIFTY-FIVE

'You were ten when we first met, do you remember that?' Jerry started talking.

'I remember.'

'But I knew of you before that. You were right to come to the station looking for your mother because of course, there was a good chance that she'd be there. I've known Liz for most of her life too. I knew she had two daughters.'

'What about the children she had before us?'

This caught Jerry by surprise, but he tried not to let her see that. 'Four that I know of,' he replied quietly.

'And where are they?'

'Her first died very young as far as I know and the three that followed were taken into care. I believe she signed over her parental rights and they went on to be adopted. Or at least, that's what I believe happened. Either way, we have no record of them. The only reason I know anything at all about them is because I got my hands on a file once upon a time.'

'I wish we hadn't been stuck with her, Jerry.'

'I know,' he mumbled. 'I wish that too.'

'But I'm glad she didn't sign us over. Otherwise they would

have separated me from Amber. But...' she cocked her head to one side, 'didn't you ever wonder about us? If we were okay, I mean? Seeing as you knew our mother so well, the thought must have crossed your mind.'

Jerry bobbed his head from side to side. 'You want honesty?'

'That would be nice.'

'From time to time I did, but not much.' He sighed heavily. 'I won't make excuses for anything because there aren't any. But I'll be honest with you about the way things are when you're a Garda. Or at least, the way things quickly become. The nature of the job means that you see a lot of what goes on in the world and you become very jaded by it all, Grace. You see little kids whose parents aren't around to take care of them or to teach them. So you watch those kids grow into the next generation of assholes, failing *their* kids in all the same ways. It's a vicious circle that just keeps on going. Round and bloody round.

'The grown-up versions of these people break the law, hurl abuse and somehow the Gardaí will always be the ones in the wrong. I remember back in the day, long before I met you, one of my colleagues, Kenny, tore a young lad out of a house one night. He was full sure the child would be killed if he stayed there. The father was going berserk and didn't care who was at the end of his fist. The boy was about seven years of age. His mother ended up in hospital, the house was trashed by the drunk old bastard and Kenny took the boy straight to Anglesea Street Station for his own protection. He was fed, Kenny found him a blanket to keep him warm and he had a sleep. An aunt came to pick him up at around six the following morning. That evening, barely twenty-four hours after he helped that child, Kenny was dragged in by our superintendent at the time. The boy was claiming he'd been abused. By Kenny.

'Camera footage from the car showed that he was brought directly to the station and was never left alone with anyone while he was there. The child's story changed several times and fell apart before long, but it didn't matter. The damage was done. Gardaí are among the most cynical human beings on the planet for a reason, Gracie. This is just one of many cautionary tales of getting involved and actually caring about the people we come across in these awful situations.'

'So what, everyone just decides not to care at all?'

'I know that's no way to do this job either. But it's just easier.' He tapped the side of his head. 'Then you came in that day, with your cheeky smile and that yarn about your school lunch.' He was smiling now.

'What made me so different?'

'I'd be told to fuck off and mind my own business by most kids, when I asked any questions at all. You put the effort in to come up with a story. All that chat... you were so innocent, Grace.'

'I was conning you, Jerry.' She smiled back.

'I know you were.' He half laughed. 'And I knew it then too. But you could have walked out the door, knocked over an old lady and taken her bag. Instead, you chatted to an ancient old guard until he voluntarily handed over all his money. But, I also knew *why* you were doing it. You didn't *want* that money. You *needed* it.'

'My sister needed it.'

'That's right. And you've always looked after your sister.' His smile disintegrated and he wondered what her mind was telling her now about Amber. Was it reminding her that her beloved sister was dead or was it still fooling her into thinking she was alive?

'Does this story end with you telling me how long you knew about my grandmother, and why you've lied to me my whole life?'

'It does. Like I said, I knew your mother most of her life

too. Remember that vicious circle I talked about? Well, Maggie was on our radar and had been for a while. The unusual thing about Maggie was that she came from a whole different sort of circle. I don't know if I'd go so far as to say that she *chose* the life she went on to lead. But I do think she got very very lost and ended up stuck in it none the less. But like that, we were aware that she had a daughter, just like we were aware that you and Amber existed. Always in the periphery until the kids themselves land in front of us, for one reason or another.

'The first time Maggie came to our attention was for prostitution. Someone at the station knew her father and contacted him, but he refused to intervene. It seemed she'd burned all her bridges by that time, so long story short, it was about the third or fourth time you came into the station, hungry, that I thought back along your family line. Liz was no good to you and I knew that Maggie was worse. So I *did* look into Maggie's parents to see if they could help you.

'What I discovered was that the mother died in a car accident before you were born and the father sold up and moved back to Belfast where he was originally from. The only thing I could find out about his whereabouts after, was that he stayed around Belfast for a few years, and then he left. No one knows where he went. He didn't have any other family and it was believed he moved to the UK. That's about as much as I could find out, so I didn't think it would do you any good to know about all that. What was the point?'

'But we had a grandmother right here in Cork.'

He nodded slowly. 'I'm not sure how much you really know about Maggie, Grace.'

'Clearly not enough, Jerry.'

'Did she ever tell you that she spent some time in the Central Mental Hospital?'

'She mentioned it. But I spent time there too. Does that make me a terrible person?'

'Of course not. But did she say why she was there?'

'What business was that of mine?'

'Well up until now Maggie needed a daily concoction of medication to keep herself on an even keel, Grace. Not that she remembered to take it half the time.' He sighed deeply again and lowered his voice further. 'Grace, Maggie killed your grandfather.'

CHAPTER FIFTY-SIX

Grace looked straight ahead and waited patiently for him to elaborate. Nothing about what he'd said was shocking and it didn't answer her question.

'Does that surprise you, Grace?'

'I killed a bad man too, remember?' she replied defiantly.

'What makes you think your grandfather was a bad man?'

'Because if Maggie killed him, then that means he hurt her.'

Jerry nodded. 'You're right. Paddy Wilson wasn't a nice person. But she also killed his wife, Charlotte. And Gracie, she *was*. She'd never even met Maggie, let alone done anything to hurt her.'

'How did she do it?' Grace asked after a short silence.

'She broke into their house one night, while they were asleep in bed. Their two children were also in the house, in bedrooms on either side. She stabbed Paddy first. Three times. Charlotte woke up and screamed and that woke the kids. They came running into their parents' bedroom just in time to see Maggie stabbing their mother. Thirteen times she stabbed her, Gracie. This woman she'd never met.'

There was another silence now, but it was heavier this time.

Eventually Grace asked, 'If he was my grandfather, then why did he have a wife and two children in another house?'

'Like I said; he wasn't a nice person.'

'I actually didn't expect an answer to that question, Jerry. I know how these things work.'

He nodded. Jerry Hughes had never felt so conflicted in his life. He was very clear on the line between good and bad, black and white. But Grace was one hundred per cent grey. He felt sure she'd killed Maggie and judging by the amount of blood on her, someone else too. Not to mention the four men she'd tortured to death. And yet his heart was shattering for her. For the child he knew.

'So why wasn't she put in prison? Why hospital?' she asked, oblivious to his turmoil.

'Maggie had had a mental breakdown not long before. She was an in-patient for about three months and after killing the Wilsons, she just... well, she wasn't in her right mind. Far from it, in fact. So it was hospital for her, but she had it rough in there. Safe to say, the treatment of patients with mental health issues wasn't what it is today.'

'Well, she wasn't always in hospital. She was better by the time we needed her. I remember her and she seemed fine.'

Jerry shook his head. 'She wasn't, Grace. You've seen how Maggie lived?' This was a loaded question, but Grace didn't pick up on it.

'So? I could have helped her.'

'But you needed someone to help *you*.'

'You said lived,' she replied quietly.

'What, Grace?'

'You said, how Maggie *lived*. Past tense.'

'That's right, I did.'

Grace didn't say anything.

'They found her just a little while ago.'

Grace nodded.

'Will we get down from here, Grace? My head is starting to swim.' He tried a smile.

'Are they all worried that I might jump off?' She looked down at the sea of blue. Flashing lights and police uniforms, where there should be lanes of traffic hurrying along the dual carriageway. Then she turned to look at Jerry again. 'Or are you worried that I might take you with me?'

Jerry shrugged, his face not giving away the pressure that he felt. 'My life hasn't been worth a damn since I carried your little sister out of that house all those years ago, Gracie.'

She lowered her head. She wanted to cry, but she didn't. 'So what are you saying? You *want* me to jump and take you with me?'

'No.' He shook his head. 'I want you to come down out of here and talk to me.'

'We are talking. As soon as we go down there it'll be all noise with that lot.'

'Do you know why they're here?'

Grace started laughing then. It started as a soft chuckle, getting louder and louder and was suddenly maniacal. So much so that it made all her features change. Added to the blood spatter, the girl he'd known for so long seemed to have vanished and had been replaced by someone, *something* else.

Jerry forced himself to smile. 'What's funny?'

She laughed harder and then stopped as abruptly as she'd started. 'What exactly do you want to talk about, Jerry? What's all this about?' She nodded towards the group below again.

'How'd you get all that blood on you, Gracie?'

She brought her hands up, which made her balance even more precarious, and again she frowned when she looked at them. 'What happened to Maggie?' she asked, as if she'd just realised that something had.

'We're not sure. But they think someone might have visited her before she died.'

Grace nodded. 'Do you think it was Paddy Wilson's family? Didn't you say they had kids who saw Maggie killing their mother?'

Jerry felt his whole body turn cold.

'Could one of them have killed Maggie?'

'We don't know that she was killed, Grace. It could have been natural causes, but we'll have to wait and see.'

She nodded again. 'Well, if it turns out not to be natural, then you need to track down those Wilson kids.'

'Where did that blood come from, Grace?'

She laughed again. 'Well it wasn't from Maggie, if that's what you're getting at.'

'Not at all. Maggie didn't lose any blood as far as I know.'

'I don't think I lost any either.' She examined her arms more closely.

'Where did you go today?'

'Today?'

He nodded.

She shrugged. 'I can't remember.'

'You can't remember?'

She shook her head.

'What's the last thing you *do* remember?'

She looked thoughtfully into the middle distance. 'Breakfast.'

'Breakfast?'

'Yeah. I just had breakfast with Maggie. On Princes Street.' She looked fretfully around the ground beside her. 'Where's my minced meat?' She swung her legs around and jumped down off the railing. She started searching the bridge frantically. 'I'm making lasagne for Amber. Where is it, Jerry? I can't make it without the mince.' She was panicked now.

'It's okay.' He pushed himself off the railing, glad that at least she was away from the edge, but he was far from relaxed. He moved alongside her. 'That's the last thing you remember?'

'Did I leave it on Princes Street do you think? I have to find it. Amber loves lasagne.'

'Grace, that was yesterday morning.'

'No. It was just a while ago. Can you help me find it, Jerry?'

'Okay. Let's get down off this bridge and we'll sort it out, yeah?'

Grace stopped searching and looked at him. Her worried face was childlike again and there she was. The little girl with the cheeky smile. But was she conning him now, too? He reached out slowly and put an arm around her shoulder. She lowered her head and leaned against him and together they walked along the flyover and back down the slip road.

CHAPTER FIFTY-SEVEN

Jerry, holding Grace around the shoulders, quickly walked her towards Mike's car. Mike, to his credit, had the wherewithal to have it unlocked before they got there. Jerry rushed Grace into the back seat and got in alongside her. Mike was at the wheel by the time the back door was closed and Martin quickly appeared in the passenger side. Both seemed relatively pleased to get one over on the ARU. It was easy for them to drive away from the scene, knowing that any fallout would be on their superior in the back seat.

'Where to, boss?' Mike asked.

Jerry was thinking. They were only a few minutes from the AMUH if they used lights and sirens. But Grace had just walked out of there and she'd possibly gone on to kill more people. As much as he wanted to, he couldn't risk it. 'Heatherhill,' he replied at last. As they drove, he fired off a text to Paul.

ON THE WAY BACK WITH GRACE. MEET ME THERE.

Without waiting for a response, he followed up with a text to Doctor Miriam Williams.

> GRACE NEEDS YOU AT HEATHERHILL
> STATION, ASAP.

That was as much detail as he was willing to put in a text. Miriam responded immediately, but it wasn't what he wanted to read.

> AT A CONFERENCE IN DUBLIN. WILL BE
> BACK LATE TONIGHT. TOMORROW?

He responded:

> ARREST IMMINENT. TONIGHT?

He tapped the screen impatiently while he waited for her to respond. If Grace was going to be charged, which seemed very likely, then without a doctor to certify her, she'd be held on remand like anyone else, and that would not go well for Grace.

'Are you okay, Jerry?' Grace asked him.

He turned to look at her. 'I'm okay, Gracie.' He turned in his seat. 'I need to take you to the station, okay?'

She nodded. 'She'll come home. I know she will.'

'Who will?' he asked softly.

'Amber. Don't worry. She always comes back eventually.'

Mike met his eyes in the rear-view mirror before Jerry's phone vibrated again on his lap.

> TONIGHT THEN. IT'LL BE AFTER NINE BUT
> I'LL GET THERE AS SOON AS I CAN.

Eight hours.

> AS SOON AS YOU CAN.

As they drove through the gates of the Heatherhill Garda Station, Paul was standing at the door waiting for them. Mike stopped and let Jerry out.

'Grace,' Paul said by way of greeting, as he opened her car door and helped her out. Paul knew Grace Murphy well and had as much sympathy as anyone for the life she was forced to lead. But right now, she was the prime suspect in multiple homicides and he couldn't see her as anything less. 'Garda Duggan and Garda Flemming will take you inside, Grace.' He looked to Mike as he locked up the car. Martin was around the passenger side, drumming his fingers on the car roof. 'Bring her to interview room one. We'll be along in a minute.'

Mike and Martin nodded in unison. They flanked Grace and started walking.

'Jerry?' Grace looked worriedly over her shoulder at him.

'I'll be right behind you, Grace.'

She nodded but looked sceptical. Paul took a pack of cigarettes out of his pocket, put one in his mouth and lit up. As he exhaled, he nodded for Jerry to follow him away from the entrance to the station.

'You've just lost all your friends in the ARU. Well done, bud.'

'I wasn't aware I had any friends in the ARU.' He didn't have it in him to banter. 'What are they saying about Maggie?'

'Early signs are that she ingested something, but we're waiting on toxicology. The two drinks cups are being tested, but Maggie is only the start of it, Jer. Liz Murphy is currently sitting at her kitchen table with her throat sliced open. The breadknife that was used to do the job was left there in front of her with a fine-sized bloody handprint on it.'

Jerry ran his hands through his hair. 'Jesus.'

'You know that print is going to match Gracie, don't you? She's still wearing most of her mother's blood supply by the looks of it.'

Jerry started pacing. Paul smoked his cigarette, giving his friend and most respected colleague a minute to get his head around this. Grace Murphy had been the case of Jerry's life and this was a horrifying new instalment. He was going to need a minute. But Jerry didn't go far.

'She has no memory of it,' he said, turning back to Paul.

'What's she saying?'

'The last thing she remembers is having breakfast with Maggie on Princes Street. That was yesterday morning.'

'Is she genuine?'

Jerry shook his head. 'I want to believe she is, but...'

Paul nodded. 'Well, to be on the safe side, she'll be out of bounds until a doctor can see her.'

Jerry nodded.

'That means no questions. Not even from you.'

He nodded again.

'But we need samples of that blood and any other evidence that might be on her.'

Another nod from Jerry. He knew all this.

'We'll get Leanne here. Did you reach out to Miriam Williams?'

'She's in Dublin. She'll be here tonight.'

'We could get someone else?'

Jerry shook his head. 'No one knows her case like Miriam. And Grace needs someone she can trust.'

'Which is the only reason why you're still allowed near her.'

Jerry looked at him.

'Because you know you shouldn't be, Jer. If it was anyone else, you'd be the first to point it out. You're far too close.'

'But I'm staying put, Paul.'

Paul nodded, but not so anyone would really notice. 'What're your thoughts on all this?'

Again, Jerry shook his head. 'I think finding Amber might have broken her. Pushed her over the edge, just like you said. They had no one but each other all their lives. For one to lose the other would be earth-shattering.'

Paul nodded. This was what he'd wanted to hear. He needed to know that Jerry wasn't too blind to see that the child he'd loved had become a serial killer. Had he answered differently, then friend or not, Paul would have booted him so far away from this case that he might never see Grace Murphy again.

'Well, the scenes can't wait until tonight and we can't wait to gather that evidence. I agree that Miriam should be the doctor on this, but she needs to send someone she can trust in her place while we get those clothes and gather what we can from Gracie. That same someone should also get a look at the scenes, particularly Liz's house and Grace's own house. Miriam might have to make do with images. There'll be plenty of them, but no harm to have a first-hand glimpse either.'

'Agreed.'

'I'll call Leanne, you call Miriam. A doc needs to get their arse in here immediately. Once Leanne tells me what time she, or another female SOCO, can get here, we can let them know whether to come here or go to Connolly Road first.'

Jerry nodded and both men walked in opposite directions, bringing their phones to their ears.

CHAPTER FIFTY-EIGHT

Miriam's phone rang out four times, but Jerry kept hitting redial until finally she did answer.

'Yes, Detective Hughes?' Her tone was clipped and the fact that she used his full title meant that she was in company and possibly wanted to kill him.

'I'm sorry, Doctor Williams, but you'll want to hear this.'

'Unless you're about to tell me that Grace is...'

'She's currently sitting in a cell, covered head to toe in her mother's blood. We also believe that she killed her grandmother today, not to mention the three men that we found tortured, killed and wrapped in plastic inside her home and the fourth one that we believe she dumped on the side of a road. All this began with the discovery of the decomposing corpse of her sister Amber in their childhood home, with one of Grace's *fresh* dinners on a table in front of her.'

Miriam was silent, but he could hear her breathing.

'How important is that conference now?'

'No one is to speak to her. I'm on my way.'

'From Dublin. Someone needs to get here a lot sooner than that so that SOCO can gather the evidence from her person.

The crime scenes should also have eyes on them. If not yours, then whoever you send up here to take care of her interests until you get here. Someone you can rely on to be thorough.'

She was quiet again, but this time he could hear rustling and then the sound of wind and street traffic. 'I'll call Cian. Where do you want him?'

'Bradford? The last time you put him in charge of Grace, he let her walk out the door and kill two more people.'

'You mean he did you the favour of finding a non-existent bed in an overcrowded, unsecured facility for a patient who was not certified *or* a prisoner of An Garda Síochána?'

Jerry gritted his teeth and kicked the tyre of the squad car beside him. Paul waved his phone to get Jerry's attention.

'Leanne is on her way here. Thirty or forty minutes.'

'Grace is *my* patient,' Miriam continued, 'and Doctor Cian Bradford is who I trust to look after her. Despite what you seem to think, Cian *knows* her, Jerry. Almost as well as I do. What happened at the hospital was outside of his control. You wanna blame someone, blame the system.'

'He needs to be here in twenty minutes.'

'Heatherhill?'

'Yes.'

'I can't promise twenty minutes, but I'll call him now.'

'He needs to...'

Miriam hung up before Jerry could finish.

'Well?' Paul asked, as they both walked towards the front door.

'She's sending someone up and she's leaving Dublin herself now.'

Paul pulled the door open and Jerry went in ahead of him. They both headed for interview room one. Inside, Grace was smiling and chatting about the differences between instant, and proper coffee. Mike and Martin were silently listening. As they should be.

'Everyone all right?' Jerry asked, trying to sound light.

'I'm trying to wangle a cuppa out of these lads, Jerry, but they're having none of it.' Her smile faded then. 'Any sign of her?'

'It's nearly lunchtime, Grace. Is there anything you fancy eating with that cuppa?'

'I wouldn't mind a proper toasty.'

'Define *proper*?' he asked. He needed to kill some time until the doc and Leanne arrived.

'Well I don't like when they toast both sides separately. A proper toasty is when you make a normal ham, cheese, tomato and onion sandwich with proper butter. Then, before you toast it, butter the outside of the bread as well. *Then* toast it. Everything will be hot and buttery, and all the ingredients will be melted together. That's a proper toasty.'

'Wow. I think I need one of those myself now.'

'Good idea. I don't know, do you eat properly at all because you don't look very well, Jerry. So many people don't realise the importance of home cooking.'

'You're right, Grace. What's your favourite home-cooked meal?'

'Prawn tagliatelle...'

'With the prawns from Aldi,' Jerry finished for her.

She nodded and smiled. 'Yeah! I got them from the English Market a few times, but they're very big those ones. I like the ones from Aldi and they're good value for money.'

'Can't argue with that.'

'Amber's favourite is shepherd's pie.' Her smile faded again.

'Realistically, it'll take me a minute to pull that perfect sandwich together, Grace. How hungry are you?'

'I'm not that hungry at all, Jerry. But I don't like skipping mealtimes either, so I should eat something all right.'

Jerry nodded. 'Okay. While I sort that out, we'll get you something clean and comfortable to wear, all right?' He looked to Martin and Mike. 'Lads, you go and sort that out, yeah?'

Grace looked down at her clothes. She pulled her jumper away from her body, her chin pressed against her chest as she checked for stains. She showed no signs of having seen any.

'I'm all right, but whatever you think.'

Martin reappeared and said quietly, 'There's a Doctor Bradford out front.'

CHAPTER FIFTY-NINE

'Do you know what you're walking into here?' Jerry's tone was abrupt and held a hint of a threat when he greeted Cian Bradford at the front desk, minus the pleasantries.

'I have an idea, yes?' Doctor Bradford sounded equally peeved.

'An idea? You'd want to have more than an idea before you walk into that room.'

'I think what Detective Hughes is asking,' Paul interrupted, 'is, are you familiar with this patient?'

Doctor Bradford exhaled loudly and shook his head. 'More than you can imagine.'

Jerry furrowed his brow. 'What does that mean?'

'It means, Detective, that I've been sharing my life with Grace Murphy's *actual* doctor for more than two decades. I know how deeply she was affected by the case all those years ago and at times, we talked through the complexities of it. Grace Murphy was a third wheel in our marriage for some time and I have a feeling she might become so again. So, am I familiar with this patient? I dare say I am, yes.'

Jerry had no idea that Miriam was married. Not that he'd

ever asked and not that he particularly cared. But he was pleased to know that this Cian Bradford had a vested interest. He wouldn't want to mess this up, for his own sake. Happy wife, happy life and all that.

'What exactly has happened? Miriam just ordered me to get up here, that Grace was about to be charged with multiple homicides. Can anyone give me more detail?'

Paul answered before Jerry had the chance. He was too wound up. 'Late yesterday afternoon, we found the decomposing body of Grace's younger sister, Amber, in their childhood home. It's believed that she's been there for around six months, cause of death looks like a heroin overdose. There were signs that Grace had been visiting the house and even delivering home-cooked meals throughout that time. She's certainly been communicating with us and talking about Amber like she's still alive.

'Also yesterday, we found the bodies of three men, wrapped in plastic and in various stages of decomposition in the box bedroom of Grace's own home. They linked to a fourth body that was dumped in North Cork a few days earlier. These men all bore some physical resemblance to Philip Munroe. All showed signs of having been tortured. Now, we're not the doctors here, but my grunt brain is telling me that Grace found her sister and cracked. *Also* today...'

Doctor Bradford raised his eyebrows.

'Yip, there's more. Her maternal grandmother was found deceased in her home, possibly natural causes, or possibly poison and Grace's mother, Liz, had her throat sliced open with a breadknife. Grace is wearing a few pints of blood, not her own, and we need her clothes to determine what we already know. She left the knife behind with a sizeable bloody handprint on the handle. SOCO are on the way to gather evidence from

Grace's person and we need you to watch out for her medical interests.'

'Oh. Is that all?'

'Are you permanently set to sarcastic mode, or what?' Jerry asked. He didn't know why, but he didn't like this guy. He was too smarmy. And judging by the look returned to him by the doctor, the feeling was mutual.

'Is this a private party, or can anyone join in?' Leanne arrived to ease the tension. Or add to it, depending on what mood she was in.

'Can we get this done, please?' Jerry asked.

'You wanna head in first, Doc?' Leanne ignored Jerry's bad mood. She held up the white boiler suit that she was about to put on. 'I have one of these for her too. If you can prepare her for what's coming and try to keep her calm. I'll give you five minutes to do that, while I organise myself here and I'll be right along.'

Bradford nodded to Leanne and asked, 'Where to?' He directed his question to Paul and Jerry mentally told himself to calm down. He was beginning to piss himself off, as well as everyone around him.

'Jerry should be in the room if possible. She trusts him implicitly,' Paul said, throwing a warning glance in Jerry's direction.

'I'd like to go in by myself first,' Bradford responded. 'You have cameras in there?'

'We do.'

'Then you can watch on if you like. But I don't want any external influences until I get a sense of what's going on with her.'

'We just told you what's going on.' Jerry again, despite himself.

Doctor Bradford smiled annoyingly at him. 'You really are

lovely, aren't you?' And he walked away towards the door leading to the interview rooms.

Paul shot Jerry another look and Jerry held his hand up. 'I know,' he mumbled. 'I'll shut up.'

Paul held the door open for Bradford and followed him in, taking him to interview room one.

'You're making yourself popular today,' Leanne said, without looking up from her kit bag.

'Don't you start.' Jerry walked away and into a back office, where he could watch and listen in on the doctor's conversation with Grace. It seemed clear that Grace was not in her right mind when she'd committed these murders. But there was something in the back of Jerry's mind nagging at him. He turned up the volume so he could hear every word of what was said, and he positioned himself where he could see her full-on. Where he could watch her body language. He needed to know that somehow, Grace Murphy hadn't been fooling him all along.

CHAPTER SIXTY

'Hey, Grace.' Bradford's entire demeanour changed when he walked into the room. The sarcastic ass that greeted Jerry out front had vanished and was replaced with a relaxed, friendly doppelgänger. 'I'm Cian. Do you remember meeting me?'

'Hi.' Grace looked fed up now. 'No, I don't think so.'

'That's all right. I have one of those faces that's easy to forget.' He smiled and sat down opposite her. 'Are you all right?'

'I'm grand. Where's Jerry?'

'He's just taking care of a few things. He'll be back in a while, but he asked me to come see you for a minute. Is that all right?'

'He's going to give himself a heart attack one of these days. He worries too much, I keep telling him that. You're a doctor. Maybe you can have a word with him?'

'Sure, I can do that. What does he worry about?'

'Me and my sister.'

Bradford nodded. 'Why do you think he worries about you so much?'

'Ah, my sister Amber goes missing a lot. She's missing now.'

'Do you know why you're here, Grace?'

'I just told you. Amber is missing and Jerry is trying to find her.'

'You've got some blood on you. Did you know that?'

She raised her hands and looked at them, seemingly without seeing.

'My friend Leanne is going to come in in a second. She'll be all decked out like she's heading on a space mission, but that's just her. She'll swap out your clothes and give you something clean to put on, is that okay?'

'You're the second person to tell me that my clothes are dirty. Jerry said it as well. But I wash my clothes, Cian, I assure you. There's no such thing as a Murphy Stench. Not anymore.'

'A Murphy stench?'

Grace shook her head. 'Never mind. That was a long time ago. We weren't what you'd call, rich, Cian. My mam didn't bother much with things like washing powder and all that.'

'And where's your mam now?'

Grace shrugged. 'She likes to do her own thing.'

'When was the last time you saw her?'

Grace blew out a long breath. 'It's been a long time now. A few years anyway.'

'You didn't see her today?'

Grace rolled her eyes and half smiled. 'Hardly.'

There was a gentle knock on the door and Leanne stepped in. She was in full protective gear.

'This is Leanne.' Bradford smiled. 'What did I tell you about the gear?'

Grace smiled.

'Do you mind if I stay while you change?'

'You can stay, but you can turn around,' Grace replied. 'I don't like anyone looking at me. And I don't know why everyone wants me to get changed?'

'Your clothes have lots of blood on them, Grace. We need to make sure it's not yours. That you haven't hurt yourself unknowingly. I'll turn my chair around and face the wall, okay?' He stood up, turned the chair and sat down again with his back to her.

Leanne placed her bag on the floor and removed a spare white boiler suit from its plastic and placed it on the table.

Grace tutted and started taking off her clothes quickly. She pulled off her jumper and dropped it on the floor. Blood had soaked through, onto her white T-shirt, which she removed just as quickly. She dropped that on the floor as well.

'Grace, can you slow down, please?' Leanne asked gently, putting a gloved hand on Grace's arm.

Grace, standing in her bra and jeans now looked highly uncomfortable. 'I want to put some clothes on.'

'I promise I'll be quick.' Leanne walked around Grace, examining her closely. She took samples from her skin and samples of the blood on her arms, neck, face and her right ear. 'Leave your bra on a while, Grace. But can you remove your jeans, please?'

Grace's bottom lip was trembling now, but she did as she was asked. 'I don't like this. I want some clothes.'

Leanne performed the same examination of Grace's legs, taking a few quick samples as she did. She also quickly checked her body for injuries but there were none. 'Okay, Grace. Take off these,' she gently touched a gloved finger to the side of Grace's knickers and bra, 'and put this on.' She held out the boiler suit.

Grace moved quickly, removing her underwear and getting dressed in the oversized suit.

'Now I'm just going to have a quick look through your hair.' Leanne was already doing this while explaining it. 'I'm going to pluck just one so you might feel a...'

'Ouch.'

'Sorry about that, Grace.' Leanne pulled another cotton bud from her kit and asked Grace to open her mouth. 'I'm just going to rub this around the inside of your cheek.' Again, it was done before she'd finished explaining. Leanne clipped some of Grace's nails into a bag and took some samples from the soles of her feet. Leanne worked quickly and chatted easily to Grace as she did, keeping her relaxed and calm. 'There,' she finally said. 'All done.' Grace sat back down while Leanne carefully placed her clothes in bags and stored all her samples carefully.

Grace complied with everything, but she looked childlike as she did. She looked scared and Jerry, watching on from the other room, hated the sight of it. But that look on her face was about the only thing he recognised in the woman before him. This woman who was drenched in other people's blood.

CHAPTER SIXTY-ONE

The day of Grace's arrest was one of the longest of Jerry's life. The two hours after Leanne finished up were spent on eggshells, while Grace was given lunch and a rest. Some wanted to let the dogs loose on her, while the higher-ups were too worried about the optics to let that happen. They wanted to be seen to give her all due care and attention, so that nothing could be thrown back at them when it came to sentencing. But the one thing they all had in common was that they wanted her nailed to the cross.

While she was resting, Cian Bradford went to visit the Connolly Road scene and had not returned.

'Where is she?' Finally Miriam arrived and Jerry went out to meet her when her car was spotted pulling into the car park.

'Follow me. Did you speak to Cian?'

'I did. I've just come off a video call with him. He showed me the house at Connolly Road. She hasn't been questioned yet?'

'No. Evidence was gathered and she's had lunch. She's resting now. I've been in and out to keep her comfortable, but she seems oblivious. She still seems to think that she's here waiting for us to find Amber.'

'Has she been told that Amber is dead?'

'No. She knows about Maggie, but Liz hasn't been mentioned either.'

'Good. Come on then.'

'Grace?' Miriam greeted her with a smile as Jerry opened the door to let them both in. Grace was moved to a cell once Leanne finished with her and if she noticed, then she didn't seem to mind in the slightest. She was sitting on the edge of the bed, staring at the floor. She still had her mother's dry blood on her face and arms.

'Hi, Doctor Williams,' Grace answered, like she was happy to see an old friend.

'How are you, Grace? Are you being looked after?'

'I don't feel too well.'

'No? In what way?'

'My head.' She put her hand to the side of her head. 'It's really throbbing.'

'Okay. I can give you something for that.' She opened her bag and took out her blood pressure machine and some other paraphernalia. 'Do you know why you're here, Grace?'

'They need to find Amber.' She squeezed her eyes shut and brought both hands to her head now.

'I'm afraid I have some bad news, Grace. They did find Amber,' she reached out and put her hand on Grace's shoulder, 'I'm so sorry, Grace. But your sister has sadly passed away.'

Grace squeezed her eyes tighter and lowered her head into her lap. She shook her head, clutching her hair in her closed fists.

'Did you know that, Grace?'

She sat up again and turned to Jerry. 'Did you check out by The Lough? She has a friend out there somewhere. She could be staying with him.'

Miriam shook her head at Jerry. 'Grace, did you go to see your mother today?'

'If she's not out there, then maybe she's in hospital? Did you try the Mercy?'

'When did you last see your mother, Grace?'

Grace was restless now, rocking back and forth, looking somewhere between confused and profoundly upset. 'Why do you keep asking me about her? She left us. She's gone. Why would I want to see her?'

'Grace, someone killed your mother today,' Jerry said firmly.

'Delaney! That's her friend's name. Did you ask him if he knows where she is?'

'Grace...' Miriam started, but Jerry cut her off.

'Is that your mother's blood on your arms, Grace?'

She looked at her hands and arms. Again, she seemed to see nothing unusual about them. She clutched her hair again, her face contorted with anguish as she lowered her head.

'Grace?' Miriam's tone was soft and she shot Jerry a look that told him to keep his mouth shut. 'Can you tell me about the men that were found in your house?'

At this, Grace bolted up. 'There are no men in my house. That's *my* house.'

'I mean, the deceased men, Grace. Can you tell me how they got there?'

'What?' She opened her eyes and mouth wide and pressed the heel of her hand into her forehead, like a particularly violent wave of pain had just crashed over her. She sat back on the bed.

Miriam applied the blood pressure machine and while it did its noisy assessment, she pulled some medication from her bag and handed it towards Grace along with a bottle of water. 'Some paracetamol. That should help with the headache.'

Miriam checked the machine and removed it from Grace's arm. Grace stood abruptly and holding her head in both hands now, she collapsed to the floor.

CHAPTER SIXTY-TWO

The ambulance arrived with miraculous speed and Grace regained and lost consciousness several times before she was stretchered into the back of it. Miriam got in there with her and it took off without delay, headed for the CUH.

'Hughes?' Paul called, as Jerry passed the front desk on his way to his car. 'Team powwow.'

'Now? I'm on my way to...'

'Yes, now. She's with the doc and I'll have a uniform head out there and keep a close eye until you get there. She doesn't look like she's in a fit state to talk anyway, so it's as good a time as any.'

Jerry stopped short of rolling his eyes and followed Paul back towards the conference room where the rest of the team had already gathered.

'Can we make this quick?' Jerry disguised his order as a question when he walked in, and he directed it to everyone in the room.

Paul ignored him and stood facing the team. 'Right, so it's looking increasingly likely that Grace Murphy will be charged with the homicides of William Jones, Joe Ferrier, Terry Reynolds, Alan Manning, Liz Murphy and Maggie Hayes. That means that, yes, the three deceased men found in Grace's home have been positively identified. That said, clearly this case will hinge on medical assessments et cetera. So one misstep from us could fuck the whole thing up and if that happens, I will personally make sure the whole country knows the name of the person who made the misstep.' He pointed at each one of them threateningly. 'Do not assume that this is a slam dunk. Treat every single detail and every piece of evidence as if it's the only thing we've got on her. Nothing is taken for granted and nothing is to be assumed, are we all clear on that?'

A mumble of yeses and yes, sirs went on for more seconds than was necessary, but Paul wasn't rushing anyone, to Jerry's annoyance.

'And if I read one word in the paper that shouldn't be there, heads will roll all over this floor. Okay, Myers, Foley; go.' Paul pointed to the officers who'd come from Maggie's house.

Linda Foley answered. 'We got to Maggie Hayes' house at just after eleven this morning. There was no response when we knocked, so Toby took a walk around the house. He was able to see her through the kitchen window. She was sitting in a chair at the kitchen table, not moving. She didn't respond when he knocked so he broke the window and let himself inside. He opened the back door for me. Nothing else was touched, aside from checking for signs of life. There were two takeaway cups on the table, one right where Maggie was sitting. They were Rosa branded cups, which would indicate that they were purchased at the petrol station up the road where they sell the Rosa brand of coffee.'

Luke Maguire raised his hand. 'CCTV shows Grace buying one coffee and one tea in the service station at 7.17am.'

Paul nodded. 'Mike?'

'SOCO wrapped up on Connolly Road. They found a large bloody handprint on the knife, along with prints in blood on the table and on a loaf of bread that was found on the floor. There were several bloody footprints around the kitchen and leading out to the hall and even on the path outside. Gra... whoever did this made no effort to cover their tracks.'

'Toxicology came back on Maggie,' Paul added. 'She had enough tranquillisers in her system to bring down Dublin Zoo. Likewise, the drink was more drug than tea. No traces of narcotics were found in the coffee and the cup is being tested for DNA. It's also been confirmed that the hair found on Alan Manning's body was that of a rodent. There was a lot of it too. Initial findings from the post-mortem indicate that he may have been cut with a sharp knife or blade and then exposed to one or more rodents. A mix of rohypnol and large quantities of magnesium, potassium and sodium sulphates were found in his system. The same concoction was found in all four of the men.'

'What's that?'

'Bowel-prep medication, normally used to clear a fella out before a colonoscopy. All four of our dead men were given enough to make their insides explode.'

A groan made its way around the room. Followed by a brief silence.

'It's only a matter of time before it's proven that Grace is responsible for the deaths of six people,' Jerry added. 'But as it stands, she appears to have no memory of any of it. She's oblivious to it all.'

'Is it genuine?' Paul asked.

Jerry shrugged and started moving towards the door. 'That's Miriam Williams' job. As of now, Grace is in the back of an ambulance headed for the CUH if she's not there already, and that's where I'm headed. As soon as she's cleared, I'd imagine she'll be certified.'

'And Grace Murphy will be off to the Central Mental Hospital,' Toby said quietly. 'Right back where she started.'

CHAPTER SIXTY-THREE

'How are you looking there?' Jerry asked Miriam Williams as he got in his car and got his Bluetooth up and running.

'We're in the ambulance bay at the CUH and it looks like that's as far as we'll be going for the foreseeable future. It's carnage in there.'

The Cork University Hospital was mentioned in the news constantly as one of, if not *the* most overcrowded hospital in the country. Trolly watch had fifty-eight people waiting on trollies as of that morning.

'Okay, someone needs to explain the situation there.'

'One of the medics has gone inside to try. But try telling the father of four with a workplace injury how much more important *our* case is, Jerry. Triage happens for a reason and right now, Grace is alive and physically well.'

Jerry was snarling in silence back at her. He didn't want or need to hear about the country's healthcare crisis. Not today. 'How is she?' he asked instead of launching into the rant that begged to be let loose. 'Has she said anymore?'

'Not a dickie bird. She's been out of it since we left.'

'What do you think, Miriam? Is she genuine do you think?'

'I'm surprised that you're even entertaining the idea that she might not be. Actually, I'm kind of relieved about that.'

He snarled again. Did people honestly think that he was so blinded by Grace Murphy that his thirty-four years of experience as a Garda just went out the window?

'Look,' Miriam lowered her voice and he could hear her footsteps and some wind again, as she walked out of Grace's earshot, 'honestly, I don't know, Jerry. It's far too early to tell. Grace suffers from post-traumatic stress disorder and as you know, that can manifest itself in many ways. Grace has, in the past, shown signs that she may be schizophrenic.'

'What? I didn't know that.'

'I'm sure there are some things that even you don't know, Detective. Grace did her time. She was treated and she was put on a treatment plan. She was monitored closely for the required duration and then less and less so.'

'Miriam?'

'Yeah.'

'Stop trying to cover your arse. This isn't about you or the system. I simply want to know your opinion on how she is right now and what you think might have happened.' There was a sudden burst of noise on the other end of the line. 'What was that?'

'Christ, I don't... oh. Things are kicking off in A&E. The medics are running in. Probably someone who didn't appreciate being told that they weren't as important as someone else.'

Jerry rolled his eyes.

'But, as you were so politely asking, I don't know yet. I need to spend some time with her, see what medication she has or has not been taking. It wouldn't be much of a leap though to imagine that finding Amber dead in their childhood home would have triggered Grace in a way that she would have had very little control over. She may well have no memory of what she's done.' Miriam was walking again, but more slowly this time. 'Either way, it's just too soon to...'

Miriam went silent, but Jerry could still hear wind and some distant traffic noise, so he knew she hadn't been cut off.

'Miriam?'

'She's gone.' The weight of Miriam's voice had changed.

'She's what? Gone where?' His voice rose with each word until he was shouting at the phone.

'I was right here. I...'

'Tell me she wasn't left un-a-fucking-tended, Miriam?' he roared, but the line was dead.

Jerry hit the lights and siren and punched his way through the city's traffic, speed-dialling Paul as he did.

Three more squad cars arrived around the same time as Jerry, but it took far too long for them to fan out and begin searching the hospital grounds. Jerry went straight to the ambulance bay to find Miriam Williams.

'What the hell happened?' he barked as soon as he saw her. She looked as though she was being eaten alive by stress, but Jerry didn't care.

She shook her head, with her phone held to her ear. She waved him away and turned her back. Jerry finally let his snarl out as he stormed up to her, took the phone from her hand and ended the call.

'What the hell do you think you're doing?'

'What were *you* doing? You left her unattended?'

'To talk to *you!*' She jabbed him in the chest. 'And she wasn't unattended. She was in the care of a fucking medic! How was I to know that his colleague was the one being assaulted inside the sliding glass doors right in front of him? How was I to know that he was going to bolt in there and leave Grace alone in the back of the ambulance. How was I to know that going two feet away was two feet too far?'

'Where was the uniform?'

'What uniform?'

'Paul said he was sending one after you.'

'Well, if he did then he was late to the party.' She gestured towards some Gardaí who were walking the car park, checking in, under and around the parked cars. 'These lads all showed up with you.'

'Shit!' Paul had walked into the meeting ahead of Jerry. He'd forgotten to send someone, and Jerry didn't think to remind him. He stood looking all around the car park and the area surrounding the hospital. He brought the phone to his ear. 'Paul, is the shopping centre being searched?' The Wilton Shopping Centre was right across the busy main road. It had a massive car park wrapped around the centre. It was a large area with lots of hiding places. And a taxi rank.

'I have six units there from all over the city. How in the name of God did this happen?'

'Well, turns out there was no uniformed escort, an assault on one of the medics and the other went to help, while Miriam was on the phone to me. So we'll call it a perfect storm, will we?'

'Fucking shit!'

'I'd say so, yes.' He looked all around again. 'She's gone, Paul.'

'How far could she have gone? She's a very unwell woman.'

'Is she though?' Jerry said, almost to himself. He knew for a fact that just about everyone who ever encountered Grace Murphy, underestimated her. She was *poor Grace Murphy*, the victim, or the *notorious Grace Murphy* who couldn't control herself. But in fact, Grace Murphy had more control over herself and her life, post-hospitalisation, than anyone else he knew. She was a survivor, not a victim. Grace survived her childhood. She survived her mother. She survived Philip Munroe. She survived the Central Mental Hospital and she survived all the stigma that was attached to her.

Grace Murphy was more intelligent than anyone gave her credit for and she knew how to get out of a situation that she didn't want to be in. Whether or not she intended to kill six people remained to be seen, but right now, she did not intend to answer for it.

'Find her, Jerry,' Paul warned, as if he'd just heard what Jerry was thinking.

Jerry hung up and returned to his car, but as he drove away from the hospital and back towards the city, he knew in his gut that Grace Murphy was exactly where she'd been for some time; five steps ahead of everyone else.

CHAPTER SIXTY-FOUR

SIX DAYS LATER – LIVERPOOL, ENGLAND

The weather had picked up dramatically over the past few days and Grace allowed herself a small smile as she sipped her coffee and watched the people around her. Some were in deck chairs on the grass with picnic baskets alongside them, while others just walked on through as they made their way from A to B. Two grown men were throwing a Frisbee back and forth like they were twelve years old and hadn't a care in the world. Grace had found a tree to sit under. She allowed herself a moment to think. Getting here hadn't been easy, but it hadn't been as difficult as she imagined either. There was some luck involved, without a doubt. But wasn't it about time that Grace and Amber's luck changed? Grace firmly believed that it had. Right around the time that Philip Munroe was dispatched from this world.

'You understand why I couldn't let them see you?' she asked Amber, who sat quietly beside her. She still hadn't spoken, but she was finally clean. Not so much as a twitch since they'd left Cork. She looked like her old self too. Clear-skinned, wide-eyed and beautiful. But still scared. Grace believed that Amber was born scared and had stayed that way ever since, through no fault of her own. 'But not for much longer, okay?' She turned slightly to face her. 'You don't have to be afraid anymore, my love. We'll have a life here. An *actual* life, me and you. Just like we were always meant to.'

After getting out of the ambulance, she'd only had to run for less than five minutes. She didn't think she'd even make it that far. 'What are the chances of someone attacking my ambulance driver?' she asked Amber now, smiling and shaking her head, as she turned to face forward again. But that was just the first stroke of luck. The second was finding an articulated lorry preparing to leave the service station on the Glasheen Road. A service station that would never usually be used by truckers, except for a slightly older one with a sweet tooth. He'd stopped for a sausage sandwich, tea, Skittles and some chewy mints. Without giving any thought as to what she might say, Grace ran up to the man as he was about to climb up into the cab, and hysterically told him that her boyfriend was chasing her. That he was trying to kill her.

'I never knew truckers could be nice,' she said ruefully. 'Did you?' She turned again to look at Amber, but she was still quietly looking in her lap. Like she always did when she was waiting for something to happen. 'It's okay, my love. None of them will find us here.' She got to her feet and wiped grass off the bum of someone else's black trousers. A woman called Lisa owned them. Or perhaps she had acquired them from someone else and passed them on to Grace. Lisa ran the women's refuge that Grace had presented herself at four and a half days ago. She decided to stick to the "woman in fear for her life" story. After all, men did want to harm her. They wanted to harm both of them and this had been the case all their lives. If anything, she was just fifteen years or so late in seeking the help that she and her sister needed.

'Wait here.' She turned to look at her sister. 'This won't be for much longer, okay? Once I get this sorted, you can come and go as you please.'

She walked towards the Hilton hotel, right beside the park and through the beautiful lobby, to the reception desk. She smiled brightly at the middle-aged woman who greeted her. 'Can I help you, love?' She pronounced it, *elp ya, loov.*

'I'm looking for Hilary Mellet.'

'She just passed through a second ago! I'll give her a call for you.' The woman picked up the phone and dialled a three-digit number. Grace liked how the woman spoke to her. Like she was a valued customer of the hotel, or a friend of a friend. A normal person. 'A'right, Hil?' Grace liked the accent around here too. 'I've got a girl,' pronounced *gail,* 'here, looking for you.' She put a hand over the speaker. 'I'm sorry, love, what was your name?'

'Gerry Hughes,' Grace half whispered. 'Lisa sent me.'

'Gerry Hughes,' she said into the phone. 'Lisa sent her.' She listened for a second. 'A'right, will do, Hil.' She hung up.

'Is that short for Geraldine?' she asked with a smile.

Grace imagined that the woman was nosy by nature but she nodded anyway. In truth she hadn't considered *Geraldine.* She just didn't want to have to keep track of any more fibs than necessary, so she picked a name that she would always remember.

'Gerry?' Another woman came striding through the lobby. She was still walking when she stretched out her hand to Grace. They shook as soon as she reached her. Hilary was taller than Grace with thick red hair cut short. She looked strong. 'Follow me.'

Grace followed Hilary back the way she'd come and into a small office at the back of the reception. She closed the door and took a seat behind her desk. 'Have a seat.'

Grace did, opposite her. Hilary seemed much sterner than her front-of-house colleague.

'Okay, first of all, you can relax. I'm not going to ask what landed you here or anything else about your personal circumstances. I've known Lisa Jackson for more than thirteen years. The woman saved my life and I'm guessing she might be in the process of saving yours too. Second of all, this is a hard job and I will be your boss. As such, I will expect you to present to work on time, carry out your cleaning duties to the highest of standards and keep your nose clean. Do not bring trouble to this hotel.

'Lastly, aside from your name, which I'm guessing is not actually your name, don't lie to me. If you can do all that, then a rate of twelve pound fifty per hour will be paid to you promptly every Friday. I'm also guessing you don't have a bank account, so I will pay you by cheque which you can cash at the bar. You will be provided with room-only accommodation for a six-month period. During that time, no one but you will be permitted to stay in that room and after that time, if not sooner, you will be expected to have found suitable living accommodation for yourself. Does that all sound manageable?'

'It does,' Grace responded with a nod. 'And I can promise you that I will be the best hotel housekeeper the Hilton has ever had.'

CHAPTER SIXTY-FIVE

TWO YEARS LATER, CORK CITY

'She's an absolute stunner, Pennie. Just like her mum.' Jerry smiled, as he looked at the scrunched-up face of the two-day-old little girl and, not for the first time, he found himself mourning the life he once thought he might have had.

'Isn't she though?' Steph beamed, walking into the room carrying a baby-changing bag that was bigger than anything Jerry had ever carried on-board a plane.

'Here comes Nana,' he said to the baby and smiled at his old partner. And his relatively new one.

'You know, I'm actually okay with being called that. I never thought I'd like it until I saw that beautiful little face.' She scooped the baby from Pennie's arms and cuddled her close, looking like she might devour her.

'Mam, I love you but I'm knackered. We'll be home tomorrow.'

With that, Pennie's boyfriend, Ollie, came in. He too looked knackered, but was beaming with pride as his eyes found his new daughter.

'Okay, okay we're going,' Steph whispered, as the baby dozed off in her arms. She reluctantly handed her over to Ollie.

Jerry put his arm around Steph's shoulder. Pennie smiled at the two of them and looked perfectly relaxed, despite having just given birth. 'You two go and have fun somewhere.' She smiled, as her own eyes began to close.

'It might kill me, but I'll leave you alone tomorrow to get settled in at home. A new family.' She beamed again. 'But Nana's coming round the day after, okay?'

'You're welcome any time, you know that.' Ollie smiled at her. 'You both are.'

As they left the Cork University Maternity Hospital, Jerry drove them straight to the River Lee Hotel.

'What are we doing here?' Steph asked.

'I've booked dinner and I've booked a room. We're celebrating tonight and it all starts with steak.'

Steph laughed and leaned against his shoulder. A warmth spread though him and he smiled. Steph had been a part of his life for so long, but with the job and any number of other distractions, they hadn't really noticed each other until recently. All the late-night brainstorms following Grace's disappearance had led from one thing to another. Jerry retired from the force not long after that and was making a relatively poor show of *enjoying* that retirement. In reality, he was bored off his head. Except for Steph. He would never be bored with Steph and he wondered how he could have been around her for so much of his life and not felt as he did now. How many years had been wasted? Again he thought about Steph's new grandchild and found himself wishing that she was his grandchild too.

'How about we skip the steaks?' She linked her arm through his as they walked through the hotel doors and into the shiny lobby.

'I like the way you think, young lady.' Jerry grinned.

Later that night, room service delivered two steak dinners and a bottle of house red to two grinning guests dressed in robes. They ate at the small round table in the corner of their room and brought their wine back to the bed.

'Let's find a good movie!' Steph suggested. 'When was the last time we lay in bed like two lazy gits and watched TV?'

'Good idea.' In truth, Jerry didn't care what they did, once it involved being right here, in a bed with the woman he loved. Neither of them had said that out loud yet, but Jerry felt that the time was coming near. He did love her. He'd always loved her, in one way or another.

'We'll just get the headlines,' she mumbled, coming to rest on Sky News. Steph, like him, became engrossed in the news and it would probably be as far as they'd get with the channel surfing for tonight.

They chatted on and off through the political news, mostly about Pennie and the baby and they tuned back in to updates on the war in Ukraine. Then the image of a man appeared on the screen and Jerry felt Steph stiffen beside him. His own blood cooled significantly, too. Steph turned up the volume.

'*Police in Liverpool are investigating the disappearance of a second man from the city centre. Fifty-one-year-old Joe Mackey has been missing for five days and was last seen in the area of the Clayton Square Shopping Centre. Mister Mackey is described as being five foot seven in height with a medium build, dark-blond hair and brown eyes. He was wearing a grey suit, white shirt and blue tie at the time of his disappearance. This follows the disappearance of fifty-year-old Will Holland, last seen on February 20th in the area of Chavasse Park. Mister Holland has been missing for more than nine weeks now. Both men are married with families, are close in age and bear an uncanny physical resemblance to each other. Police believe the disappearances are linked.'*

There were two pictures filling the screen now and neither Steph nor Jerry had moved a muscle since the report began.

'Police are asking anyone with information as to the whereabouts of these men, to contact Merseyside Police at the number below. A press conference is due to be held tomorrow morning at 10am.'

The two men staring back at Jerry and Steph from the corner of their ever less-enticing hotel bedroom looked so alike that the Merseyside Police had seen the connection immediately. But Jerry didn't have it in him to consider the length of time it had taken him.

'It's her,' Steph mumbled. 'It's Grace.'

Jerry got slowly out of bed and started getting dressed.

'Jerry, no.' All the joy of the day had vanished from her face and was replaced with something far less shiny.

Jerry looked at her with sadness and regret. 'I have to, Steph.'

'What are you planning to do?'

'This is on me. I need to bring her back, but... come with me?'

She shook her head, disbelieving. 'No.'

Of course she couldn't go. He was stupid to ask, but he had to.

'Jerry...?' Steph's wide eyes were pleading with him.

Jerry knelt on the bed and tenderly kissed the top of her head. 'I love you, Steph.'

Her face told him that she wanted to kill him, but her tears let him know that she loved him too. She pulled her knees to her chest and lowered her face into them, while Jerry put on his jacket. She turned her head away and didn't say goodbye when he left carrying a lifetime of regret.

He walked through the lobby and out into the dark wet night and he cried tears that he'd been holding back for years. Out in the car park, his phone rang. Clearly someone else had been watching Sky News and had come to the same conclusion.

'What?' he answered abruptly.

'Jerry... are you okay?'

He gripped the phone tighter to his ear and squeezed his eyes shut. He doubled over on himself and it took a few seconds for him to straighten back up. Then he fell seamlessly back into step.

'I'm okay, Grace.'

THE END

ACKNOWLEDGEMENTS

I've loved every minute of writing this book and I'm so grateful to everyone who has supported and encouraged me along the way. I'm especially thankful to everyone at Bloodhound Books, especially Betsy, Tara, Katia, Hannah and my lovely editor Ian for their expertise and guidance.

To my brilliant agents, Nicky Lovick and Madeline Cotter at WGM Atlantic who have championed me, and this book from the very beginning.

Sincere thanks to my old friend, Brian Slevin. Just one of the incredibly decent people I had the privilege of serving with. Now, many years later and answering to the name Garda Slevin, he's been so generous with his time in answering my many procedural questions. Any inaccuracies are purely down to me.

To the fantastic community of Irish writers, who support, encourage and lift each other up at every given opportunity, especially Amy Jordan for the copious amount of coffee and bubbles when required. And Vanessa Fox O'Loughlin (AKA Sam Blake) for being a listening ear and a wealth of knowledge and sound advice.

To the best little girl in the world, Emily; thank you for making me laugh every day and for always assuming that there's nothing I can't do. (Long may that last!) And to Dominic for always being there.

The friends who have inspired me all my life, Yolanda, Louise and Anne-Marie. Everyone should be so lucky.

Finally, this book is dedicated to my lovely dad, Ted McNamara and my equally fantastic father-in-law, Billy Dunne, both of whom had to leave us in 2023. They were champions for the underdog, great friends and dedicated family men. There's nothing about them that won't be missed.

A NOTE FROM THE PUBLISHER

Thank you for reading this book. If you enjoyed it please do consider leaving a review on Amazon to help others find it too.

We hate typos. All of our books have been rigorously edited and proofread, but sometimes mistakes do slip through. If you have spotted a typo, please do let us know and we can get it amended within hours.

info@bloodhoundbooks.com

Printed in Great Britain
by Amazon